Praise for Meliss

Sick at Heart

'Imagine a man-hater's dream date: a mother-fixated, child-hating, wife-bashing, schoolgirl-seducing fiend. There you have Alex, the handsome devil of *Sick at Heart*. Elegant, spare . . . compulsive'   *The Times*

'The language is beautifully chosen to show the damaged mind of Alex as it really is, in a story that will haunt and disturb'   *Birmingham Post*

'Alex is barking mad; he is also intelligent, plausible and, ultimately, pitiful. His mother is lip-smackingly monstrous. I defy you not to enjoy meeting both of them in a shivery kind of way'   *Image Magazine*

Cold in Earth

'Her writing is clear and intense. Her characters . . . are each convincing and complex . . . You put the novel down feeling thoroughly chilled, and aware of a strong new author'   *The Times*

'A quietly chilling account of the destruction of a family. The story unfolds in the journals of some of the people involved . . . it's a difficult technique to employ successfully, but Melissa Jones has brought it off with deceptive ease'   *Sunday Telegraph*

'A near brilliant first novel'   *Kirkus*

'Intelligent, suspenseful work, offering something to both mainstream fiction audiences and mystery fans'
                    Publishers Weekly

'A dark compelling tale of disintegrating family life'
                    Frances Fyfield

SICK AT HEART

Melissa Jones

ORION

An Orion paperback
First published in Great Britain by Orion in 1999
This paperback edition published in 2000 by
Orion Books Ltd,
Orion House, 5 Upper St Martin's Lane,
London WC2H 9EA

A CIP catalogue record for this book
is available from the British Library.

Grateful acknowledgement is made
for permission to quote from
Fools of Time: Studies in Shakespearian Tragedy
by Northrop Frye,
© University of Toronto Press, 1967

ISBN 0 75283 427 4

Printed and bound in Great Britain by
The Guernsey Press Co. Ltd, Guernsey, C.I.

For S. J.

I would like to thank my husband,
my parents and my agent, Clare Conville.

'Be a child o' the time.'

SHAKESPEARE, *Antony and Cleopatra*

These letters are a faithful record of my past life before it was poured out and I came here. Although I've been asked to put it all down on paper, I write the words for myself. They keep me company. I write what I know to be true, which is all that can justly be asked or expected of me. I think what I've written is what could be described as an apologia, which should on no account be confused with an apology.

A Letter to my Mother

Love is not love which alters when it alteration finds.

Darling Mummy,

Even writing these words makes me want to cry, hurts me in the eyes. How dear you have always been to me, how dear, how sweet, how cruel. That was a long time ago. It was a long time ago when you were cruel. You were the first of my three cruel women.

Remember how we used to read together, so many books, so many evenings? Stories. We loved the big fat nineteenth-century stories, the ones that solved everything, left us satisfied. There was the one that began, *David Copperfield* I think it was, with this question: would the hero be the hero of his own life? If it didn't start like that, it should have done. And I remember saying to you, 'How could someone *not* be the hero of their own life?' And you laughed and kissed me and said you hoped I would never find out. I have to tell you now that I have fought for it, my life, to be the hero of my own life, and I have failed. I think, after all that has happened, we can safely assume that, if only that. You know most about it. You were the first to rob me. You've been a bit like God, my God, giving life, and taking it away. (Not like Susannah's God, the one with churches and rules, but a God just for me.) It is easier if I don't think about it now, being only a spectator at my own life. But that's wrong. What I mean is, that I am *a* protagonist. It is just that I'm not *the* protagonist.

You were my first hero, heroine, it doesn't matter. You were the only one. I didn't know a man, let alone a father. It was just you and me in our own paradise, and how I loved you. I loved you so much that I wasn't even conscious of it, could not have

5

said to a stranger, 'This is my mother, I love her.' It was just you, part of me, the other me. You, the elemental force. I haven't written for so long, even for myself. My poems were a long time ago, a long time. I know that I'm telling you things you already know, but it doesn't matter. This letter is not written for you, it is written for me. (Or that's what they say.) If I can't be the hero, I will be the author. I will write you. I will pin you down with words, I will make you stay with me, I'll hold you and hug you and kiss you, and I'll hurt you, I'll hurt you with words. Except I don't want to hurt you. I'm sorry I wrote that. Can you forgive me? I've forgiven you. I'll never say this again, but we both know I've so very much more to forgive.

There has to be a beginning to our story, and for me it always begins with rain. The sound of rain falling on the house, around the house, outside the shutters and dripping from the terrace roof. We used to close the doors to the terrace, and put towels on the floor, because the water would stream in across the tiles. The house was cold and dark and damp in the rain, soft, dim, and there were draughts from under the doors, through the windows and shutters, rising up from the floors. There aren't draughts like that any more, not in London, not anywhere that I can find. We didn't have any electricity, so it was candles and lamps and the big fire in the sitting room, with our chairs pulled close to it. Reading our books or quiet to the sound of music, we had music sometimes. It's odd that I remember the rain, when really, in the South of France, there was so little of it. Autumn and spring rain mostly, or those wild cracking summer thunderstorms that split the sky. In summer it was a dry dusty life we led, so we loved the rain. Falling asleep in your beautiful brass bed with its old linen sheets and the lace pillow-cases with the shutters tight shut, it was so dark, and so safe, with the blackness, and the sound of the rain. Morning rain was beautiful too, waking to it, peaceful, clean, the sun on wet earth so bright, all those reflections; or that sudden furious shower in the afternoon, like drawing a curtain between us and the outside world. I suppose I remember the rain because then I really couldn't go outside. We didn't even have an animal, no dog or cat to share our life with. Just ourselves, and the incomparable beauty of the place, ours and only ours. Hot skies: the smell of lavender on the acres around us, in the scratchy earth. Above us, our hill village, our bread, milk, fruit and wine village. The track that led through the sloping fields, the woods and prickly hedges, to the village, I could tell you about each rut and hole and bump in it, and our stone farmhouse, closed at the front, open at the back, looking out across the valley, at the hills and trees. Beyond, and far out of sight, the sea.

The kitchen: flagstones and an old wood-burning range, huge empty fireplace with a hook for where the pots used to hang. It was an ugly room and dark with small windows which were too high for me to reach. No fridge, we had no fridge in those days. We used to keep plates of food under fly-covers in the clammy pantry. Our sitting room, our dining room, your study, all with their thick walls and high windows, were like little cosy cells. And the long terrace facing the view, with its lawn of poor faded grass, and the terraces below us, sloping away, all these were precious, our domain. Upstairs, we slept in your room, I never thought of it as mine. There was also a bathroom, with a rough floor, and some empty bedrooms up there, unused. We came there when I was three, so I didn't remember England at all. You came with me to be alone, by yourself, to write. You came, as you were so fond of telling me, because you wanted to die. But we made a life there that was so beautiful and safe you never wanted it to change. No, that's wrong. I'm confusing you with me. I never wanted it to change. It was you who was restless. It was you.

I'm giving the impression of always being with you, us

7

locked together in perfect love, but it wasn't like that at all. We were both so very alone. I would wake beside you, that's true. In our sleep we were the closest. I remember you turned away from me on your side, your breathing back, your hair, the whiteness of your nightdress, all within reach, but not visible, hardly visible, because of the shutters at the windows. I don't remember stroking your hair, or your skin, or the cotton of the material, because I would have woken you, and you might have been angry, but I wanted to, always. And the wanting, I'm convinced, surpassed the doing. I used to lie feeling you there, closing my eyes and seeing the world outside. Would it be hot, would it be bright or grey, if bright, what sort of bright? By the sounds of birds I could tell what time it was, and then when I was so awake I couldn't lie still any longer, I would get out of bed quietly, take my clothes and dress on the landing, creep downstairs and open the shutters on the day.

You liked your breakfast in bed. I used to go to the village to get bread, hot baguette, fresh, through the dew, through the promise of the morning which seemed to say that everything belonged to me. It was my hillside, my sky, all the earth below me, all the curved space above. I used to put a flower on your breakfast tray, or a stone, or a feather, something. And you had cool butter and good strong jam and hot bread and thick coffee. I had mine downstairs. You used to say breakfast was a very private time for a woman, and I've never forgotten it. No woman I have ever spent the night with has been able to say that I have not been considerate to her in the morning. After coffee, you smoked a Gauloise. I could smell it from downstairs. You washed and dressed and came down to work in your study. There was only a table and chair in there. Nothing to distract you, you said.

I went to school in the village, although you tried your hardest to keep me away. You said that schools corrupted young souls and destroyed innocence. You were quite lighthearted when you said that, but I remember it. School days I always came home for lunch. You were silent because you had been working. I brought it home with me: rough pâté or cheese, salad, fruit from the market; misshapen, beautiful fruit, not like the waxworks we eat now. You would always be silent so I contented myself with watching you, trying to work out what you were thinking. You didn't like talking to people, sharing yourself with anyone, and you hated going to the village very much, but that was all right. I could always do the things you couldn't bring yourself to do. It was my privilege. At the weekends we would go for walks, beginning hand in hand, before I left you to explore. After a while, when I was out of sight, you would go home to read your book, on your bed, rest and sleep. Or you would sit on the terrace and write letters and smoke, your writing rapid, the hard pages covered in ink blots, spatters, dashes. We had no telephone in those days. I've believed in letters ever since. Words written down are more permanent. They can't lie the way voices can. We had a woman who came to sweep the floors and clean, Mathilde. I liked her. She taught me how to cook. I think she was sorry for me, because I was such a cautious little boy and rather thin. I had no friends. She used to worm me quite a lot, it was her cure-all – it made you laugh.

You always changed your clothes in the evening, put on powder and rouge and lipstick and scent and brushed out your hair. Sometimes you let me brush it for you. I think I was clumsy but you were patient. That was for drinks' time. In those days it was pastis. I used to mix it for you in a tall glass with a long spoon. I can't smell it now, that strong aniseed, without feeling sick with longing for you. For you as you were then. I can't begin to describe your beauty, your heavy grace. I won't try. We ate olives. I drank wine and water from when I was about twelve, just to keep you company, you said. And that's when we used to talk, when you used to tell me who I was. 'L'Heure Bleu', you called it, the blue hour, that gloaming time, and that was the name of your scent. It had vanilla in it, and flowers. The smell unfolded itself over time. The blue hour was a perfect description, twilight was blue there. You'd stare into the shadows, your finger dipped in your drink, then in your mouth, and you would suck it, suck the alcohol from your finger. You would put your fingertips on your lips, stroking them. You touched yourself, I remember, often, stroking your own soft throat, or the inside of your wrist. You did this while you thought, as if it helped you to remember your own beauty, your own charm. And then you'd tell me who I was.

I began with you. You were the youngest child of a youngest son. You had two brothers. Your father had been born into property and money, and as a younger son, had seen himself grow up to leave them behind. He was given an income from his family, and that's what your family lived on, or lived beyond, in a house on the family estate in Shropshire. 'There's a great deal of mud in Shropshire,' you used to say. Genteel poverty, you called it. Good phrase. Your mother was what was known in those days as a disappointed woman. Patiently, gently, endlessly, she whispered in her children's ears: one boy would become a barrister and the other a doctor. They would be eminent, wealthy. And as you were only a girl, your task was to marry a rich man. Because you were beautiful, and proud, and silent, displaying your beauty shyly, knowing its worth, her wish came true, and you were married to my father, Max. You've never said his name without a form of reverence in your voice. He was something other, my father. He was, in your own words, in your low voice, simply divine. You were married in London, swathed in satin and lace, gleaming and disguised. You were nineteen. I keep the photograph in my wallet. Even though you were a beauty, it was what your mother called a match. Max came from a 'good old-fashioned' family, he was handsome, he was rich. He was a made man, something in publishing. He was fifty when he married you. You have never described it as your marrying him. He had had many mistresses, many affairs, but he married you because you were pure. That was how you rather coyly put it. He was only faithful to you until I was six months old, less than two years. You tried to bear it, you bore it until I was three, and then you left him. You were a silly romantic girl, your words, and you left him, and you came here with me. You never asked him for money. I think you thought it would be vulgar. I think you believed he would follow you. Instead, he was busy losing most of his money, gambling, and he had no wish to see either of us again. You still chose to adore him. You chose it, I think, because some part of you knew that if you hated him, it would destroy you. You would have no reason to go on living, because your marrying him was the only thing that defined you, that you believed you had ever done for yourself. You wrote to your mother for money; she sent you secretly what little she had, and you dedicated yourself to a life of mourning. From the earliest age you instilled in me the glamour, the utter desirability, of the unfaithful man.

You told me about the house where I was born near Kensington Gardens, how you used to push me along by the Serpentine in my pram, that I was the most beautiful baby the world had ever seen: green-eyed and dark-lashed like him, like my father, like Max. From you I inherited the full mouth and dark colouring, the pinks and browns of my face; your face, my face, it doesn't matter. You told me that as a baby I had terrible tummy-ache and couldn't bear it if you put me down, so you held on tightly to me almost all the time, 'as if you were a teddy bear'. My daddy was away at work, and so we'd lie in bed dozing together in the mornings in that Kensington house. You'd lose yourself in the sunny patterns on the walls and make plans. You'd gaze at me. Eyes closed, I was the flawless mould of a perfect baby, wise and old. Eyes open, I was bewildered and alone. You stroked me and explained that this was the world (Kensington, to be precise), and you were my young mother and I was your all. Once I'd learned to recognise you and smile, you'd brush my face with your hair and stroke my nose, you'd kiss my ears and the unprotected part at the top of my head where there was no real skull. You'd stroke my little legs, my little penis and my little balls, and the bulge of my stomach tight with milk and wind.

Sometimes it was all too much for you when I cried and you'd push me through the streets in my pram, crying too, and everyone would stare. When I was older you pushed me under the blossom trees and you'd say, 'Look, blue sky. Look, blossom – look, birds,' and I'd kick my legs with violent excitement and you'd laugh. We had baths together. You liked me to be close to you all the time. You loved my father, but he was so old, so busy and tired, not the same as us, so preoccupied. He thought pregnant women were ugly and breast-feeding women worse. I liked your breasts much more than he did, so you attached me to them most of the time (which was quite unfashionable then. Fortunately, there was no one to interfere.) My father was busy seducing his secretary, as you were later to find out. You were much too young to have had a clue about anything then, you used to say.

Rocking me with your foot in my white-painted cradle, or asleep on the bed beside you, you'd sit up, pillows propped behind you, and write your stories, scribbling them frantically on the backs of envelopes and in the margins of newspapers and magazines – until at last you found the courage of your convictions and bought your first pad of paper just for yourself. You didn't have a typewriter until I was a year old and you'd sold your first story. 'We were never spoilt in those days,' you said. You couldn't cook so if Daddy's friends came for drinks and didn't go home (because you were so beautiful and they were so drunk), you'd make them scrambled eggs – until my father lost his temper and you began going out to restaurants, which you hated because you had to leave me behind. My nanny didn't understand me the way you did and left me alone far too much, you said. As soon as I could walk I toddled everywhere after you, my hands in your skirts, almost tripping you over (not that you minded, you said). Not long after that I toddled after you to France, which was heaven because we were always happy and together and no one else could come and disturb us.

You used to promise me though, whenever I was sad about it, that when I was a grown-up, handsome man, I would see my father again, and he would be so moved, so moved, he would – he would – what was it that he would do? I was never quite sure, but something like cherish me for ever, and never let me go. I would have dissolved into a happy ending. There would be nothing further to write down. I loved those evenings, your face in the lamplight, your golden brown, high-cheek-boned, high-foreheaded, wide-jawboned face, your brown eyes, so dark, iris and pupil the same colour dark, and your thick heavy hair. You didn't look at me very much. But I looked at you, honey-skinned, velvet-eyed, dark-haired mother. *My* mother. When you did look at me, it hurt, but it hurt in a perfect way. Your sorrow made you even more beautiful to me. It was so permanent, so enduring. Your gaiety, always short-lived, brittle, frightened me.

So there we were like two birds in a cage. You were my world and I was your creature. It was a very long time that we were like that, there in that rented house which I thought was our own, but because not very much happened, sometimes it seems like only a year. One year, where the patterns of the seasons, of our days, followed from one to another, simply, and the year just repeated itself over and over, beginning from when I was three and ending when I was fifteen, when you met Gerald, when the time that had Gerald in it, the time labelled with his name, began. It's not surprising that you met Gerald, even married him. What is surprising is that you didn't marry again earlier, when I was much younger. But then you have always been a surprise to me, a continual surprise. How did you meet Gerald? I don't remember, I just know that one day it was you and I, and the next, you and I and Gerald. All I remember is you coming back from Draguignan one afternoon in the car, April or May it must have been, and the sound of you slamming the door very hard, and walking quickly into the house, calling for me excitedly, your shoes going tap-tap on the stone floors. I was outside, and you called me in. I felt afraid, I remember that, as though something terrible had happened. You were carrying a parcel, tied with string, and you said, 'Alex, look, look, I've bought these beautiful sheets. They're for you, would you like to open them?' And you smiled, eager, a taut mouth, as if you were afraid I might suddenly become a naughty child and start kicking and screaming, as if you had forgotten that I was fifteen. I didn't say anything, but took the parcel from you, and you said, 'The sheets are for you, so you can have your own bed, your own room, now you're a grown-up boy.'

'But I've always slept with you.' You sighed a sharp little sigh, and shrugged in an ugly way, I remember that.

'I think it's time you had your own room now. You can choose which one you want, but the one down the passage will be the best. It looks over the view, and it's the largest.' There were three other bedrooms besides hers, upstairs. The one she had chosen was the one furthest away from her room. I didn't understand her. I knew it was important to her, to hurt me, and turn me away, though, so I just agreed with her, I mean with you. I agreed with you, and that was that. But that wasn't the beginning. I'm confused. You must have met him before that. I

can't think why or how. Yes, I do – of course I do. He was a
journalist, and he had come from London to interview you
about your book. I haven't written anything about your work
yet, but that was how it happened, and he was staying at a
hotel quite far away, near the sea. He was lanky and tall, and he
wore glasses. He had a loud, explosive laugh. He came and
took you away with him in the car. He had a bottle of vodka in
the glove compartment and he used to drink from it. He
offered it to you, but you said no, you told me. Your serious
drinking hadn't started then. You laughed at everything he said
and everything I said at that time: as if you'd suddenly made a
discovery, and it was that nothing mattered, and that you were
alone, and it was all incredibly funny. You started to feel alone
when you met Gerald because of how much he wanted you. It
was distorted, his desire. Only my love has ever made you feel
good, part of something, right.

He tore you away from me. He ripped you away from me,
but you started it. It was what you wanted, as though our
twelve years together had been a private interlude that you
could end without my consent whenever you chose. My life
had been an episode for you. I was, 'The time I lived alone in
the South of France with my son Alex. It must have been until
he was about fifteen.' I don't know if you would now say, 'I
was very unhappy then,' tears in your voice, or whether it
would be, 'We were so happy, it was such a peaceful time.' I
don't know what you would say now, Mother. Imagine it.
Imagine I'm a stranger and tell me what you would say. All I
know was that it was a tawdry affair. You were another chaste
beauty for another middle-aged man, the only difference being
that you knew that then, and that's what made you laugh. It
was a pretence at cynicism, knowing the world. What you
really were was disappointed and tired of being alone. You
didn't love him, not for a second, I'm sure of that. I endured
the nights without you without complaint, listening to the

night sounds from the hills, from the trees, because that was what you wanted, and I wanted you to be happy. I was very cold under my new sheets, I remember. I remember shivering with cold. The room held no memories for me, no treasures. You'd bought me a washstand and a picture of a bunch of flowers. My evenings were lonely. I lived for the mornings, when I could run to the village for the bread for your breakfast, and bring you your tray, when I would see your face again. All those morning rituals became fast, frantic, because I was so desperate to end the time without you. Sometimes it was too early, and you would turn over in bed with a sigh, and say, 'Come back later,' and I'd sit down on the stairs with your tray on my lap in despair.

All the time: weeks, months, I don't know, I didn't know Gerald. He was just a tall man who came and took you away in the evening, and who brought you home late at night. I don't think he ever got out of the car. I don't remember being introduced to him. If he stayed I don't remember hearing his footsteps on the stairs, your quiet laugh, the opening and closing of your bedroom door. I don't remember any of that, although it must have happened. He must have stayed for secret waking hours. But he didn't take your sleep, your sleep which had been mine and only mine. I didn't know what a lover was. I didn't know what a lover did until ten o'clock one morning when I went into your room without knocking, went in with the breakfast tray, backwards, pushing the door with my hip. I didn't knock because it was so late, and I was impatient, and wanted to see you, and you had overslept. Turning, holding tightly to the tray, I saw you both, Gerald and you, sit up in bed, as fast as puppets, jack-in-a-boxes; you, cotton and lace, you, I didn't look at, but only sensed; it was him, his bare narrow chest and frightened eyes, it was Gerald I discovered. You said, 'You should have knocked,' and he said, 'It's quite all right.' He had a hoarse voice. The air smelled of

16

cigarettes. I think he said, 'Now's as good a time as any,' or something lame like that.

'Alex, you must meet Gerald,' you said, 'I'm going to marry him.' You smiled at me. I stood there, holding the tray, your servant, your silent servant. You got out of bed and took the tray from me and put it on the dressing-table, moving to open the shutters, just a few inches, and I stood there, looking at Gerald, who was looking now at you, and you said, 'Run along, darling, I'll be down soon,' as if he wasn't there, except you would never have spoken to me like that if we had been alone. I turned and walked down the passage to my room and you said something I couldn't hear, and he said, 'Quite the little ragamuffin, isn't he?' and you murmured something else. I don't remember what happened after that. I think he got dressed and went away. I don't remember him staying.

You told me only a few years after that that you had never thought about marrying Gerald until that moment when I came into your room and found you. You had felt so ashamed, as if you had committed some adultery, and the only way you felt you could be justified in having this stranger in your bed was if you had been going to marry him. No minor infidelity would do, no small adultery was worthy of either of us. It was the first thing that came into your head, that's all I know. I don't remember thinking of you at that moment, which was rare because I never thought of anything else as a child. It was my own pounding rage and trembling, the physical feeling I had, of passion and anger and no thought. I couldn't speak or move. If I had been older or younger I would have rushed at him and tried to hit him and kick him and hurt him, but because I wasn't a boy, because I was nothing (a ragamuffin), I did nothing. Alone I stood at the window and looked at the hillside and cried, and I hung my head and put my hands over my eyes and mouth and made no sound. I felt as if I were nothing. You made me feel as if I were nothing.

Thin, pale, tall, stooping Gerald came and took us in the car
to the sea. He rolled back the top of his car and the wind blew
the dust from the road in our faces. It was a bright June day.
You wore a chiffon scarf and no makeup. Your face was brown
and clean-looking. I wanted to kiss it. Gerald wore a hat, a
beaten-up Panama hat and a white linen shirt, as if imperson-
ating an Englishman abroad. The shirt was open at the neck,
he had hair on his chest that was grey. His chest was narrow
and the place where his shoulders joined it, around the
collarbones, was hollow. He looked gaunt, and he didn't smile.
He always seemed preoccupied by some intricate, painful
problem. At the beach the water was calm and still. We had
brought our picnic basket: hard-boiled eggs ('How English,'
he said) wrapped in a napkin, and salt and pepper in paper
screws, and bread, and meats, and cheese. Peaches. A bottle of
wine. We had a dark blue parasol and a tartan rug. You spread
his towel on the sand for him. I think that was one of the rare
things I've ever seen you do for another person. You wore a
bathing dress. Bikinis hadn't reached our little life. You lay
together in the heat, in the sun, moving into the shade as the
sun became hotter. I lay beside you, bare, in the sand. I knew
you wanted me to swim or walk along the beach to the rocks
and out of sight but I couldn't leave you. I wanted to
understand.

'What a beautiful life this is you have,' said Gerald. Did he
think this was how we usually spent our time? You said
nothing, lying on your stomach, gazing into the sand. 'A
wonderful place to grow up in,' he said to the air, squinting up
at the sky. He sat, his hands around his knees, in a knot.

'It will do, for now,' you said. This hurt me very much. You
hurt me very much, again. I closed my eyes. A breeze came up
from the sea.

'You'll be wanting to go to a proper school soon,' he said. I
think he did look at me, that time. 'So you can have a

profession,' he went on. You continued your examination of the sand.

'I'm going to be a poet,' I said.

'Oh, I see.' He emphasised the 'see' in an insulting way. Do you remember, Mother, how we used to talk about it? You had said how hopeful it was of me. That was exactly the word, and you pronounced it with a little lilt in your voice, you lifted the word.

Now you said, 'It's a difficult way to earn a living. Do you want always to be poor?' And you sounded so anxious, Mummy, anxious and sad. 'I don't.'

'You won't be marrying me for my money,' said Gerald, moving his hand to touch your cheek. I could not speak. I must have seemed so stupid. I couldn't play the game. You played it, though, Mother, didn't you? In that glare, which shimmered on the water, I walked away over hot sand, and straight into the sea, and swam out, hard. I had always paddled, and ran in the shallows, and watched you watching me and laughing, but that was a different time. New rules, new ways. From the deep water I could see you both talking, first languidly, then you sat up and turned towards him. You put your heads together, that is quite literally what you did. Gerald glanced out at me, but you didn't. More laughter followed and you put your face up to the sun, and closed your eyes, tilted back your head. Strange days.

In the car on the way back I said, 'Are you really going to get married?'

And he took your hand, and trying to catch my eye in the rear-view mirror, said, 'Yes.'

You didn't say, 'I hope you'll like it,' or 'We thought we might.' You didn't promise me anything. You didn't soften your will, your new desire, your new plan. There it was. You only said, 'Yes,' just as he had, 'Yes.'

You went to Draguignan to get married, to the *mairie*. You were ashamed to do it in front of the people we knew, in the village. He wanted to do it right away, but you delayed because you were so particular about the dress. Your mother had chosen your first wedding dress. You wanted this one to be yours. No white silk or satin, this time, no lace. In your excitement you were like a child who wanted a dress to make you an adult. There was a dressmaker in the village with whom you had earnest exasperated conversations. Gerald went to Paris and came back with magazines and dress patterns which you crumpled up and threw away, but you spent hours with the pictures from the magazines, hours and hours and hours shut away in your study. Your beautiful low voice became very clipped when you spoke to me, if a drawl can become clipped, and you hurried around the house as if you had a great deal to do. You had a tiny child's frown when you looked at me, or spoke. I was a trouble to you. It worried me how much I seemed to pain you, so I tried very hard not to do anything wrong. I was as polite as I could be with Gerald, who seemed to have taken up a permanent position on the terrace, reading or just staring into space. He went back to his hotel in town after supper to sleep (he was getting nearer and nearer like an inevitable disease), and to write the column he had begun to send home. I was as gentle as I could be with you, and I left you alone with him, going out for whole days with my notebook and pencil and eating a bread and cheese lunch on the hill. Either that or I was at school. But it didn't work. I couldn't please you because I couldn't disguise my suffering and that hurt you. You have always been far too sensitive, Mother. So you ignored me, and concentrated only on the dress. In the dress you invested all your hopes for the future. Into the line of the dress across your breast and waist and the length of your leg, you believed your future to be entrusted. It seems odd to me that you had any hopes for the marriage at all.

But you did, and even though your wedding was a personal disaster to me, I cried at the sight of you in that dress because you looked so young, and it was such a skimpy thing. After all, it was 1965, so there need be no smart little suit for you. I remember its scooped low neck, its flared bias-cut skirt, its bold silver-grey colour and cobweb feel. Do you remember the bouquet I made you of cornflowers? I wanted red roses but didn't know where to get them, and I didn't want to ask anyone to find them for me. The flowers were a private, a strictly private, present. You looked like a girl. My girl-mother, your hair untidy in the breeze, exuding a vague sort of glamour, a strained glamour. How I could have kissed you and clasped you in my arms.

The night before the wedding you asked me to come to bed with you, 'Because I'm afraid.' I changed the sheets first, so they were clean and new. We laid the dress out on your chair that night and the silk stockings, and put your mother's pearls to hang from the mirror on the dressing-table. I brushed out your hair for you and we didn't speak. We packed your case for your wedding night: new nightdress and dressing-gown, folded in tissue paper with a sachet of our own lavender, a dress for the next day, your shawl. In the morning we added eau-de-Cologne, rosewater, all your private things, and your tortoiseshell brush and comb. It was a strange ritual, but right that we should perform it together. Through most of the night we lay awake in bed, dry-eyed, without touching. I don't know which of us felt more afraid, which of us more power-less. Is it that if someone wants you, Mother, you have to surrender? Is it that your mother's teaching bites so deep that you entice a man, out of reflex, according to how you were brought up, and then you marry him, because that's also what you were taught? Those weren't the questions I wanted to ask you that night. Mine were simpler: why are you leaving me, Mother? Don't I make you happy any more? I hardly dared move at all that night because I was afraid you would know what a helpless witness I was to your fear. You already knew about my grief. I couldn't hide that from you. Before he had come, if you were afraid in the night, or suffered, I would hold your hand, or put my arms around you, bury my face in your hair and murmur nursery rhymes to you that you had once whispered to me. If it was very bad you said you had a pain in your heart, and I would put my hand over your heart and try to soothe the pain away. All those things I could have done that night, but I didn't dare do any of them. I don't know why, but I shared your paralysis, just as I had always shared your restless, agitated nights, as a little boy. I would have given anything to make the next day go away, but I couldn't. We waited, quietly, for it to approach, and when it arrived, we went to meet it.

Gerald sent a taxi to the house to bring us to Draguignan. The wedding was at noon. We had swallowed a little coffee but couldn't bring ourselves to eat. I had not even gone to fetch the bread that day. You stood on the stone floor of the bathroom, and I washed you with a cloth, carefully, very slowly. The sun streamed in. You held up your hair so that it didn't get wet. You were shiny with soap and water. Outside the window no birds sang. The wind was getting up, that whistling August wind, the mistral, it was beginning. You shivered and I patted you dry. I dressed you in your cobweb dress and your shining shoes, and again I brushed out your hair. The sky had darkened by then. I sat on the bed while you powdered your face and you put the colours on your cheeks and mouth, the greys and blacks on your eyes. All my life I have loved to watch you make up your face. It is like a glorious game, and it makes you feel more mine, always, because I witness it. I wore a white shirt and a tie, and a dark suit we had bought together.

'You look ridiculous,' you said. 'You look like an undertaker.' It was quite true, I did. The wind lifted itself around our little house, encircled it, surrounded it, as we waited for the car. All our lives, Mummy, we have been early, because you taught me there's nothing worse than being late. You smoked a cigarette. We closed all the shutters and locked all the doors and stood on the front steps, you with your suitcase beside you, like a child being sent away to school, me the stern parent, grimly undergoing the farewell, holding an incongruous bunch of flowers.

At Draguignan the leaves shivered on the trees. There was more dust. Gerald waited on the steps, a flower in his buttonhole. I gave you your cornflowers to carry. He smiled at you as we walked towards him, and he nodded at me, saying, 'How's our poet today?' I think I said that I was well. He took you by the elbow, and you hardly looked at him, climbing the steps carefully, as if you were injured and trying not to fall. I followed behind at a respectful distance. He seemed very tall that day. The actual ceremony was extremely short. There was confusion when I had to run out into the hall to find witnesses – two officials – and bring them in. I wasn't sufficient witness for it to be legal. I stood behind you and wept as the business was concluded, your voice husky, saying the peremptory, 'Oui,' Gerald's flat and without emotion. I try to remember the room, even the man's face, and I can't. I simply can't. You gave me the flowers to hold while he put the ring on your finger, and I was still holding them when we walked out into the day. I never gave them back to you. I think I took them home with me. The sky was still darkened by the wind. We drove in Gerald's car to his hotel where we had lunch, oysters and champagne. Then you went upstairs to his room, and he followed after he'd said goodbye to me. I wanted to walk the streets and find a café and drink coffee and brandy, I longed to try brandy, but Gerald had arranged for the car to take me home, and I was still a child, so I obeyed. I didn't want to make things difficult for you. When you came back the next day you

23

were still drunk and did not want to meet my eye. After that, there were four of us: you, me, him, and the drink. The drink sustained you, even me, sometimes. Or we believed that it did, anyway.

So that was the end of us, of the love in solitude, all the drowsiness, the headiness of it. After the wedding everything felt sharper. There was no beauty in our life, it was bled dry. What we did together or said to one another was a violation of our sleepy life, its innocence, and every word between us in front of him was like a graceless little play. At the beginning you tried, following me with your eyes, pleading in the small things you did, the glances you gave me. You asked to see my poems, and where I had been on my walks. You consulted me about what music to play, and what book you should read aloud. You read to both of us. No longer was my head in your warm lap, your hand lying idly in my hair. My place was outside the circle of the fire and lamplight, closer to the window, a half-lit world of my own. Gerald fell asleep when you read aloud. It made him uncomfortable, I think, or maybe it was too comfortable, I don't know. Perhaps it was just that he was drunk. But every morning, every, every morning, I went to fetch the bread, just as always, walking in the mist, dew, sun, rain, and home to make the coffee for your tray. I didn't take it in to you any more, just knocked and left it outside the door like a waiter in a hotel. Gerald used to come down and pour vodka shots for you both into small glasses. It was his first action of the day. 'For the digestion,' he'd say. The drinking began at breakfast. At eleven it was pastis. At lunch, wine. After lunch, brandy, a sleep and then vodka, then wine and brandy again before bed. Sometimes you didn't come out of your room until lunchtime. The door would open, letting out the stale air, and you, heavy with sleep, with his touch, with his weight, with the drink, would stumble down the passage to the bathroom. He liked to drive away in the car sometimes, and be gone all day. He must have been drinking in the bars in Draguignan or even as far away as the sea and St Tropez. Even though he was gone you did not go to your desk to write, but to the terrace just as if you had been with him. I wish I could say that your slovenliness made me long for you less. It was true that I had no tenderness for you, that I was angry. But I still longed to lift the hair, damp with sweat, from your sour-smelling neck, and kiss the bone beneath the skin with all my strength. You'd stretch yourself as you drank, and sigh and groan as you had used to do in your sleep, and I wanted to go down on my knees to you and implore you, beg you, to stop. But I didn't. I left you there, alone, as you'd left me.

As I write this, I see you, my remote, fragile, extraordinary, beloved mother, I see you down those years and I realise how desperate you must have been. At twenty-two, to come to France, with a baby, a little child as I was then, to make the journey quite alone, to find the house, settle me in it, to look at it straight and say, 'This is it, this is what I have chosen and will endure.' You were desperate but you must also have had great courage to be alone in that first dusty summer world with just a child. Or perhaps it was because your fear of life with my father, any other people, was so great that it seemed easy, the stone house on the hill, the empty sky. If your family pleaded with you to come to them, you never told me about it. Certainly they never visited, and only the occasional letter came. You wrote dozens more than you ever received. The more I think about what you did the more extraordinary it seems, the less I can explain it. It would have made better sense if your craving for solitude had been that of a great artist longing to be alone to create. But it wasn't. Painful though it is, we both know your books weren't very good. I don't think they would even be published now: whimsical historical romances, riddled with poetic dialogue, anachronisms, false emotion. All the plots awkward reworkings of the ancient theme: damsel in distress, cruel but misunderstood hero, set amongst towers and bloody battlefields, treaties and masked balls. I have to tell the truth here, Mother, you had no talent at all. But how you loved it, shutting yourself up with your trite fantasies. For the real thing you read me Georgette Heyer and Barbara Cartland. We loved those books, thrilled to them. I still read them now, when I want to relax. Our rule was to read one Dickens, or Trollope, or Thackeray, followed by one romance. (You weren't keen on so-called 'serious' women writers. You said they were too angry.) We alternated them because you said we had a responsibility to the classics. That's what you said, a responsibility. I'm trying to work out whether you felt a responsibility towards anything else, but I don't think you did.

But I'm losing the thread. Where have I got with my story, our story, the story? Beautiful heroine cruelly rejects son for a loveless marriage to a wicked stepfather. Fills her bed with the tall body of the faintly ridiculous, drunken Gerald. Descends into alcoholism. That's about as far as I've come, isn't it? Did you marry him because he was good in bed? That honourable betrayal reason doesn't hold any credibility for me. I don't know. I must stop being so angry. I mustn't be angry with you. So we were married. You were married, I mean, and I, like Cinderella, cooked and cleaned for you both. There was quite a lot of cleaning up which I couldn't leave to Mathilde: vomit, ashtrays to be emptied, even stained sheets and clothes to be scrubbed and scrubbed by hand. I'm sorry to remind you, Mother, but there it is. And I was always running to the village for you because you had run out of drink, or wanted something special, brandy or an *eau-de-vie*.

You would have terrible rows after his drinking binges, when he stormed out and then came back. I think they were the only thing about your life with him you enjoyed. You ranted and raved (soft-voiced Mother), and threw things at him, and you called him a drunken lecherous bastard, a cheat, a bully, a coward. And he called you a bitch, *saloppe* (French swear words were also used), even a cunt. Then slobbering reconciliations and the slamming of the bedroom door. I won't detail these things. They demean you. At least he never hit you, I would have killed him if he had hit you. Hitting you was my prerogative, as your son. Forgive me, Mother, I know it was wrong of me, but you provoked me so, you made it hard for me to do anything else.

Do you remember how it started? An autumn evening, late September – you were on the terrace, it was quite dark and coldish, you wore a silk dress and your arms had goose-pimples. You never kept yourself warm. You had on the garnet necklace my father had given you, and you sat drinking, sipping a martini. I'd made it for you because I knew exactly how you liked it. (I kept the vodka in the pantry, as cold as I could.) I was making up the sitting-room fire, and had just got it going, when you called me outside.

'My precious, I want to talk to you,' you said. I felt uneasy about this term of endearment, but out I went to you, heart beating, burying my suspicions, and you reached out to take my hand. I stood over you, blocking the light from the doorway, which had shone on your face.

'Shall I bring the lamp?' I said. 'It's getting dark out here.'

'No. I want to talk to you,' you said, tightening your grip on my hand and looking into my face almost with yearning, a strong, swelling emotion. I should have gone away to fetch a chair, or sat on the floor at your feet, but I just stood looking at you. I was so moved, overwhelmed by your look and the chance to return it and touch you at the same time, with no Gerald there to watch us, or interrupt. You smiled at me. 'I'm so sorry,' you whispered. I had to lean closer to hear. (Such an old trick, Mother.) My heart expanded, I remember feeling that, and began to beat. 'None of this has been fair. All these changes.' It made me giddy because we were so alone.

'Your marriage,' I said, to make sure that that was exactly what you meant.

'It's so difficult for you.'

I couldn't speak. My mouth was dry. At last, I said, 'I miss you.' Letting go of my hand you reached up to me, and I stooped so you could put your hands on my face, which began to burn as my tears fell on your skin.

'Don't,' you said, 'Don't cry.' I touched your eyelids, the hollow of your eye sockets, your eyelashes, the firm skin of your cheek and the tip of your nose, and you smiled. I put my hands on either side of your face, bent down and kissed your mouth, your lips trembling and moving, opening like a rose. That was my first kiss. How else could I describe it but as the most tender, the most perfect moment we have ever shared? After we had kissed I smiled at you, knelt at your feet, buried my head in your lap, as I had always done, every day of my life, and you put your hands in my hair, as you had always done. We were quiet, quite still for a long time. I wanted to kiss you again, but did not dare. I wanted to stroke and kiss the belly where my head was resting. 'It's all right now,' you said, after some long time.

'Yes.' I stayed kneeling at your feet, my head in your lap.

'It must be all right between us,' you said, 'because I'm going to have a baby.' My ear was against your belly, the side of my head pressed against it, hard, as you said those words, as they vibrated through your body into the quiet evening. In my belly, your belly, that exquisite curve between bone and beautiful bone, lodged Gerald's child. I raised my head to look at you, and when you looked into my eyes, doubt, even fear, flickered there. 'Aren't you going to say anything?' you said, still trying to smile.

I got to my feet, and you stood up too, fast, and I said, 'How could you do this?' I was not angry then. Because you are magnificent, you didn't quiver or hang your head, but stood there, quite firm.

'Is it so terrible? A brother, or a sister, is it so terrible?' you said.

'Terrible? It's –' The only word was dirty. 'It's dirty.' Then I was angry. Then, I wanted to hurt you. You made as if to strike me with the flat of your hand, but I caught it, got hold of it, and I caught the other one. You were breathing hard and furious and I shook you, holding you by the wrists. I shook you and shook you, and you didn't resist me, I remember that, didn't try to hold yourself still. I gathered up your hands, I brought them to my mouth and I bit them hard. I didn't know what I was doing, but I kept biting you, in a fury. I bit you until I was sated. You didn't resist me or try to take my hand away. You gave in to my rage, let me play it out, hanging your head, unresisting. You must have been in pain. Perhaps you were so angry you didn't feel it, I don't know. You had no right at all to be angry with me, we both know that now. When I stopped and let you go we were both breathing hard. And as I looked at you, at your fearless eyes, defiant, your beautiful emotion, my fury subsided, and all I felt was tenderness. It seemed like a sickness, a frailty in you that you couldn't overcome, your marriage, your pregnancy. I wanted to bring you to your senses, but it came over me then that I was powerless, and I felt sick at myself. I had always protected you, made sure you were safe, and I felt I had to go on doing that however much you provoked me. We stood looking at one another, you rubbing your hands, one against another, and you said, 'I forgive you. Now disappear and leave me alone.'

Your slippery baby was never born, though I did see it. You had time to think about it and you knew what you had to do. Thank God I was on hand – as it were – to help you. It was really quite disgusting and I don't want to go into the gory details again. Suffice to say that you were lucky I was so devoted and prepared to help you out. I didn't lose my nerve even with you panicking and carrying on, awash with self-pity and coming out with all kinds of viciousness. The right thing isn't always the easy thing, however much you love someone. I hated to see you suffer – but, Mummy, you got yourself into that mess, and sadly there was no escaping the pain it caused us both to get you out of it. But let's not dwell on old quarrels. It was too long ago.

Sadly, Gerald knew what he had to do too. He approached me one morning after breakfast, shambling into the kitchen where I was washing up the things. He was useless at coming into a room. You must have been still in bed, you weren't well after losing that baby, not for a long time. He said something about a short walk, 'before it gets too hot', and would I like to join him. He talked as if he were imitating a nineteenth-century gentleman, which made me want to kill him. (Perhaps that was what you liked about him, his pretentiousness, perhaps you believed it. You've always been susceptible to the phoney and false, after all.) His eyes had a ghastly habit of constant flickering, as though he were trying to find something he had left somewhere, a bit like the eyes of the blind. He was sweating, even in the cool of the house, and his sweat smelled of alcohol. He hardly ever came into the kitchen because it was principally my domain – you used to laugh and call it my lair – and it shocked me to see him standing there, tall and stooped, as if I didn't know him and was meeting him for the first time. There he stood in his dirty shirt, his clouded glasses, his crumpled trousers, a dishevelled stranger who looked as if he had been walking for miles and sleeping in his clothes, looking for some precious lost thing. I almost felt sorry for him, felt sorry because he had no place with us, and I would never soften towards him, sorry because he had chosen the wrong woman, because I was stronger. I don't like feeling sorry. He muttered something more about the little walk, and I think I just went with him without a word. We stood side by side on the terrace looking at the sunlit morning hills and I almost forgot him, confronted by their beauty.

'You love it here, don't you?' he said, a clumsy attempt at disarming me.

'It's all I know.' I did not want to talk to him about the things I loved.

'You didn't think you'd ever have to share it all, did you?'

'I thought you wanted to go for a walk.' I set off away from him across the grass and down one of the scented scrubby paths, making sure that I chose one so narrow he could not walk beside me. The hill slopes down steeply, and I could hear him sliding a bit on the stones and loose earth, and swearing. I pretended I couldn't.

'I say, could you slow down a bit?' I ignored this, stopping only when we reached a small plateau where there was a smooth stone, a boulder. I turned and leaned against it, watching him scramble down, staring at his feet, the house above and behind him still closed.

'Would you like to rest here?' I said. The stone was already warm in the full glare of the sun. When I walked alone I avoided it, leaving it to the lizards, stopping only when I could paddle in a stream or sit under an umbrella pine and rest my back against it and look up at its branches and the sky. He sat down gratefully but I remained standing.

'Is this one of your haunts?'

'I'm not a ghost,' I replied. I must have sounded so adolescent.

'I used to be a great one for walking,' he panted, 'as a young man.' He wiped his forehead, smearing the sweat. His nose was red. 'I should have brought a hat,' he said, squinting at me.

I was sweating too, but I was young and brown and strong. I was part of it all. He was the interloper. 'Look, Alex,' he said, abandoning his attempt at a sympathetic wander around his subject, 'I love your mother very much. You know that, don't you?' I said nothing. 'And I'm trying to do my best for her. I'd like to do the same for you, if you'd let me.' I could have said, 'What do you have to offer me, or her? Nothing.' I could have said, 'I don't want anything from you.' But it would have sounded petulant. Instead, I counted to myself the length of the pause. I reached nine. He was so nervous, he plunged on. 'Even you have to admit that she was in a terrible state when we met. All that drinking –'

'What do you mean? She never drank until she met you!' He looked at me, and he looked as shocked as I was, but I hurried on, 'You've made her drink.'

'No, Alex, that's not how it is. You know that's not true.'

'What about all you drink now?'

'We drink, I'm not denying it, but not in the way she drank alone, when she'd pass out on the floor and you'd have to help her up the stairs. She's told me all about it – you don't have to pretend. She's very ashamed about all that, you know, she wants it to be different for you now.'

'What are you talking about?' I felt winded, weak in the legs and chest, and cold. He shifted towards me, and I sat down beside him on the rock.

'No son likes to see his mother so unhappy. I know you did your best for her, and I'm grateful. You've looked after her all your life, and that's difficult for a child.' His voice was horribly confidential, familiar.

'I don't understand you.' I said this slowly, as if he were an idiot. 'We were perfectly happy before you came. There was no drinking.' I had to tell him this, Mummy, because I thought I could correct him, make him understand how it really was. Now that I know more about alcoholics and their delusions I know that there was nothing I could have said to him, but then, ignorant and young as I was, I just thought he was insane. I didn't think it was a deliberate lie, designed to confuse me. I didn't think in detail about him, I thought about you and me and how we were living with this mad person and how terrifying that was. I wondered if he was trying to persuade you of the same things.

'It's natural for you to want to defend your mother. It's admirable. There's no need for us to talk about it any more now, or ever again if you don't want. Let's talk about you.' He seemed to be gaining a command of the conversation, of me, that I hadn't known he was capable of.

'All right.' I tried to sound calm, myself.

'You need the chance of a good clean start in life. This is wonderful here, it's superb, but you'll want more than this when you're older. A life of your own, friends of your own age, the theatre, concerts, art. Your life is just beginning. You need an education, so that your occupation, whatever it may turn out to be, is one of your own choosing.'

I looked down at my hands, scratched and rough. 'You're going to send me away, aren't you? And there's nothing I can do about it.'

'Try not to think of it as being sent away. Try to think of it as a chance.'

'Who's going to pay? We've never had any money.' He was surprised when I asked this question, but I knew he wouldn't be talking about it all so definitely unless he had the practical part all worked out.

'Your mother has written to your father.'

'My *father*?' This was unbearable. My father, distant, divine, mourned, of whom I was a constant and glorious reminder, he had been brought into our lives now, only as a way of separating us.

'Yes.' He had the grace to look – briefly – ashamed. 'And he

33

thinks it's as important as we do that you have a proper education.' My father, Max. It was like someone back from the dead, stepping, breathing, from the pages of one of our books. 'He's happy to bear the expense.'

'Will I meet him?' I wished I hadn't asked that question. I'd forgotten about him for so many years, but in that second I had a complete vision of him and I wanted it so much.

'I can't say. You must ask your mother.' Mother. I had forgotten you. Did you want me to go away, truly, in your heart? I wasn't going to ask Gerald that.

'You've worked it all out.'

'You'll be home for the holidays. This isn't done to make you suffer, believe me.'

'You want her for yourself. I can understand why,' I said. I stood up and moved away from him. 'When will I be going?'

'September – next month.' I started to walk back to the house, up the path, and he must have watched me, but he didn't try to follow. He wasn't as helpless as I had calculated so feebly. He knew he had me for an enemy, right then, but I'm sure it didn't matter to him at all. I thought about running into your room, going down on my knees to you and begging you not to make me go, but I knew you must have decided it all in your own heart, and you've never gone back on a decision in your life, however bad it was. The right or wrong of it has never affected you, it's always been your own strength of purpose that matters more. I would have been ashamed to beg you, I couldn't have. If you didn't want me, if I had failed you and you had decided to send me away, I had to accept it. You are treacherous, Mother. You think you are high-minded and honourable and I suppose that's true too. Certainly you are the hero of your own life, you've always made sure of that.

When I had to leave you – when the time came – I felt as if I were abandoning you, which was ludicrous, because it was the other way round. I was so used to caring for you. It had been my life, and I was so full of grief and pity. You seemed so helpless with that man bleeding you with his drinking and his lies. I worried about how you were going to manage, who would cook for you, who would keep order in the house. Gerald waved his arms around a lot and said you'd have to hire someone, and I asked whether my father would be paying for that, too. I wished he'd hit me but no one answered me – I got the big ignore. Later, you whispered something to me about Gerald being commissioned to write a book, memoirs of his life when he had been a theatre critic (another fat joke). You said that if it had enough rich and famous people in it, it would sell well. I couldn't imagine Gerald even being so much as nodded at by a star of the stage or screen, but you said something about his having been a 'celebrated wit' (what a pathetic expression), and invited everywhere, which was even more bizarre. I had a glimpse then of the context you'd invented for him, the London glamour you'd chosen him to represent for you in your exile. You had been a beauty. People had photographed you. Now you were getting fat, and looked – frankly – liverish and sickly, your skin sallow and your hair dull, you'd begun deluding yourself that Gerald would provide for you. I tried to tell myself that this wouldn't be how I would remember you when I was far away. I tried to believe that it would be your radiance and your languor, and the generous music of your voice. I wanted to remember you as the vision of loveliness that had once surrounded me, and belonged only to me.

The actual moment of parting, without a second alone, without one look or one kiss, is not even worth recording. You, standing in the sun beside the car, Gerald restlessly revving the engine, my eyes on your face, you looking now at Gerald, now at me, with a curious, blank expression, and as we drove away, turning into the house before the car had even turned the sharp corner and heaved itself into the road. I half expected that under the strain of such a cataclysmic separation as this I might just cease to exist, die suddenly from the violence of it. I think that might have been my last boyhood fantasy. After that the world was cold and real and unforgiving. Since that day you've only ever permitted me glimpses of the light.

I stayed at school until the next summer, waiting to hear from you. You didn't write me one word for nearly a year. At last a telegram, from Gerald. 'Your mother needs you. Come.' Hardly his best literary effort but thankfully one of his most succinct. I flew to Nice and you met me at the airport: a vision of beauty, exhausted, thin, sober.

'I think he's left me,' were your first words. 'God – it's so good to see you. You're so tall.' I'd grown taller than you.

'It's better than anything,' I said.

'He's been gone nearly two weeks now. I'm alone.' This, with a kind of exultation as if you'd accomplished a miracle. 'I got a telegram from him yesterday saying he'd sent for you.'

'Do you think he'll come back?'

'It would be far better if he didn't.' You said this looking over my shoulder nervously, as if searching for an image of him. I was afraid to ask you more. 'But I don't want to talk about him.' You focused on me. 'Let's talk about you.'

I sat at your feet beside the fire – the July evening was cool – which meant that I had to sacrifice looking at your face for the comfort of being so close to you. We'd feasted but I have no memory of what we ate.

'I expect you'll fall in love soon,' you said. 'Sixteen – it's about the age.' You were drinking wine, but only sipping at the glass.

'Why do you say that – as if it didn't matter to you?'

'Of course it matters, darling. I was simply saying –' I turned round so I was on my knees before you.

36

'You're teasing me.'

'Yes, I'm teasing you,' you said, and smiled. In the light of the fire your face was flickeringly clear to me. You were smiling, but you looked sad. I could have said so many things to you. I could have said, 'I'll never leave you, Mother,' or 'I'll love you always,' but I sensed that nothing I could say would be enough. It made me feel half angry, half glad that I understood you. 'You were born wanting the impossible,' you said.

'What makes you say that?'

'Because I want the impossible, too.' You leaned down towards me and I reached up to touch that part of your collarbone which your necklace left uncovered as it separated itself from your skin. You shivered when I touched you and closed your eyes. It wasn't easy at all, it was difficult. Were you to gather me up or should I pull you to your knees in front of me? Kissing your neck made me cry. I knew you were moved.

'Tell me you'll always love me and never leave me,' you said.

'I'll always love you. I'll never leave you.' The words tumbled out.

'I love you more than – Take me to bed.'

I'd thought I wouldn't sleep at all, but I slept deeply. The moon shone outside, the creatures moved in the darkness, the clouds hurried across the sky, but we didn't move, you and I, because we were complete. It was a sleep of the dead, with no dreaming, shutters tight shut, door tight shut, you and I wrapped up. When I began to hear sounds I thought they were in my head, a dream, like a giant's footsteps, the heavy monster of dreams, pounding up the stairs and against the door. I stirred and turned, burying my head in the pillow and you. I licked my lips and they tasted of you. The air I breathed smelled of you. In the dark there was a monster's roar and a sudden weight on my chest, in the dark a hand groping over my face. I was awake. Gerald was on top of me, astride me, pulling me from my side on to my back, scrabbling at my face with his hands and scratching at it. He was breathing and wheezing uncontrollably, uncontrolled. You must have woken beside me, but I don't remember that. I could hardly breathe. He kept panting.

'You fucking little bastard,' he shouted. 'She's *my* wife.' He put his hand inside my mouth, as if he were going to put his fingers down my throat. I bit him, but that just meant he started to pummel me with his fists in the side and head and kidneys and I couldn't defend myself. I didn't even try to throw him off. I don't know why I felt so weak, as if all my body were water. He didn't pummel me for very long before he seemed tired and sort of slumped on me as if I were a lilo in a swimming-pool. Thank God he was drunk. You must have started screaming by then, but I can't say I'll ever remember. You were on your knees, trying to pull him off me. Eventually you ran round to my side and stood there while together we pulled him away. He appeared to have passed out. Shaking, you held on to me, feeling my face and chest and saying, 'Are you hurt? Are you hurt? I'll kill him for this,' and I, shuddering, said, 'No, no,' and you lit the lamp. Gerald the dishevelled was passed out across the bed and my face was scratched and bleeding. Not a pretty scene but no disaster either. You clung to me, but you didn't cry, just questioned me.

'What are we going to do now? He knows about us, he knows.'

I said, 'Why should we care?'

But you wouldn't let it go. 'How could he come here, how could he hurt you?' as if it were all an amazing, unlikely, extraordinary thing; instead of what it was, understandable, inevitable.

I tried to make it real, I tried to shock you out of it. 'How does it feel to be fought over?'

'Don't joke, it's disgusting of him, vile. How dare he?' You were trembling and cold.

'It's all over now. Come here. I'm going to dress you.' I put your nightdress back on and your ancient cashmere cardigan (how I love it) and some socks. Patient, sad, shaking, you submitted. I knelt down and patted your knees. I couldn't resist kissing the inside of your thighs. 'I love it that you're mine now,' I said.

'What's the matter with you?'

'It's all right. He won't wake up.' I could have pushed you back and climbed into you again only a second later, but you were sharp, your voice like a scandalised maiden aunt's.

'No. Come on, darling, no.'

'Soon?'

'Soon.' You pulled your nightdress down in a quaint sweet gesture. I kissed each foot once and promised you I'd be sensible.

'You mustn't be afraid,' I said. 'He's sleeping it off. He'll be sorry when he wakes up. We'll go downstairs and have coffee. We'll feel better.' But we didn't do any of those things. You stood up, determined. You pushed me, backwards, out of your room. I only had time to say, 'So is that it? You'll take him back?'

You frowned, squinted at me, past me. 'He's my husband,' you said.

It was only a few hours until morning and I didn't sleep but sat up staring and longing for you in a way I never have done before or since. I just wanted to be in you, with you, in that adolescent way, that desire which is purely a longing for oblivion. But enough philosophy. I say now I'm sure I didn't sleep, but then it's entirely possible I'm wrong. Certainly there are gaps in my memory. I could have dozed. The next thing I remember properly is the sound of your tears, and my heart yearning to comfort you. I wanted to press the backs of my hands against your eyes, stop the tears from falling. That was my lover's instinct, but as the boy who had always looked after you, I knew exactly what I'd have done: fetched a cold flannel from the bathroom, wiped your helpless face, patted it dry with a clean towel. I knew how to comfort you and it seemed absurd that you wouldn't let me. But you stopped crying and I must have fallen asleep. I woke again to the sound of silence, but so fast and so completely that I knew there had been a noise. I didn't feel afraid any longer but elated without knowing why. Then the half-familiar, heard-in-dreaming sound came again. Bump, like a sack of something, a heavy load being dropped. Then shuffling, and a groan that could only have come from you. Out of bed in an instant, I was in the passage, black as night except for the shape of you, your back to me, candlelight coming from the open door to your room, your arms clutching the sleeping Gerald's ankles, pulling him towards the stairs. You heard me but didn't turn round, saying, 'I'm not having him in my room another second,' as if he were an ugly piece of furniture you couldn't stand the sight of.

'Mummy, it's late – why don't you wait till he wakes up?'

'No.' You were negotiating the right angle at the top of the stairs, your hot face tilting towards me. I couldn't see you clearly, but you seemed as confident and sure of yourself as a sleepwalker.

'Wait, let me take his arms, he'll hurt his head going down.' You said nothing, retreating down the stairs so his head slid towards the top step. 'You can't just pull –' I stood over him in an instant, as if I'd been catapulted. His eyes were open and there was blood pouring from what must have been the back of his head. 'He's hurt — let me –'

'No,' you said, yanking his ankles so his head went bump on to the next step.

'You can't just –'

'It's too late – he's dead.'

'What?'

'I killed him.' The hem of your nightdress had blood around it. You were panting like an animal but your expression was bland. 'Got to get rid of him now. You can help me.'

'He's bleeding on the stairs.'

'Don't care – don't want him in the house ever –'

'All right. But first – just wait.' I ran to my room, took the pillow-cases from my bed and tied one around his head like a Mrs Tiggywinkle bonnet. While I did it I felt a rush of joy. There was no doubt about it, my sworn enemy was dead.

'You're wasting time.' You pulled him down the steep steps, stopping at the bottom to wipe your forehead. 'I'm hot. You weren't meant to wake up until I'd got rid of him.' You were out of breath.

'Now what?'

'I don't know.' Gerald in his little red bonnet was crumpled and incongruous, more ill at ease than ever. You smiled a little smile at me, and almost shrugged your shoulders. 'I was going to throw him down the hill.'

'He'll be found.' You didn't seem to understand this.

'Let's just get rid of him. No one will think any –'

'Yes, they will. We'll have to take the car.' I don't know why neither of us got dressed. If we'd had any sense we would have done. You in your nightdress, and cardy (you'd taken your socks off), me in my night things, barefoot. It was too unexpected. If you ever murder someone again, Mummy – give me fair warning. It was that time of night when we could have been forgiven for thinking it would never be day. I was terrified because I knew that was misleading and the sun would come up before long. Leaving you standing by him, sighing irritably, I scampered to the car (thank God he always left his keys in it), and drove round to the front steps. I had the forethought to realise we didn't want him bleeding on the ground, and besides he was too heavy to carry any distance at all. He was incredibly heavy, even for both of us. We laid him down on the back seat, you got in beside me, telling me to hurry up. The car strained in first gear up our short steep driveway. The sound of that engine was the loudest thing I'd ever heard – will ever hear. It was cold, but we were very hot. It was peculiar – our hot hot energy – how clear it seemed, our purpose.

The road starts out flat, winding only slightly, hewn from the side of the hill. Going towards the village in the other direction the sight of it is superb, driving out as we were doing, it's all behind you, so there was only the road and our breathing. We had to wait until the village was well behind us and the road began to drop steeply, coiling back on itself on the way down to the next village. The drop was on the left and we were on the right so we had to choose a blind corner where drunken Gerald might have swung out, only to lose control and career off the road into the pit. After all, it was an accident waiting to happen. It had happened before, cars had come off that road before. We drove in silence, only our sidelights on, the one and only car, ours the only light in all that country darkness, darkness that began to soften horribly as the minutes passed.

'Are you going to make sure the car burns?' you asked me, in a remarkably detached way. As if I'd know – as if I had all the answers and were in control. Didn't it cross your mind that I had no idea how to make it all look real, convincing, justify your faith in me? All I knew was that there had to be a fire or we were doomed. At the first respectable hairpin, we stopped, parking the car across the road, which was dangerous enough. I dragged the increasingly hideous Gerald out of the back seat, with your help putting him over my shoulder like a baby being burped, then deposited him in front of the wheel.

Blood continued to seep from his head – we took away the soaked pillow-case. I got hold of him by the hair and slammed his head against the steering wheel a good few times. I got the vodka bottle out of the glove compartment, emptied it on him (there wasn't much left), cracked it in half and gouged his chest where his shirt opened at the neck. If he were found it had to look real. One blow to the back of the head was nowhere near real enough. I did all this for you while you sat at the roadside, your head in your hands. It was strange to be pulping him at last, strange and not unpleasant. He'd had no right to you. He'd never had any right. Doing that helped me to understand that it was all really happening and it made me very happy.

The next thing I remember was the sound of the birds and your voice saying, 'Hurry – no more time.' In silence we tried to put his hands on the wheel, slammed the doors, let out the handbrake and we pushed that car over the edge of that road with our last remaining strength. It tumbled and crashed obediently. For a long moment I thought it wouldn't burn, but thanks to a rare stroke of providence, burn it jolly well did, with a ripping sound, a roar and a terrible smell. You took my hand and as we looked at it together I can't say I was sorry. 'How are we going to get home?' you said. We couldn't risk walking along the road in our bloody night things in the early light. We took the first path we found – thank God for all my wanderings, I knew how to navigate home the shortest way, and I did, you holding on to me, allowing yourself to be led. It was like being a bizarre kind of goat-herd. We found the house like an old friend in the wet morning, and you groaned going up the steps to the terrace while I went around the front to let you in. I hadn't locked the door. I wanted it to feel clean and undisturbed, but there was blood on the floors and I had to boil a saucepan of water and get on my hands and knees to scrub it up.

'No peace for the wicked,' you said, smiling, as you picked your way over the slippery stones.

'Take off your nightie – I'll burn it.'

You took it off and handing it to me said, 'Thank you for helping me. I'm going upstairs to lie down.'

'I'll bring you some coffee.' You didn't answer, just turned your naked beautiful back to me and went upstairs.

It was a deliverance. I'll never look at it any other way.

Last night I had a dream about you. We were standing on our hillside, the house behind us. We were holding hands. I knew I was there but I couldn't see myself, either naked or clothed. The sun was coming up, the sky was hard and bright, the birds were singing their hearts out and there were butterflies and flowers. You said, 'If this goes, everything goes,' and we gazed at it all in wonder. Almost as soon as you'd spoken, the sun opposite us began to sink in the sky, the trees and hills around us and in the valley below began to fall, as if the whole world was sinking to its knees, being crumpled like a piece of paper. The trees toppled, the earth quaked and dissolved and a tidal wave came up from the invisible sea. The sea was over the land. As all this began to happen, you pulled me by the arm and we flew away, sharply rising out of the chaos, hand in hand. Like angels we dipped and rose, dipped and rose, down to the surface of the water, and up into the sky, describing an arc like a rainbow across the horizon, but rising and falling, mingling with the falling stones and branches. The dark water became bright and transparent as we flew down into it and among the fish and coral and waving fronds of the sea. I felt complete and not frightened, holding your hand. I knew what it was like to fly – absolutely we were flying – and we were safe. This seemed to go on for a very long time and no time at all, until once more we were standing on the side of our hill and the other hills beside us and in the valley were rising out of the sea and taking their rightful place once more. The sun was rising, and a great bright calm came over us. You hadn't said a word to me but just kept hold of my hand.

They try to make me say different things about you: explain my scars. You and I were the only ones there together. You and I are the only ones who know what it was really like. Where my front tooth is chipped – that wasn't your fault – I tripped trying to drag you up the stairs becuase I didn't want you to wake up in the night and not know where you were – you hated that. We looked after one another. That's how it went.

The marks on my thumb – Kitty called them the roots of a tree – from dropping the frying pan with the potatoes and onions – also not your fault. We had to eat. I was too small to reach the stove and accidents will happen. The other scaldings were much more minor. 'Doing things you're not old enough to do again,' you'd say, kissing it better.

I'd get other people to help me. Mathilde's husband split the logs for me. Bringing food from the market was just a run up and down my favourite path. And I wasn't always busy. You couldn't always find me – I did day-dream. That made you angry – understandably – you were worried. I liked to explore the network of paths around the village, the little gates. It was a village under siege in my mind. I'd stand in the gateways and look up at the cold stone, the ribs and gargoyles, and pretend I was a sentry on watch. The village sat on the hill like the prow of a ship on a hundred-foot wave. On summer days the hot silence of the hillside would change to cold under the wide gates, on the shadowed streets, and it was cool under the plane trees of the narrow market. But the fierce heat always found me out in the end, just as the cold did in winter, so sometimes

I'd sit in the church and think. Everybody knew me. It was incredibly safe. I tried to explain that when you were terrified I'd come to some unidentified harm and so angry with me tooth and nail that I cried with terror. Cuts and bruises, pain, loneliness, fear, shame – they're part of every childhood. I don't know why people try to imply that mine was so extraordinary, so marked.

By myself, I'd name things. My favourite path – our path, I won't tell you what I called it even now – so green in spring, so green and steep and lined with nettles and brambles and those extraordinary scrambling roses which burst out at me every spring in a blur of colour so delicate that when I turned the corner and saw them each day – even though I was expecting them – they'd make me smile and want to brush my face in them. Roses won't let you do that – it's why they have thorns. They say, 'See me only, try to hold me with your eyes' – but it isn't possible. There's one particular pale pink one which used to tumble through the skeleton of a tree as easily as a weed. I loved that one and named it after you. Susannah thinks she's the only one who cares about flowers. It's not true – but how could I love an English flower after those?

There were very few other houses then. Ours was a ruin we made live. Now that the paradise is lost, Parisians are coming, even English, putting chi-chi apartments into the walls and renting out the 'villas' in summer. I'm sure you can't see that everything's changed yet but it's only a matter of time, and I fear it dreadfully. I'd never go there now. Why do people take the places they're given and desecrate them in a rush to give everyone a piece of the indivisible? A wilderness can't be conquered and bought and sold. It has to be inhabited, tenderly and gratefully, and treasured, then returned and surrendered. Estate agents and property developers – I could kill them all.

In all this world, I've always felt I'd be strong enough for anything, except the possibility of your death. Then – I've felt sure – my life would end. It's been the greatest of my constant fears. In spite of everything, thinking of you now still makes me feel safer. Now that there's no more Susannah and no more of the girl, it is just you and me again in my mind, and I don't have to apologise or hide anything from you. There may never be a return to the rain on the roof, no shutters, only bars, but I long to know, I do know, that somewhere in the world there's a room, with the old brass bed in it, the sheets of lace and cotton, the lost warmth and slowness and beauty, and you. Between us there is silence, the silence of having exhausted all the world and its people, and come home.

A Letter to Susannah

Is a memory something you have or something you've lost?

Darling Susannah,

I don't know why I use a quote from a Woody Allen film for you – you never liked his movies, funny or sad. You've no sense either of humour or of tragedy, no feeling for culture, but you were always forcing us to go and see everything (as if I didn't have enough to do in one day) in case it was mentioned at one of those interminable dinner parties we so rarely attended. Opera was the only thing I could stand because there was always time for a good sleep. But I'm being facetious. I love opera, especially when the heroine dies of something nasty and squawks with beautiful self-pity. Those have always brought tears to my eyes.

Darling – at sixteen you were such a sweetheart. My sweetheart, my girl in the black velvet hair-band, my girl with her heart-shaped locket for every day and her charm bracelet for best, Penhaligon's Bluebell and even lip-gloss but no eye makeup because that would have been an unforgivable sin. You were a tall girl, a long-legged girl, a slender girl, a fair girl. You never had beauty but you had fineness and grace. You had breeding. You were the first girl I ever called darling. Thrillingly, you were darling, the darling of delight. And I still feel delight when I think of you, because you are so fine. Even though I've found out such terrible things about you, I'm still immensely proud of you. After all, I won you, I won you for ever, past the happy ending into eternity. And I know it's conceited of me, but I don't think you'll ever belong to anyone else. I'll never love anyone else in the same way, with that feeling of unworthiness, awe. Even though, Susannah (in your own words), you were not clever, interesting even. It was your gentleness, *gentillesse*, as my mother persisted in calling it, but sweetness does just as well: it was that peculiar sweetness and goodness in you that would have made any husband of yours feel both honoured and ashamed.

You slipped through my fingers like water. I could never grasp you. I'm still furious about it. You said you were mine to have and to hold but I think you lied. Not on purpose, of course, you'd never have lied on purpose. I used to look at you, and wonder who you were, feel your strangeness. I'd say, 'What are you thinking, Susannah (tasting your name), feeling? What's happening in your heart, now?' You'd smile and say, 'Nothing,' or if that failed to satisfy, you'd blush and say something like, 'I was just wondering how strong that new rose of mine might really be on a north wall.' That was your one passion, gardening. I've chosen the word passion carefully. You weren't passionate about me, ever – or anything human, unless you count the boy. I'll admit freely that I've never felt any passion for you, I didn't think it was necessary. To quote you, 'I didn't think it would do at all.'

I wish I could forget how you took the hopes of my youth and trampled on them, and remember only how proud and delighted I once was. I could feel very happy and not so cheated any more. I will make an effort and try. Let's remember our first meeting, shall we? To quote another one of your girlish expressions, 'Oh, do let's!' It was the autumn after I came back from France. I was seventeen. Mummy had said that we had not left the stone house for ever, but I knew that we had. She would never live there again after what had happened and I felt a kind of revulsion at the cliché of it all as we drove away and I couldn't see the road ahead for tears. We didn't have many things, most of them had been sold to pay the debts, hers and Gerald's. She'd laughed and said that now we were gypsies again, as the men came and took away the furniture and I strapped our remaining possessions on to the roof of the car. A procession of villagers came to see us off and I had to make sure there wasn't too much crying. People pressed our hands silently and there were no promises made. She swore she wouldn't let the house go but I knew I'd have to put my foot down with her once we got back. Then I was too tired, absorbed in keeping her supplied with *vin rouge* and vodka from the passenger seat all the long drive back to England. I still spoke better French then than English, but my father had managed to get me into the right sort of school and had written to say that he would continue to pay. Mummy would be stuck in some family cottage in Shropshire until I could start earning money to get her out of there. They wouldn't speak to her though, furious with her for squandering her tiny inheritance and shaming the family name through drink and my stepfather's death, a source of mystery and scandal. It was a mess.

We met at the races. My new friend from school – Oliver the incredibly rich and amazingly popular – took me on one of our exeat weekends. We were going to meet some friends of his and there would be girls. Oliver said I'd be a hit with the girls because I was so good-looking, and that would make things easier for him because my glamour would rub off. I felt guilty that I'd avoided going to see Mummy – I just couldn't face it. School was bad enough without home at the end of it. We went to Chepstow races, 'Which are actually in Wales,' Oliver said, and it rained all the way there. We didn't have anything to eat but drank whisky out of his flask, fantasising about ham sandwiches, steak and kidney pies, and fruit cake. We couldn't see out of the car at all and had to drive so slowly we missed the first race. I've never been interested in horses, but I liked National Hunt racing straight away because it was so different from Ascot and polo where all you did was parade up and down admiring the women and showing off. Here there was mud and a fug in the bar and strange people with peculiar noses which looked as if they were putty attached to red-veined faces, and everyone had waterproofs and the horses steamed when they sweated. I wouldn't like it now, but then it was new and different so I got carried away, betting and losing and laughing. By the fourth race my hands were feeling raw but I was still absorbed in the ritual of pre-parade ring, paddock, race and the final twirling of the horses on their silver hooves when the jockeys dismounted in the winner's enclosure and everyone clapped. Oliver's friends were a crowd of people in hats and old Barbours and you were one of them. You had a red nose and I couldn't see your blonde hair because it was tucked into your collar, but I could tell that you were slender and tall and I noticed you concentrating on the horses particularly (because you were so shy), and talking in an inaudible voice to Oliver about their conformation. The sound of your voice was low, almost languid, even the interest in your eyes couldn't force you to hurry your speech, trip over your words. I think we watched from the stand and your horse came third and after it had passed the post you sneezed and I said I'd offer you my handkerchief but I didn't have one.

'You're catching cold. Let's go into the bar for a drink.'

'I'd rather stay here,' you said. Very uncharacteristic of you to disagree with me, when I look back. I went to get Oliver's flask, and when I poured you a measure you drank it quietly, looking down. I wanted to get you by yourself so I suggested going right down to the fence to watch the last race. Everybody else was complaining about the cold and rain so I knew they wouldn't want to come. 'I'm game,' you said, and smiled. I remember taking you by the arm – quite unnecessary – and guiding you over the slippery grass quite a way from the stand down by the rail. The only other person there was a photographer standing mournfully next to his shooting-stick and gazing into space. There was hardly any wind or rain by then, but everything was wet, and the trees in the distance looked soft even though they were bare. 'You're not wearing a hat,' you said.

'I like weather,' I said. I think I started telling you all about France and the wind and rain and snow and how I liked to be out in it, and the rocky paths and the winter cold. You looked at me carefully.

'But you live here now.'

'Yes. I wish this bloody race would start.' I was looking around and stamping my feet.

'Are you always this impatient?'

'If I want something. Absolutely.'

'They're under starter's orders and they're off!' echoed the megaphone.

Oliver came stomping up. 'Can't see anything from here. Whose idea was this anyway?'

'Mine,' I said, and you laughed, which was a very musical sound. When the horses came up to the fence at last, fighting to win, and reaching for it in a flash that was so fast I wanted another chance to take it in – jockeys shouting, concentrating, horses stretched, pounding, colour and noise – I forgot every-thing, and turned to you as they galloped away with a sound that went into the earth under our feet, and I saw your face was white, elated but still, and as you looked back at me a feeling of calm mastered me, just for that second.

In the car on the way back I said to Oliver, 'Who was that girl? Susannah?'

'That's my sister. Hands off.' Then he nudged me, saying, 'Just kidding,' and we both laughed and started singing. Honestly, Susannah, I'd had no idea.

Autumn that year was particularly bright – blazing. I'd taken up cross-country running and used to run early in the morning before school, when the grass was still slippery with frost, and the twigs and leaves crackled beneath the thud of my feet. Breathing was a piercing pain that made me feel more alive, my cheeks and nose felt as if someone had cut them with a knife, my eyes watered and stayed wet with the beauty of it. I came to love those grounds, but it took a long time because there was no wildness in them, the wildness I'd loved. Every morning I ran through that monument to the Age of Reason, which made no impression on me of any kind at all. I was obsessed with you, and that was the beginning and the end of it. You didn't have to do or say a thing to prove yourself: I was hooked. It was not that I wanted what you had, I wanted what you were, the innocence of it. You made me feel my own lack. Meeting you had made me see for the first time how alone I was.

On that year's New Year's Eve, your house in Holland Park glittered with lights, they dazzled from every window, but no sound seemed to reach the street until the black front door was opened. I expected it to be a servant who opened the door, but it was Oliver. The servant stood behind him to take the coats.

'Hello,' he said. 'Come inside and have a drink.' He looked around, vaguely. 'I can't think where Susannah's got to.' It was late, and the party was already going. A huge dense Christmas tree towered over the long drawing room, reaching as high as the ceiling, and it was deep, almost touching the fireplace, hiding the road completely. Its thickness and darkness made it seem as if it were only one of many on the edge of a forest. It was gaudy with fluttering streamers and tinsel and ornaments of paper and glass, but none of these things made it any less wild. It was splendid. I stood there, contemplating it, feeling I had to be careful not to slip on the parquet floor. Oliver found me a glass, and asked me if I wanted to be introduced to anyone. When I said no, he stayed with me a few minutes and then went away to greet someone else. People were talking loudly and drinking champagne. When you're seventeen, you think it's a party like any other. Now I'm thirty-three, I know I saw a collection of soft-cheeked children in black tie drinking champagne and there's something comical about that. There were plenty of girls grouped together, not knowing how to stand up straight, wearing tight revealing dresses they seemed to wish they hadn't put on and were trying to ignore. I felt that they wanted me to talk to them but I couldn't move. There was no fire in the grate, just pine cones, stacked up. Perhaps your parents believed we couldn't be trusted with fires. Waiters came by with drinks on trays. There were sausages on sticks and cheese straws, smoked salmon. There were olives and pieces of cheese. In the back part of the room, on the other side of the folding doors (thick with coats and coats of cream paint – years' worth), long french windows revealed a garden decorated with fairy lights. I thought it looked like magic. To the side, against one wall, beneath an enormous oil painting of a dead animal, a long trestle table was being laid with a late supper. 'Late supper' was what Oliver had called it when he'd invited me. He'd said, 'Drinks, with late supper and dancing.' I remember deciding that the kitchen must be in the basement and wondering if the dining room was also down there or whether it was on the other side of the hall along with the library and morning room. I felt there had to be a library and a morning room. It mattered to me, to my idea of you.

But these peripheral thoughts were all distractions from the main idea: where were you? Where, Susannah, were you? As I stood there, my back to that vast Christmas tree, the french windows opposite me were flung open (there must have been eighty feet of marble from one end of the room to the other), and you appeared, the illuminated night behind you, laughing and shivering. There were two girls and a boy with you, a blond, stupid-looking boy. You were laughing, which was extraordinary. I had always pictured you as the tall, cool girl I had met and frozen into images that were still and peculiarly without life. I could hear you laughing and talking, excited and clumsy. Someone behind you closed the door. You had on a dark blue silk dress with big sleeves and a big skirt, terribly conventional, and a string of pearls. I think the dress was meant to show off your figure but you didn't really have one. You saw me and pretended you hadn't, which I took to be a very good sign. But before I could walk over and speak to you I was hit with an emotion, like a punch in the stomach, which made me feel giddy and brought tears to my eyes. I hadn't known how anxious I'd been to see you. I knew it mattered, but I hadn't understood how acutely. I felt panic because you seemed further away than when I was at school running in the woods, carrying you with me. I felt sickeningly aware of how much time had passed since I'd first seen you, a whole season. I knew you remembered me, but that was all I knew about you. The rest was meaningless. In that time of hesitating, some tedious boy I knew at school came over and, shifting his weight from foot to foot, started muttering about what a jolly good party it was. Then someone else appeared, and suddenly I seemed to be surrounded by all the shy people in the whole world. I felt unable to escape, inhibited because so many of the faces around me that night were familiar. I didn't talk to them at school, and wasn't going to start talking to them that night, either. The only ones who were interested in me were the boys who felt – rightly – that I was more glamorous than they were. Getting rid of people was a skill I hadn't yet acquired.

After what seemed like an hour, where the more champagne I drank the more clear-headed and despairing I became, I found myself in the supper queue.

'There are chairs next door if you want to sit down,' shouted Oliver. 'We'll dance after supper.' I wasn't looking forward to that. I didn't dance, as you know, still don't. I caught a glimpse of your shoulder in front of me in the queue, then your pale back as you carried your plate out past the tree into the hall. I felt unable to follow, despite catching a little glance – which I think was aimed at me – over your shoulder as you walked through the doorway. You were giving me all the right signals, and I was being an idiot. I had some vague idea that I would find you once the dancing had started, when I'd be protected by the noise. I made myself promise that I would, as I stood in one corner balancing my plate and wolfing down cold turkey and ham.

A little tap on my shoulder and your low voice. 'Alex? I thought it was you.' It was my turn to blush, blush and chew, turning to face you, while you smiled. You had the advantage. You were prepared.

I swallowed and said, 'Hello, Susannah.' I'm so busy always telling myself what you weren't: not beautiful, not clever, not brave, not strong, that I forget what you are, or at least, were to me then. In your serious eyes, there was light, the light they've always held for me and only me. It made me feel very moved, very large, very tender. I existed for you, I felt, I was real to you, I mattered to you. All I could say was, 'What a beautiful house.'

'Yes, it is, isn't it?' You weren't proud, you answered me automatically, agreeing with me as if it were irrelevant. You always behaved as if these material things didn't matter at all, while it was unspoken that you couldn't live without them. In that way you were inseparable from your context. I couldn't achieve one without the other.

'You look lovely,' I said – why, I don't know, I felt so wet, saying it.

'I'm pleased to see you again,' you said. I think I nodded. It was so brave of you to keep looking up at me. I remember feeling that.

'Could we go somewhere and be by ourselves?' I said, wincing at my clumsiness. 'I just want to talk to you.'

'Of course.' You took me to a room at the back of the house, across the shining hall. It was rather shabby.

'I've thought about you –' We stood close together, my back

to the door. I couldn't even wait to get into the room properly. I felt in a great hurry, as if we might be interrupted and you snatched away. 'Thought and thought.' I took hold of both your hands and you blushed slightly around the throat and neck as well as over your face. I couldn't believe that you weren't trying to escape me.

'So have I,' you said. I think I stroked your little cheek and your chin, and then I kissed you – not in fire or fever, not in a stealthy way – I kissed you as reverently as I could. I didn't think of that word then or even know it. You, timid, laid your cheek against my cheek and I touched your hair, and I felt a second of fullness, being where I wanted to be. You gave me an extraordinary trust. I think you laughed then, not a girlish giggle, or anything shy, you laughed and said, 'Now I've done it!' which I thought was charming. 'I think I'm meant to make it more difficult,' you explained, and I said, 'It's simple.'

You said, 'Hold my hand.' We walked to the window and looked out at the garden. The lights were still there, but there were no people.

It's always seemed strange to me that we left that room after that, threw away the privacy, the chance to be alone. I think it was because I didn't know what to say to you, what would be the right thing. I'd made the most important move, I'd kissed you, and I didn't want you to know me well enough to decide that you'd been wrong to choose me. Back at the party, you were ambushed by the crowd and, with your perfect manners, gave yourself up to it without any attempt to escape. I stayed close to you, either beside you or behind you. I was your companion that evening, we were in our private world, created out of separate fantasies, entirely our own, and everybody else was outside it. I can't describe what passed between us because it's impossible, but in the silence we both surrendered our most private dreaming selves to our idea of the other. It's a terrifying thing, the way lives are decided in seconds so short.

But I didn't think of that. I felt all-powerful and unbeatably strong.

I came back the next day: New Year's Day, my new life's day as I felt it to be. You opened the door with a pale smile and no words. You looked transparent-tired, exhausted-happy. There was a commotion of floors being swept and polished, carpets being hoovered, the scented stale air of the night being destroyed. You took me downstairs to the kitchen and made me a cup of tea. It was exquisitely mundane. Your hands, getting the milk bottle out of the fridge, stirring the tea-bag in the mug. I'd imagined it would be china and tea-leaves, but it wasn't, it was tea-bags and mugs.

'There's nothing to eat,' you said. I flattened you against the oven, kissed your hair, your face, your neck. 'I like your coat,' you said. I don't know what we talked about, sitting at the kitchen table, certainly nothing important. I found out many small things about you: you didn't like shopping for clothes, you didn't like seafood, you liked walking and riding, but not sports at school, you'd had a pony of your own (Thimble), your parents owned a racehorse, you hated having your hair cut, you didn't like crowds. Your A levels were English, French and History – all girls' were at that time. I wanted to find out as many things as I could, discover them quickly so I could think about them later, by myself. You were in the middle of packing to go away the next day. I didn't mind because I knew my longing for you would outlast any holiday that any parent could devise.

I was allowed to take you to dinner before going back to school. I had to borrow the money. That ghastly restaurant – full of those pinstripes and their wives – why did I take you there? We were children. Your black dress and pearls were too old for you. You said something about your parents not thinking I was a good thing. What a slight that was for Mummy, though I didn't show that I minded it. I tried to explain to you how extraordinary she was, and you said, 'I'd like to meet her.' (How like you, never to say 'love', when you can say 'like'.) You spoke calmly, without curiosity or desire.

It was awkward for me, that first year of you. We were only seventeen, so we had no power. I had no claim, I couldn't make you belong to me in any way. I wrote to you, your parents let me see you, but not often. I used to thank God for Oliver. He initiated me into the rituals of upper-class life as if I were an orphan or a vagabond, kept me connected to you, and I liked to flatter myself he was grooming me for my entry into the family. He pretended it was amusing when I told him I didn't know my father or his family or any of my half-brothers and sisters, and that Mummy's family wouldn't speak to her. All I had was Mummy, and you kept begging me to take you to Shropshire to meet her, but I wouldn't. Equally, I didn't want to know your family properly until I had something to show for myself, prospects at least, if not money. If you'd had a sense of humour it would have made you laugh as I couldn't possibly make any money for at least another four years. When we did meet it was unsatisfactory. I always said the wrong thing. You didn't like me to try and kiss you, I knew I shouldn't and I didn't really want to, only felt I should. I tried to make you laugh, impress you by bragging about my marks at school, how I was doing my A levels in one year so I could go up to Cambridge early. I boasted about the distances I could run – and you'd smile, but I didn't dare tell you how unpopular I was, and that Oliver was just about my only friend. If I told you how lonely I was without you, you'd only sigh.

In the summer you went away with your parents, and I went to Mummy. In August, though, you refused house-party invitations to Scotland and Cornwall, and stayed at the house in Holland Park. I slept on someone's floor. The days were sultry hot and dirty. I watched the dirt of the city smudging into a sky pale with dust and cloud and I felt my heart should have been heavy with longing for France, the stone house, home, but it was not. The city was holiday-empty, the bridges over the dirty river were delicate and empty, and I could see you. The streets were abandoned, and we drove them in your car like conquerors. You took me to see a lot of gardens, and I had to be polite about them, even though the flowers were hot and tired. But I was proud of you because you knew all their names and you explained to me about design and symmetry and the architecture and planting of a garden. You knew what was vulgar and what was not (I had no idea), and you bent and showed me roots and leaves and didn't mind if your shoes and hands got dirty. You were delightfully unselfconcious when you were absorbed in your gardens. You told me that your mother had given you part of one of the walled gardens in the country to have as your own and that you wanted to make an arbour, and when we could you promised we'd go to the country gardens: Forde Abbey, which was enchanted, Hidcote, Tintinhull, Sissinghurst and Knole. We couldn't go then because it was too far, but when we were grown-up we could go.

You weren't frivolous. You were so earnest that I stopped being frightened of boring you. I always knew you'd make a good audience. 'You're my summer girl,' I'd say. I'd sing to you and invent rhymes to make you laugh and tell you about all the jewels you'd have when we were married, and the rooms.

'And the gardens,' you said once, 'don't forget.' That was the first time I felt sure you wanted to marry me too and I caught your wrist and kissed it. When my results came I had three As, which meant the world was all before me. I couldn't have felt better. It was the first step towards our marriage.

Unable to bear the idea of a year off (a year off from what?) without being able to afford to travel, I went straight up to

Cambridge that autumn. The sooner I could get my degree, the sooner I could be making money, and the sooner I could marry you, Susannah. The sooner I could marry you. That thought was in my mind last thing at night and first thing in the morning of every day at that wretched place. I have absolutely no sympathy with people who become and remain obsessed by the glamour and romance of Oxford and Cambridge. For a start, if you imagine all the swots you ever knew at school, they're there, behaving as if they own the place; add to that all the boring *nouveau* middle-class people who want to pretend they're the *jeunesse d'oré*, enacting their fantasies by floating about in punts, or carousing in the quads late at night with a pretentious immaturity that still makes me weak with loathing, you have a good picture of what it's like. Then there are the tutors, smug, lazy, and intent on sleeping with their students while stabbing each other in the back, added to that a bureaucratic infrastructure of petty, prurient old men whose idea of civilised living bears comparison only with a prison camp. Combine this with all the future giants of journalism and the BBC networking their socks off, plus second-rate actors and artists prancing about as if they're already at the RSC and the Tate and you've got a cocktail of barbarity. The place is a hotbed of petty intrigue, hearsay, and misery, and in this claustrophobic world, shabby, insincere, derivative minds and personalities thrive. Their annual unleashing on the world is an unqualified nightmare. I'm no egalitarian and, as you know, I adore my privileged life – the life that place gave me – but I'm too much of a misanthropist not to have hated it. I loathed it. I despised the self-congratulatory ethos which held that if I didn't like it there was something wrong with me. People killed themselves because they believed that. I was miserable, lonely and angry, reeling with visions of the place I'd lost and the girl I loved. But I didn't hide from that world. I joined it. I went to its parties, rowed on its river, was a member of its

Union, wrote its essays, went to its libraries, looked at its pictures. And I whiled away my time with girls. Every girl I kissed only made me feel more acutely how irreplaceable you were to me. You remained irreplaceable, believe me. Those girls were nothing. Part of them wanted to know how it felt to be nothing, I'm sure of that, and they sure as hell found out. I didn't believe it could harm you in any way. I wish you had believed that, Susannah. In later years I'd say to you that if there was anything you could salvage out of fifteen years – I begged you – let it be that.

When I left for Cambridge, my last sight of you was a muffled figure on the platform as the train left the station. And while I was away I always thought of you as standing still. I visited Mummy and I visited you. But I didn't want you to become part of my life there. It would spoil you, stop you from being my glittering prize. I see you now as I thought of you then: as I imagined holding you in my arms, my princess of gold and white, of cool skin, and I wonder if you could have absolved me then, like the little saint you were, taken my wickedness away, righted all my wrongs. Once I believed that you could, but I know now I didn't try hard enough to deserve you. I was bound to you then because I'd promised myself to you as a boy. We were children betrothing ourselves – there's something inviolate in that.

You were faithful to me, you waited. The first summer my father died. He had left me a small legacy but I didn't go to the reading of the will. If I had, I'd have met the six other children he'd fathered in the course of what I will politely describe as his chequered career. I despised him and my mother then, and I believed you understood why and how painful that was for me. We never talked about it when I saw you again. I craved your silence because it made me feel so peaceful, almost like how I imagine prayer might be, and being blessed. There's always been a touch of the saint about you, Susannah. Which leads me, in not too roundabout a way, to your martyrdom.

The first (father dying) summer the telephone on my staircase was out of order, so you, in a rare impulsive act, drove from the country house to Cambridge to see me. It was a watery misty Sunday and you ran through the quad and up the stairs to knock on my door, calling my name, almost crying with fright in case I wasn't there. (With your female antennae you were already regretting turning up without warning.) I answered the door with a towel round my waist in a state of considerable irritation. I'd been in bed with someone called Cassandra, only answering the door because the knocking wouldn't stop. When I saw my straight and perfect girl crying with humiliation I wanted to shake you for being such a fool as to drive all that way for no reason but to give yourself pain. You forgave me, though it was unforgivable. The second time you found out about another girl was right before my finals and that time you didn't forgive. Your mother took you abroad for a long time, and I went back to my life. Somehow I didn't feel that it would really affect our plan in the long term and I had other things to think about. There was a great deal on my mind. When I came down from Cambridge, I was almost surprised to find you weren't there as the train came into Liverpool Street. I was afraid then. Through Oliver I got you to agree to write to me. Other people mightn't understand why I didn't try to see you. But you and I understood it – I was convinced. Words were all I could offer you anyway, for the time being, and words are pointless without money, so I settled down to my job in the City. Everyone I knew who'd gone into the City said it was nothing to do with talent, only a certain skill and being willing to work like a dog. I had one aim: to make enough money with which to earn – sorry, wrong word – afford? persuade? impress? Whatever. To marry you. And I know you couldn't always bear the comparison, but it was expedient I made money for Mummy, as well, who was practically destitute.

Memory and anticipation are wonderful things. It's like Mummy: while she knew she had my father to mourn she could face anything. While I had you to worship, you to hunger for, no job was too menial, no day at the office too long. In spite, or perhaps because, of all the money to be made, there's an apprenticeship to be served in the City, and I served mine with passion. My dedication was total. There was something very comforting about it, like being a worker-bee, humming away in the hive, part of a giant enterprise. Except that everyone was doing it for themselves, while pretending it was 'for the team'. But that's human nature. We are way beneath the altruism of the bee. I had a sense of purpose, and I felt sheltered, beneath the low ceilings, bathed in artificial light, staring at those figures, surrounded by clocks telling me the time all over the world, neon bulletins with the latest news from Reuters. It was a bit like a nursery school. The others were certainly childish, boisterous, comfortingly and indescribably banal. I knew I wasn't liked or trusted, but I didn't understand how to make that better. Clients always liked me, if not my own colleagues. I thought if I was good enough at what I did that wouldn't matter, wouldn't get in the way of my success, which turned out to be only partly true.

Weekends I hated most. I couldn't think of anything to do, usually ending up chasing some girl or other. I've kept your letters. They're touchingly dull: finishing school (they called it secretarial college), occasional skiing (which you hated), more finishing school, the lakes, house parties, sailing, presents, garden visits, Busby the dog. (You'd lost interest in Thimble, or grown out of her, I never asked.) At least your parents weren't trying to educate you any further. I'd never seen the point in that for you. There you were, dancing in the light, while I toiled in the dark. Imagine, Susannah, my single room.

On the chest of drawers, your photograph. In my wallet, a fragment of one of your letters ('All my love, Susannah') folded in with my pathetic amount of money. Picture the single bed, its rumpled sheets, my few belongings strewn around the floor. Friday night, drinking with the boys from the office, Saturday night, a party, perhaps a girl, Sunday – reading reading reading. Weeknights, takeaways and videos. It was a half-life. If it had happened to me now, now I'm stronger, I wouldn't let you banish me. I would simply stop it from happening. But no – thinking about it, I see I'm wrong again. You've always been stronger. You've banished me again, and you've succeeded. This time, there's no possibility of a reprieve, no hope at all, this time, you're gone for good – for ever, which, however one chooses to look at it, is a very long time.

I knew that you'd promised yourself to me once with your whole soul. I didn't rebel against our separation because I acknowledged that time had to be served, and I believed that the greatness of my punishment was equal only to the strength of your love. If I were to be rewarded I couldn't show weakness. If I'd written to you about my fear, my longing, I'd have been weakened in your eyes, so my letters were brave and strong, bulletins from the front. They were a sign of my patience. For three years I wrote letters to you and you wrote letters back. When I was on my bicycle cycling into the office, and the city was clear with dawn, this is what I wrote:

Dear Susannah, I am making my fortune, and I am alone. I can't see the window from my desk. Sometimes I think I might be going to be good at what I do.

Dear Susannah, I'm tired. At lunchtime I'm too excited and sick to eat. I drink coffee and Diet Coke. I don't trust anybody. My stomach burns.

Dear Susannah, I bought a new shirt. It is pale pale

blue. Now I have three.

Dear Susannah, sometimes I can't sleep I'm so frightened about tomorrow. I know now that I'm good at meetings – I'm charming. Clients trust me. I annoy the yobs in suits by putting semi-colons in my reports and quoting Latin.

Dear Susannah, there's a wind through the City and across the river when I cycle home in dust or dark. The fairy lights on the bridge seem frivolous. I go slowly past the big houses on the hill and I look in at the windows of the families – their books and the colours on their walls.

Dear Susannah, the pavements are cold.

Dear Susannah, are you in the world? Don't let your parents take you away from me.

Dear Susannah, I am making my fortune and I am alone.

These letters were the songs in my head. These letters were never sent. But I knew from those that were written and sent what you did and where you went and you knew the same things about me. I was afraid I might not have enough time before the morning would come when I'd open the paper and read about your engagement and you'd write and say you had not had the courage to tell me first. But those were only the bad days. When the world was beautiful, when I could see no one, only sky and buildings, and the blood flowed in my veins so I could feel it – I knew you were part of the future, that you were listening for me.

The month before my twenty-fourth birthday, I owned my first car and had moved into my own flat in Battersea. I painted the kitchen aquamarine, the bathroom indigo and the sitting room orange with scarlet floorboards which I'd stripped myself.

'Are you going to ring her up?' said Oliver.

'I haven't seen her for three years.' But the time was right. I had money in the bank. I wrote: 'Dear Susannah, please come and have dinner with me in my new flat. Name the day. Alex,' in big scrawly writing on a large piece of thick cream paper and I sent it in an envelope that was lined.

I was lucky you'd chosen a golden evening with slanting long light so I could open all the windows and the colours glowed. I made rabbit pie and chocolate tart. The food was too wintry but I decided not to mind. I bought champagne, truffles and white roses. The flat was on the top floor of a rather busy road, even if the bell had worked I wouldn't have heard it, so I left the door open for you to surprise me. I put loud happy music on, then turned it down in case it didn't fit your mood, your vision of my repentant self. I was just turning away from the speakers when I saw you standing in the doorway.

'Shall I come in?' you said. I wanted to cry I was so happy to see you.

'Yes. Yes.'

'But, Alex, what have you done to the floor?' You tried to laugh a little as you walked across it. All I knew was that you'd spoken my name.

'It's red.'

'I can see it's red.'

I wanted to take you by the hand and lead you from room to room, make you touch all the colours, but I knew that would be wrong, that I had to be more humble. You looked solemn and distant. Your hair was longer than I remembered it. You wore a summer dress with a pale pink cardigan over your shoulders because it was September. You didn't wear any jewellery but there was a touch of makeup – that was new. I couldn't wait to get my hands on you.

'Come up on the roof.' I persuaded you to climb the dark

stairs, and you were amazed surfacing in the evening light on my mini roof-terrace with its grubby views.

'You've put trellis up.'

'Of course. Nothing on it, though.'

'And these –' The roof was crowded with pots and pots of fuchsias.

'They're the only thing I could find that I liked. I thought you'd know what to do.'

'You can't just have fuchsias,' you said, surveying them seriously. 'It's so – over the top.'

'But they're beautiful, aren't they? I don't care – the garden's for you.'

'I don't know whether to laugh or cry.' But at least you looked at me then. I ran and got the champagne and gave you a glass. We drank in silence and then you said, 'What about the girls?' Abrupt, in a forced light voice, standing up straight among the nodding fuchsias.

'Oh, girls –' I tried to smile, dismissing them, hating my own frivolity, exuberance, longing with all my heart to be forgiven and the moment to be over. But you had to have your pound of flesh. You turned your back on me, crossing the small space to the other side, looking at London as if you were gazing out to sea.

'I couldn't bear it. When I found you – it nearly killed me. I think it would kill me if it happened again.' I followed you – just to touch your hair with the back of my hand – just to brush it. You didn't turn, but flinched.

'Live with me. I'll do anything for you. We don't have to be engaged, even. If you don't like it you can leave me, and –' You turned to face me – sharply.

'What are you talking about? I thought we were going to be married – all this time.' You put your hand up to your mouth, astonished, like a little child who'd let its secret slip, your eyes cartoon saucers. I'd got you.

'If it's what you want.' I went down on my knees to you. 'I'll never want anyone else this much.' I felt you begin to tremble and heard you laugh in a way that was more gentle and soft than I'd heard even in my dreams and you stooped and touched the top of my head with your cold fingers. I put my hands up and buried my face in your stomach as it curved in to your hip-bones. 'It's decided then,' I said.

Of course it was pandemonium after that. Your parents were astoundingly vile about the whole thing, as if I were some kind of monster. First they said that it was impossible, then that I'd have to wait another two years. You, in tears, threatened to run away, and I had to have that 'long talk' with your mother. It was this talk that made me realise she was the head of the house not him and the fact that she didn't even mention his name made me see he didn't really exist for her. And that was the way she treated me, as if I didn't exist – or if I did it was simply as an instrument through which to make you 'happy' (by gratifying *her* every wish). You've always wanted to know what happened that day; now I might as well tell you. I tried to get her to meet me in a public place, some hotel bar or park, but she was having none of it. She chose a time when she couldn't offer me a drink, Saturday morning at half past ten. 'I'm far too busy during the week.' (That's the sort of thing you get from a career woman.) You weren't even there to wish me luck, she'd sent you away on some errand or other. She led me into that room at the back of the house where I'd kissed you on New Year's Eve. I tried to console myself by thinking of it, but without the party glamour it was even shabbier and felt depressing. I didn't know what to say because there were no preliminaries.

'I understand you want to marry our daughter.'

'We're engaged, yes.' I didn't want to sit down but she made me, glaring at me until I did. She used the old trick of sitting on a high straight-backed chair while I fell backwards, ludicrous, in a slimy old armchair. She's so fat it's disgusting – those tiny hands and the iron-grey immovable hair. I looked for your face in hers, just about found it, your nose and rounded cheek, but not the delicacy of your jaw and forehead; those either came from your father or had been obliterated by her own greed.

'It's difficult that you say, "We're engaged". It's polite – the done thing – to ask the parents first.'

'She's over twenty-one.'

'Why be so defensive about it? Is it because you thought we'd say no?'

'Yes.' It was easier to admit than to deny. The garden sun was in my eyes, another trick (gleaned from the Gestapo) but I didn't show that I minded by changing my chair or asking for the blind to be pulled down. Her bulging silhouette was about all I could see in that room. I rested my eyes by looking at the books and the terrible china. I hadn't noticed it before, but lack of taste and money really is a terrible combination. They could have smartened it up a bit.

'If you won't answer me, at least look at me.'

'I have answered you.'

'Shall we approach it another way? Presumably we both love Susannah.' That 'presumably' was unbelievably insulting.

'Of course.'

'And we both want what's best for her.'

'We might have a different opinion about that.'

'I think I should explain. Susannah is – isn't – she's never been at all healthy. She won't talk about it but as a child she had problems with her kidneys, it's weakened her –'

'She's told me.' You hadn't, but I wasn't going to let her get the better of me. She didn't believe me anyway.

'Then you understand she's what one might call delicate. She needs plenty of sleep, good care, a reasonable amount of exercise.' She might have been talking about one of her animals for all the picture she gave me of you. It was all invented rubbish anyway. 'She's very private about it – doesn't like it to be mentioned. It hasn't helped that Oliver's so – robust.'

'That's one word for it.' She didn't smile. My first attempt to joke with her was to be my last, I think.

'She adores her father, she finds it hard that we don't –' (long pause) 'get on. I don't want her to rush into anything. She needs to be taken care of, and whoever marries her has to understand that and be prepared.'

'I do understand that. I've been taking care of my mother ever since I could walk.'

'Is that so?' She didn't ask any more about Mummy so I knew then that she'd already found out what she wanted about me, presumably from the mothers-of-eligible-daughters' grapevine. As if she'd read my mind, she backtracked, pretended to be interested. 'You used to live in the South of France?'

'We only came back a few years ago. My mother needs my support now more than ever. I've never let her down.' I thought it would have been vulgar of me to say that the support was financial, but I'd implied it to show how responsible I was.

'Susannah's money won't come to her until after we die.' That was so insulting: she thought I wanted your money for my mother.

'That's not an issue.' It was the politest I could manage to be.

'Our deaths, or Susannah's money?'

'The money has nothing to do with it. I love Susannah.' I'd promised myself I wouldn't end up saying that, but I did.

'I'm sure you do. But is there such a need to marry so young, so quickly? Especially nowadays. You're only twenty-four – your life's before you.'

'I've already waited seven years. She wants to be my wife.'

'And that's so important to you?'

'Yes.' It was exhausting, her relentless manipulation of me towards the false and unworthy. I pulled myself out of that bloody chair and stood over her. Her face had hairs in all the wrong places – in the midday light I could examine every ugly pore. 'Will you give us your blessing?'

'I can't do that.' She blinked at me like a white rabbit. 'We haven't even begun to talk about the religious question.'

'That's all decided. It's whatever Susannah wants.' I felt much more myself, upright, on my feet. She couldn't stand up because I was so close to her chair I was practically on top of her. 'I appreciate your concern about Susannah. All I can say is it's my turn to take care of her now.'

That wasn't the end of it, of course. All hell continued to break loose. She was so snooty about the ring – and that was only one of the things she tortured us about. (I think you were ashamed of her behaviour, though you never said so.) I couldn't afford a good enough diamond, so had bought you a tiny sapphire surrounded by seed pearls which she said were bad luck. She wanted to give you a family diamond, which we could have set. I think you wanted that but I said no. It hurt, because I'd chosen the ring and made weekly down-payments on it for as long as I could remember. The jeweller and I had almost become friends. I promised I would buy you an eternity ring when I could afford it. I admit I wasn't a pliable, or even tactful, future son-in-law, but I had to start as I meant to go on. From now on you were mine, not theirs. That's what a wedding ceremony is all about. Primitive, but there it is. Man is an animal, after all. I must say, you were surprisingly resilient in all this. (A taste of things to come.) It ended with your glorious ultimatum: 'Either make him welcome or lose me for ever' (I can still hear your quivering voice, saying it), so make me welcome they eventually did. Your mother drove us mad about every detail: we had to have a year's engagement (shortened after intensive negotiations so you could have a June wedding), she chose the trousseau, the wedding list, the flowers, the church, the dress. You decided not to mind, but in your heart I think you minded very much.

About one thing we stood firm, our darling little cottage house in Clapham. I bought it as a surprise, during our interminable engagement, while you were still living with them, mortgaged myself up to the eyeballs and beyond. It was worth it for the sight of your face – I'll never forget your fussing and frowning over the furniture, the choice of decorations, every little thing. It was pretty, that house, and much subtler than my bachelor flat. It's only a pity that the garden was so small, but you never said a word about that. It's extraordinary, looking back, that we were so happy while all this was going on. It was like a perpetual Christmas Eve. I just couldn't believe I was going to marry you, that we were going to wake up together every morning, and go to sleep together every night. There would be no more painful nights alone. You were going to cook me dinner, and we could go on holiday together wherever we liked, and buy things together, and no one would say no. I was in a state of absolute wonder. You were pale and tired, the strain showed in your expression, and in your eyes, but you were so sweet to me, so kind. You'd put your arms around me, and I'd say, 'You're kinder than God,' and you'd say, 'Sssh, blasphemy's no way to start married life,' and I'd explain to you it was Rupert Brooke, and you'd say, 'Even poets mustn't blaspheme.' But it became a joke between us none the less. You wore white shirts with high collars, you must have had an awful lot of them. You smelled so clean. You actually smelled of soap. I used to fall asleep imagining your clothes folded in the drawers and hanging in the cupboards of our newly wallpapered bedroom, your necklaces suspended from the mirror. It used to make my head reel. You'd say, 'It won't be like that, it will be ordinary.'

I'd say, 'It will be ecstasy. Ordinary ecstasy,' and tickle you and you'd laugh.

Lying in each other's arms one night you said, 'I don't want to leave it too long to have a baby,' and I couldn't answer for a while because I'd never given it a thought. Then I said, 'I suppose it'll be all right if you're there too', which seemed to satisfy you.

I wrote to my mother as soon as we were engaged. She'd been the only bride I'd ever known, but of course, she'd never been mine. She wrote back, only one word, 'Come.' It was impossible for you to imagine how terrified I was about your meeting Mummy: physically terrified, with acid in my stomach and water in my bowels.

'But I'm so eligible,' you said. 'Such a nice girl.' Uncharacteristically insensitive of you, I must say.

You tried to touch me but I shrugged you off. 'You don't understand.'

'Then tell me.' I think we were bundled up, sitting on a rug somewhere, I can't for any money remember where. (Note: subject having memory lapses about crucial events of the not-so-recent past. Sure proof of insanity.)

'Don't be unfair. I'm trying.' In those days you talked back.

'How do I explain about Mummy?'

'All right – I'll start with what I already know. She was a great beauty –'

'She'll tell you that a hundred times.'

'She drinks and her health's not good. She's alone in the world. She doesn't have much money. You love her very much and would do anything for her.' I didn't acknowledge that last emotional-insight part at all. 'Also, I know it was only you and her for a very long time.'

'Now Gerald's dead I think she wishes it still was.'

'Which is why you think she won't like me.'

'I have no idea whether she'll like you or not. She's a constant surprise, which is exceptionally tiring. She's still writing: unpublished drivel as opposed to published drivel.' (Contrary to received opinion I'm capable of being very objective about Mummy.) 'That and drinking are her only occupations. She cries a lot. She'll frighten you. She might even change your mind about marrying me.'

'Don't be so morose, Alex. You're practically pouting. Wait till she sees the ring. That'll cheer her up.' You were such a sweetheart in those days.

'Driving to Shropshire is an impossible bore. She can come up to London on the train.'

At the station Mummy sat on a bench wearing a grubby mac and smoking a cigarette. Her days of standing were long gone, but it was before her stick had entered our lives. She'd made a big effort with the makeup, far too much. She looked like a corpse (rotting with alcohol from the inside out), but on that day she was starting off sober at least. You didn't hesitate, but strode over to her like the country girl you aren't, holding out your hand and saying, 'I'm Susannah. How do you do?'

Mummy, her skin muddied with makeup, eyes like violet bruises, skin like yellow parchment, stood up and smiled like a little girl. 'At last,' she said, open-mouthed, her tongue suspended (like a lizard's) in delight. I hated seeing her like that, through your eyes. Why did her soft brown hair have grey in it, why were her famous cheekbones obliterated, why was she bloated and old and why had it had to happen? I wanted to say to you: 'This isn't her. This isn't my mother.' She took hold of your hand and grasped it with hers, and not by a glance or anything in your eyes did you show how horrified you must truly have been.

We had lunch in some quiet old-fashioned hotel. Cigarette smoke and scent wafted across the table as a fading signal of the past. She drank two bottles of Chablis but they seemed to have no effect on her apart from a slight clumsiness with the crockery, which made her giggle girlishly. 'I know I'm an old woman now, but I was a great beauty, once, my dear. When he was a little boy.'

'I've told her, Mummy.'

'Don't be sharp. You're embarrassed by me. It'll make me upset.' She was practically wagging her finger at me like a pantomime dame.

'I don't think so,' you said, mildly, so kindly, with your warmest smile, and she turned to you, beginning to ignore me in favour of you, the more respectful audience. Patiently you endured her life-story: her great love for my errant father, her infatuation with the dreadful Gerald who'd led her astray and squandered all her money, the diversion which to her was writing books and, of course, her greatest gift in life, her son, 'growing up together' in the unsurpassed beauty of Provence. She really overdid her French Rs there as well.

All I said was, 'Mummy, you're not an old woman. You're forty-three.'

'Darling, you know it's rude to discuss a woman's age,' you said. You'd reprimanded me in front of my mother. I couldn't believe it. Calmly you carried on dealing with the third degree: did you want children, if so how many, and how soon? Would you keep working? Would you stay in London or did you want to live abroad? You were non-committal in reply, but never dismissive. You were a marvel. When lunch was over I had to leave you and go back to work. (I'd already lied about being with a client.) 'We're going to have a little stroll. Look at the shop windows,' you said.

'Then you'll be a precious and put me on the train,' said Mummy, patting you. And off you both went, arm in arm.

'It's official, she adores you,' I told her after the next day's debriefing by telephone. 'You're, "a lovely girl".'

'Honour thy father and mother,' was your pious reply, accompanied by a smile. You were far too proud of your success.

Such infrequent meetings became part of that engagement year. The more successful they appeared, the more furious and irritated they made me feel. And I could never explain why.

I didn't want a honeymoon because it would mean weeks before I could take you home. But I knew you'd judge it unthinkable not to have one, so I submitted. I was worried about what we would do with ourselves. I've always hated holidays: nothing is accomplished, there's no routine. The worst thing about it all was how conventional you were about the whole idea, wanting me to surprise you with the destination, so I couldn't just leave it to you to organise. (Not that you've ever been able to organise the smallest thing.) I'm not sure I made a good choice: France was out, you'd already been to every city in Italy, Spain was too barbaric – the same went for Turkey, most of Eastern Europe and Russia, I couldn't bear the idea of cocktails and crooning in the Caribbean – all those paradise islands seem to me to be infinitely dull – so I chose Vienna. At least it was civilised. No beaches, plenty of luxury, buildings to go and examine inside and out. But I was still pretty bored. You were good and quiet, on your best behaviour. You wouldn't eat the cakes or even taste the hot chocolate, though, which was an awful bore. It showed so little appetite for life.

I felt rather embarrassed by our wedding night: doing the things with you I'd done with all the other girls, and were so new to you. You didn't understand that my euphoria about marrying you was anything but physical. Not that you said anything. You looked puzzled by it all, still polite (while we were actually making love, which I found extraordinary), and then you cried, 'Because I love you so much.' 'Don't worry, darling, you'll get used to it,' I said. I think you felt virginal desire for me, which I hadn't expected and you didn't know how to express. My happiness came when lying with my head on your marble stomach I could listen to your breathing, so regular, so calm. I felt connected to something intricate and precious then, something blessedly outside myself, unassailable. All your ways of touching and holding me then were so innocent, so natural. I loved them. Usually I don't like to be touched. In a casual way, I can't bear it. With you at that time it was good. But the trouble with you and sex was that it stopped you from being a girl. Our wedding night marked the irrevocable end of your girlhood, which saddened me, if it didn't sadden you. The Susannah I took home to Clapham wasn't the girl I'd courted and married, not the one I'd walked through fire to possess. Already you were different, you knew me. You'd seen me impatient when the waiter took too long to take our order, irritable if you spoke to me while I was dressing, unmoved by the churches you loved to wander through. I've never liked walking around absorbing things. I like to take a taxi from A to B.

And in return, I discovered your vagueness. I'm not sure why I'd never noticed it before. You were always late, even for dinner in the hotel when we didn't have to go anywhere, reading a book or a newspaper when you were meant to be getting ready; or unable to decide what to wear, dressing and undressing and leaving your clothes over the backs of all the chairs. At first you were serene in the face of my irritation, then uncomprehending, at last distressed, but it didn't make any difference to how you behaved. You remained as vague as ever. And you wasted so much time talking to people: the bellboy, the receptionist, the doorman. You could have answered twenty questions about all their lives by the time we went home. You didn't seem to understand that they didn't matter, you were always pulling the background into the foreground and giving it your whole attention. 'Don't fuss, Alex,' you'd say, in your low voice, when I told you to hurry up. You'd frown and smile a little and say, 'You really mustn't fuss.' That's you, gentle, but stubborn stubborn stubborn. I had imagined that you would do your best to accommodate me, as my wife I expected it, but right from the beginning you insisted on your own way. I suppose I shouldn't have been so surprised. If a woman can banish the only person she really loves for three whole years, she's perfectly capable of ignoring him when he tells her she's late for dinner. I think your parents must have spoiled you utterly, because you seemed so astonished at being criticised. It was really very strange.

What frightened me was that – despite your inadequacies – I felt I needed you more than you needed me. I couldn't work that out. I wanted always to be with you and never let you out of my sight. I wanted us to be in perpetual harmony. I needed us to be as one, required it, and when you behaved the way you did I was genuinely wounded. 'I never meant to hurt you, Alex,' you used to say. 'It's just that I didn't think you'd mind.' This when you came back from shopping an hour later than you'd said you would, or left your hair down when I'd told you how it enhanced your looks to put it up. When you made me angry, helpless with anger sometimes, my hands a fist in my pockets, you'd give me your soon to be familiar blank look, your intransigent look. That look, Susannah. That look and your silences have presaged all of our many troubles.

On our somewhat strained return, you settled into the little house with ease. But you were astoundingly lazy. I came home from work after my first day back at the office and found the hall still crowded with suitcases and hand luggage, duty-free bags, the sitting room littered with newspapers and magazines, you curled up on the sofa with one of them, looking up and smiling at me. Midsummer sun streamed into the room.

'Hello, darling,' you said, your expression satisfied, almost sleepy, content. 'How was your day?' and you laughed at your own question, as if it were the height of wit and invention.

'It was fine.' I stood in front of you. 'Why are you laughing?'

'Because it's our first day of ordinary married life and I'm happy.'

I took off my jacket and tie, emptied my pockets of change, went into the kitchen to make myself a drink – all familiar rituals, everyday, comforting, they helped to steady me. 'If you're making a drink I'd love a glass of wine,' you called.

That really got me. I didn't have time to put down the ice tray, but carried it with me back into the room. 'Am I your servant?' I asked. 'Susannah – am I?'

You remained curled, coiled like a soft, boneless thing. You frowned your little girl's frown. 'Of course not.'

'Then why are you giving me orders?'

'I thought – as you were in the kitchen –' Another aggravating unfinished sentence.

I sat down beside you and tried to be patient in my choice of words. 'Let's look at it this way. I come home from a day which started at quarter to eight. I've been on the phone from then until now. I haven't had lunch. I've struggled home through traffic, longing to get home to my wife, and what do I find? I find the hall and sitting room strewn with mess and, judging by the immaculate state of the kitchen, nothing in the oven for my dinner.'

You curled your legs closer towards you and looked down at your white hand. You played with your engagement ring, moving it around on your finger, another habit quickly to become all too familiar. 'I didn't think of it like that,' you said. 'I thought we could go out.'

'You don't think we might have had enough of restaurants, for now?'

83

You looked up at me with your child's eyes. You said, 'I always seem to be doing something wrong.'

'Why do you think that is?'

'I'm thoughtless.'

'You could put it that way,' I said.

'I'm sorry.' I couldn't say anything. You weren't looking at me, and I just felt so miserable. 'Do you forgive me?' Then you looked up. Your expression was tender. 'I'm awfully tired after the journey. I'll tidy up tomorrow. Are you terribly disappointed in me?'

I sensed there was a teasing note in your voice, but I didn't want there to be, I wanted to ignore it. I decided I would. 'Are you really sorry?' I tried to keep looking stern, but it was difficult.

'Of course.'

You held out your arms and I fell to my knees and buried my head in your lap. 'What am I going to do with you, Susannah?'

'I've a confession to make,' you said. I could hear the words vibrating through your body. 'I can't cook.'

After that it was Prue Leith's cookery course and a cleaner who came twice a week. You were very industrious at that course and I liked it because I always knew where you were. We ate the things you'd made during the day, and at the weekends you practised pastry and soufflés and God knows what, and made the most appalling mess. But because you were trying, I didn't mind. I was only angry when you wouldn't try.

Soon you began to drop little hints about what a shame it was to be stuck in London at the weekend and wouldn't it be lovely if we could get out into the country now and again? Finally you said, 'I think we should go down to my parents' this weekend.' I asked you if you'd forgotten how much I disliked them. You said you hadn't and expressed the hope that

84

perhaps now we were married, 'some understanding could be reached'. I think those were your words. It would have been churlish of me to refuse. After all, I wanted you to be happy. It would have been preferable if you could have been content to find happiness within our marriage rather than outside it, but I was very young, I suppose still very much in love, and I couldn't say no to you. The trouble with your parents is that they are so pompous, so full of themselves, so convinced that they are better than everyone else. And they hate each other, but they're too conceited to admit it. Their hatred for everybody else is greater than their hatred for one another, so they stay together. And, of course, there's the Catholic thing. Honour your promises and all that hypocrisy. You've never understood that I resent them principally because their clinging to one another made you so unhappy from when you were a very young child. Take the wedding, for example. All they could do was quarrel about it: she wanted London, he wanted the family chapel, she wanted a hundred guests, he wanted two hundred and fifty, and on and on. I detested all that family-chapel nonsense. My family's just as good as yours, but yours made me feel like some kind of upstart because I found that landowning rigmarole rather ostentatious. You challenged me at the time – uncharacteristically, I thought then – by saying that if it were my family and my land, I'd be just as proud of it as they were. The point is, and I don't mind admitting it, I knew my past could hold up to any comparison, it was just that not being able to invite my father to the wedding, and Mummy and France and all that, put me at a disadvantage.

After the full feudal nightmare of the country wedding, the idea of going back to those mullioned windows and draughty corridors, dirty carpets in the bedrooms and the all-pervasive smell of dog didn't exactly fill me with glee. I know you've said (in a rare moment of criticism) that my delight in comfort can verge on the *nouveau*, but frankly, I don't care. Give me gold taps, enormous radiators and plush towels any day. Plus, the Suffolk countryside is so flat and bleak. I like hill country. And I knew you'd want to ride that old pony of yours, Moonbeam or whatever its name was, and I'd probably have to have a tour of the acres with your father. Oh, Susannah – I don't think you spared a thought for me at all. And I was always thinking of you. You just wanted to go back, go back to your old home.

At dinner on the first night you were unusually animated, chatting on and on about your cookery classes and how much fun they were, and the other girls there, and where they lived and what they wanted; things you hadn't bothered to tell me. Your mother said something about that all being very well but when were you going to find something sensible to do? She sounded very hard, determined about that (this from a woman who's never been able to cook, or thought it in the least important, either). There we were in that dismal dining room with its dark shining furniture and those ancient heavy red curtains, and you said, 'I have thought of something, actually.'

Haughty old mother said, 'Have you?' and your father nodded in an excited way, and I said, 'Hold on a minute, we haven't even discussed this.' What were we eating? Some revoltingly overcooked beef I think it was. I felt sick.

You looked at me, almost excited, and said, 'It's still just an idea.'

'Well?' said your father, ignoring me. You all ignored me.

'I thought I might start a gardening business,' you said. 'Designing and planting. There's a girl at cookery class, Claire, who's also very keen, and you know there are so many people in our part of London who'd love to have a classy-looking garden, even if it's only a terrace.'

'What an excellent idea!' said your father. (I have to write it with an exclamation mark, I've no choice.) Stupid old fuck. 'You've always been so clever at it.' For once, your mother agreed with him, and you all began chattering on, falling over yourselves to agree with one another as if I were invisible. 'The beauty of it is, there's no capital to put up. You can't lose,' said the blithering idiot.

'You'd be giving up time to do drawings, but what else have you got to do with yourself?' said the she-wolf.

'Be my wife, for one thing,' I said. 'Being my wife is what she's got to do with herself.' I really wasn't looking for a row, and tried to stop my voice from shaking, but it was so hard with them insulting me so unashamedly. You were opposite me, pink-faced, bright-eyed, leaning forward as you spoke. You had forgotten me until I said that.

You all turned your heads to look at me, and your father said, 'That goes without saying, old chap,' and your mother backed him up, adding, 'I'm sure she's a very good wife to you, but it's hardly an occupation.' (I wish you'd seen fit to offer me the same kind of support.) Her words sounded like a reprimand, as if I too were one of her children – terrible thought.

'No – no,' I said. 'Why can't it be an occupation?' my voice shaking and loud.

'Perhaps we ought to leave the subject alone,' said your father, not looking at me, and there was a kind of shamed silence before your mother started on about some party she'd planned to give at Christmas. I couldn't see anything but your face, its blush, your quick look at me, then back at your plate. I was so hot. I wanted to shake you. I wanted to shout, 'How dare you talk about our life to them before me? How dare you even start such a conversation?' I was hurt, but it was the rage I found hard to control. I controlled it.

When we were by ourselves, I didn't trust myself to talk to you about it. Not one word. You made a speech as you brushed your hair in front of the mirror, avoiding my eyes. 'I'm sorry, truly sorry, that I was so thoughtless. I shouldn't have said anything to my parents before discussing it with you. It's just an idea. Really, I'm sorry.'

'We'll talk about it when we get home,' I said, my back to you. You made a little sound, a sound of bewilderment and sorrow. I think I surprised you by making love to you that night, more passionately than before. It felt good being on top of you so you couldn't move.

Almost straight after that delightful incident Mummy tried to kill herself. It was awkward at work because I'd already taken so much time away for the wedding and honeymoon. I had to tell them it was a family emergency, which was unpleasantly compromising. We were in bed with the papers on a Sunday morning. I have such a clear picture of our bedroom then: small and papered yellow, with a Laura Ashley border around the walls (it was the fashion), daffodils and irises. We still had that bed with the cane headboard, and there were pretty moiré curtains at the windows, with black-out blinds behind them as an attempt to help me sleep. (It failed.) Those pleated lampshades were a bugger to dust. (The last thing I wanted to have to do before I went to sleep was dust them, but you were so lazy I had no choice.) The second bedroom was a dressing room then so there wasn't the impossible slum that came later, with the baby. The blinds were half up, yellow paper masking the dull autumn morning. We should have been happy, but I was irritated by something. I think it was some noise in the street, that bloody motorbike from across the road revving and revving, and you were asking whether I would like the radio on, and I was saying I couldn't read to voices talking. I wanted to get up. Lolling in bed is just not for me. But that moment of aggravation seems idyllic now, coming as it did a fraction before the doctor's call. He said she'd cut her wrists, they were bound up, she lay in the dark, she asked repeatedly for me and wouldn't be moved. Of course it wasn't the first time, it was just the first time in England, the country of our new start.

While I was talking you had your hand on my arm. It wasn't soothing, but stiff, and your touch was making the doctor's voice fainter, Mummy further away. When I put the phone down and told you what had happened there were tears in your eyes, they sprang up – it was instant pity you felt. That was how I knew you didn't truly care for her – why should you? I had no pity. You were asking questions: 'When? Why? How? She will recover, won't she? Won't she? How terrible, how terrible.' I couldn't say anything. I fetched the honeymoon suitcase and just stood and looked into it without knowing why. You tried very hard then to do the right, English thing. Pity was followed by coolness. You put your broderie-anglaise dressing-gown over your broderie-anglaise nightdress, you assembled my shirts, my socks, my night things. I stood and looked at you and you said, 'Go and call about trains. Then bath and dress. I'll drive you to the station.' Above all, I was thankful you didn't expect to come with me.

Mummy had jerked me out of your bed and into hers, at least in my mind. I had such an image of her, lying in our bed, wanting only me. I saw her, she was the only thing I could see, and I was so angry with her. All the way there I was angry and feverish and that was how I wanted to stay. But I couldn't. Perhaps that was why you felt sorrow, for me as well as for her.

God, I'm sick of finding my women on the floor – so so sick of it. Her wrists were bandaged. A doctor and a nurse were with her, furious, because she wouldn't be moved and they were afraid to leave her alone. I was furious too. They left soon after I arrived. She was crouched, hiding, bunched up like a spider. There's a limit to the amount of times a son can find his mother after a suicide attempt before he simply feels tired.

'If you don't get up off that floor now you never will again.'

(This was to become one of her favourite stories later, as you know.)

'I want to die. It would have been better if I'd died.'

'You don't want to die. You want a better life.' It's amazing what rubbish a man can spout when it's called for.

'You hate me.'

'No. I love you. More than anything else in the world.'

'You've got Susannah now.'

'She loves you too. We both love you.'

'I want to get out of here. This mud. These lanes.' Big pause while I felt her thinking. We both knew that this was the real reason she'd got me out of bed.

'All right. I'll take you home with me to London on one condition. If you break it I'll never see you or speak to you again.'

'Anything,' muffled, snotty, repulsively hopeful.

'Stop drinking.' It took another forty-eight hours to convince her of that, but the bargain was made.

In my one call home you sounded strained and anxious and I resented you for not trying to hide it. Your calm authority hadn't lasted, and I was disappointed by that. Because I wasn't unfair to you I didn't tell you I was disappointed and I tried not to show it. When I said I was bringing her home, you said, 'Home?' and I said, 'To our house, of course.' I still wonder why you were so deliberately obtuse, almost obstructive. I told you she would be staying with us until I found her somewhere, and you said, 'Naturally,' as if there were still some question in your mind. You were so baffling, Susannah. Unfortunately, there's a time limit on the glamour of mystery in the woman one loves.

Seeing you on the platform at Waterloo with your straight, tall back, your pale hair and your timid smile was the most extraordinary shock. We'd almost forgotten you. I hadn't expected you to meet us at all. I saw you immediately, because in all the crowd that milled, you stood absolutely still, you were a slender little tree, a sapling. You greeted me with only a touch of your cool hand, a kiss on both cheeks. You held out your hand to Mummy, who gazed at it, puzzled, before taking it. 'I hope that's the last time we'll be so formal,' she said. She looked so small and fragile compared to you. I couldn't think of a thing to say to you, I don't know if you felt that. I have no idea what you felt that day, Susannah. I've come to understand that great emotion makes you hold yourself especially still, so perhaps you were overjoyed to see me. You've never told me.

You'd put flowers in our dressing room at the house, bought a bed and made it up with proper sheets and blankets. You knew I couldn't stand duvets and correctly assumed that Mummy would feel the same way. Nothing much was said. You'd made a stew, carefully prepared and uninspiring, like all your cooking. The house was tidy. 'So this is where you live,' said Mummy, adding absentmindedly, 'How sweet.' I had to go back to work the next day.

In bed you whispered to me, 'What shall I do with her tomorrow? What shall we do?'

'I haven't the faintest idea,' I snapped, then I think I explained to you how weak she was and there wasn't much she *could* do. 'Get her some books,' I said. 'She'll sit and read.'

'What will *I* do?' was your reply. I was really irritated by then.

'What do you usually do?'

Muffled, you said, 'Mostly, sit and read.'

'You'll be companions, then, won't you?'

Trouble in paradise began something like this: Saturday breakfast, you were freshly washed and dressed, but you looked tired, nervous almost. Mummy was in the bath. We sat over the breakfast things and you fidgeted with your knife on the plate.

'Are you and Mummy having nice cosy chats?' I said, sensing you craved a conversation.

'Mmm.' You looked up at me.

'What's that for?' I said.

'What?'

'Little-girl lost – that little-girl-lost look.' You looked down again, as if unsure how to answer me.

'I only –'

'What?'

'It's nothing.' You looked at me as if some terrible wrong had been done you. 'It's just – she comes into our room and sits on my bed in the morning after you've gone to work, and –'

I couldn't restrain my irritable reply. 'Why shouldn't she?'

'I feel a bit uncomfortable.' Your lowered eyes confronted me. You fiddled with the butter knife.

'Uncomfortable how? Intruded on?'

'Yes – intruded on.' You looked up, relieved that you'd been understood.

I couldn't bear it. 'Don't criticise her to me,' I said.

'I wasn't – I didn't.' So like you to deny it, so duplicitous. How is it, Susannah, that you, Miss Goody-goody, were such a liar? Your insinuating tone, it made me wild. You only had to say one word, give me one look, to make me wild.

'Stop – stop it!' I reached over and tried to take the knife from you and you dropped it, let it go.

'I'm sorry,' you said, reaching across the table to take my hand. 'Let's not quarrel.'

'I have no desire to quarrel with you.' How many times have I said these words in our fifteen years, and how many times have you actually listened to them?

'Please listen. I like her very much. It's only that, if I could – if I could understand her – she says things I don't understand. Private things one wouldn't think she knew about you. She

92

says you'd do anything for her – that you'd make any sacrifice for her.'

'I'm sure she does. I don't care what you understand or don't understand. She's my mother, she can say what she likes. Susannah, look at me.' Obedient, you looked. 'I just can't listen to you criticising her. Do you understand that? I want you to take a deep breath if you feel bad words coming. Can you do that? It's made me so angry, you see, and I can't bear to be angry with you.' I was relieved I'd managed to put it so clearly.

'I don't –' You tried to speak but I don't think there was anything in your head.

'It's not her, Susannah, it's you.'

'Yes.' You said the word in a child's voice.

'I don't want to scold you.'

'No.'

'Let's give this a try, shall we?'

'Yes,' you said, looking up at me. 'I'll make you proud of me.' Frankly, that was rather an ambitious promise.

You wouldn't leave the subject alone. You were obsessed with Mummy's habit of coming into our room in the morning and sitting on the bed. You wouldn't let it go. During the week she'd climb in with you, at the weekends she visited us both. It was harmless – perfectly natural – she was family after all. Your next protest went something like this.

'How's everything with Mummy?'

'Fine.' (I'd already learned to flinch from 'fine'.)

'What do you mean – fine?'

'It's just that – I feel a bit –'

'For God's sake, Susannah, you obviously feel more than a "a bit".'

'When she – I'm in my nightie and –'

'She's my mother.'

'I know.'

'And it's my house.'

'Yes.'

'She's only trying to get to know you. Come on – you started so well.'

Sudden courage. 'I can't have it, Alex. Her living here is one thing, but –'

'No pets allowed in the room.'

'Try and understand.'

'That you want me to reject her after all she's been through?'

'It makes me unhappy.'

'Oh, well, why didn't you say so before? I'll just get my magic wand.'

'You never used to be so sarcastic.' (Pouting and tearful.)

'Do you realise how difficult this is for me? Do you ever think?'

Silence, your most potent weapon, followed by, 'Our room should be private.' In the end I had to give in and tell Mummy off and it was very nasty indeed. Your will – contrary to the impression you liked to give – was frequently stronger than mine.

You both claimed I'd been unfair to you, and I felt a fool for just expecting it to be all right. We were all miserable. Mummy, because she was alone and still very weak and in a strange house; me, because I felt powerless and frightened; and you, you because you were so spoiled. Like a real brat, once you had my ring on your finger, you changed towards her. You couldn't, wouldn't, just get on with it: care for her, be a wife to me. You were unnatural with her, over-polite, over-solicitous. If she asked you questions, tried to chat, you answered her in monosyllables. If she were downstairs you stayed in our room (negotiated as a no-go area), or went out for long periods of time. You wouldn't talk to her about me, and that had become her chief pleasure. It's all she ever wanted to do, and you denied her. You – young, strong (or so we thought), pretty, all your life before you, denying an old woman (as she insisted on describing herself), employing every trick of passive resistance. Ostensibly you remained thoughtful: buying her her favourite things to eat, delicacies and chocolates, tempting her, feeding her up, taking her for short walks in the park, but all along you were denying her what she most needed so that she could recover – talk about me, even you and me, especially you and me. Things like my taste in ties, shirts, even boxer shorts, how I was sleeping, whether we were trying for a baby. (Perish the thought.) She wanted you to tell her how much in love with me you were. In different ways, through different intimacies, she wanted you to love me with her, she wanted you to do it together. Your refusal – your lowered eyes or pursed lips, your infernal blushing, or the fiddling of the right hand with the rings on the left, all these attitudes blocked her. She couldn't understand why you'd stopped wanting to be known by her. If she'd talked to me about it at the time I could have explained that as far as I could see you didn't want to be known by anyone. It made me so angry, watching you day by day, guessing what I didn't see. Poor Mummy – in desperation she even asked you questions about your gardening, only to be met with, 'Yes', 'No', 'Perhaps', 'Sometimes', 'It depends'. I didn't hear either of you laugh for the whole three months of her stay.

The situation became untenable. Such was your intransigence. Weekends were quickly taken up with the search for somewhere for her to live. I longed for the time alone with her, without you. It was such a relief, running away with her into the country, different towns, villages, looking for somewhere she could love again, which would restore her. (Thank God I could afford it by then.) Constraint was left behind and we talked and laughed and made plans. I love plans. She was never bewildered by my feelings and wishes the way you always seemed to me. You didn't acquit yourself at all well then,

Susannah. But in the end it came right. We were happy with the cottage we found. Kent is a difficult county, beset by all that is twee, but if you look hard enough you can be lucky and at a good price. We both recognised the cottage immediately as the place, we didn't have to say a word. It was the best solution, a refuge where we could be alone when we needed to be. Only two hours from London, at the edge of a village where she could walk to the post office and shops, woods close by. The rent was affordable. I could go and stay. She could begin a new incarnation.

It's all beginning to look like a catalogue of crimes against you, and you're no longer here to defend yourself. Not that I think you could. The more I remember, the more I see you had good reason to feel ashamed. Your laziness and indecision, your unkindness to Mummy were only the beginning. I could never understand what you did all day. As far as I could see you could pass a whole morning by reading the paper. I'd call you after breakfast, I'd call you before lunch, and you'd say, 'I'm still in the same chair, darling, there's no news,' in that uncommunicative drawling voice you had. When I was at work you were hours on the phone. By the time I finally got through you had nothing to say to me.

You cared nothing for the house, but you got a man in to paint the garden walls white and put up trellis. You wanted to put mirrors on the back wall to make it look bigger, but I wouldn't let you. It was a horrible lapse of taste on your part. Brick beds were built. That spring you began to plant: a laborious business. I came home and you wanted to show it to me, although it was already dark. You put on the outside light with a great show of triumph and said something like, 'I've moved the philadelphus.' That was all you had to show for an afternoon, one philadelphus surrounded by feet and feet of bare and perfectly prepared soil. Rows of unplanted plants leaned against the wall outside the back door. You'd planted the same shrub the day before, and that day you'd moved it.

I said, 'Why haven't you planted any others?'

'I couldn't. It's complicated. I have to draw up a plan.'

That God-awful graph-paper plan, I can see it now, you poring over it on a Saturday morning, your coffee untouched. 'I don't want to do anything wrong,' you'd say.

I'd shout at you, 'We can't be the only garden in the street with brand new beds and nothing planted. It's absurd.' And you'd look up at me with such a face of suffering, as if you were alone with this terrible absorbing problem and I was some kind of Philistine – it was unbearable. I'd lose my temper, threaten to plant the bloody things myself and you'd cry. I've never known a woman cry so easily. I'd try to explain to you that it was only a silly little hobby, other wives did it all the time. They planted their gardens and their husbands praised them and that was the end of it. How could you expect to turn it into a business when you couldn't even plant your own flowerbeds? You'd nod, and say, 'I know.'

It was either the garden or the catalogue shopping. You loved your catalogues: clothes mainly, nighties and dressing-gowns, but anything would do. You'd send off for things and then send them back. You put in hours queueing at that post office. I'm surprised you didn't have your own window. But you liked it, you liked doing that. Real shopping appalled you, unless it was with a girlfriend, usually that cooking friend of yours, Claire, and usually at Peter Jones ('Because it's so unthreatening'), and you were capable of spending hundreds of pounds in one afternoon. You didn't like shopping with me, accusing me of deciding too quickly, and being extravagant – that from you. I made you nervous, you complained.

Before I'd even realised it, we'd been married a year. With you spending so much of my money, I needed a promotion.

The ghastly thing about my job then was that I was only one salesman in a team, I had no real power, no autonomy. Colleagues less gifted than I was were moving up to head teams, and I was staying put, ostensibly because, 'You're so good on the phone.' The head of the sales desk was that Essex man, Lewis. How well I remember him, with his red stripy shirt, slicked-back hair, shiny face. (There were actually people like that then, and I had to deal with them every day.) He was so big, so barrel-chested, so unashamed of taking up space. I couldn't stand him. He had twice my bonus every Christmas and didn't know what the word ubiquitous meant. I'd never seen the point in ingratiating myself with him, because it was his job I wanted, but the man above him was too distant to approach and always kept himself out of my way. Eventually I felt I'd have to make a play to get close to Lewis in the hope that he'd use his influence to get me moved sideways at least. I lay awake at night worrying about whether it would be less of a punishment to endure Sunday lunch with him or Saturday dinner – finally plumping for dinner because it was more formal and less as if we were pretending to be friends. There had to be a limit to how far my desperate hypocrisy would stretch. I thought we should have another couple as well to balance it out a bit, put on a show, make him and his wife feel they were moving up in the world. Claire and her husband Will were the only people I could think of. Both presentable, I could be sure of that, properly brought up. I kept telling you that Lewis would be impressed by you because you were 'posh', but at the same time I didn't want him to look at his wife after looking at you and hate her for being so common: a delicate balance to aim for. One of your best qualities is how unaffected and sincere you are, so I knew you wouldn't try to make them feel inferior. It was just that nothing could change the fact that they were. We all knew it. At least the house couldn't make him feel envious. We'd done it up with tarts' curtains but it was still only a gentrified workman's cottage – there was no getting away from it.

You kept bleating on about what you were going to cook. In the end I had to choose for you: melon and Parma ham, roast chicken, chocolate mousse. What could have been easier? Of course I could have done the cooking myself, I'm more than capable of it. But I wanted you to do it, as a proper wife should. I went out that day, I couldn't bear to be with you while you fussed. I think I drove down to have lunch with Mummy. When I came back at about six o'clock I was afraid, kicking myself for being so late. I just couldn't believe you'd have been able to cope, fully prepared to throw myself into a last-minute rescue mission for the next hour and a half. It was very silent. In the wet June evening the house felt sad. No clattering in the kitchen, no sounds at all. I called your name, and after a while you answered from upstairs, a faint greeting, an almost casual hello. I began to fear that it was worse than I'd thought, that you hadn't even started, that you were lying down. I charged into the sitting room: it was immaculate and dainty, cushions plumped, fireplace mirror gleaming. In the kitchen the table was laid, flowers arranged, napkins washed and ironed. The oven was on, the chicken in it, the vegetables prepared in their saucepans, mousse in the fridge. It was as if fairies had been working.

Upstairs, you were indeed lying down, but the curtains were open, you had no headache, no attack of weakness. You were wearing jeans and one of your pretty white shirts, which looked a bit big for you. An empty water glass was on the bedside table next to you, and you smiled at me.

'I was afraid you were ill,' I said.

'No, not ill. Just a little tired.' You sat up, pale and clean. 'Shall I go and make you a cup of tea?' you said. 'Would you like one? How was your mother?'

I wanted to cry. Instead, I took your hand and kissed it. 'Everything's ready? I'm so relieved.'

'Did you think it wouldn't be?' You said this casually, as you got to your feet, looking around you vaguely, as if it weren't important, but we both knew that it was.

'Of course not. I'll have a bath. A cup of tea would be good.' You went and made me the tea and left me to dress in private, discreetly going back downstairs. When it was your turn I lay on the bed and watched you at the mirror, doing your face, brushing out your hair.

'What are their names?' you said. 'I mustn't forget their names.'

'Lewis and Deborah,' I said.

'Lewis and Deborah,' you said, over and over, 'Deborah and Lewis,' as you brushed out your hair.

I'd thought it would be vulgar to offer them champagne, but we had everything else, gin, whisky, wine. Deborah wore a long peacock blue dress, high heels of the same colour and dangling earrings which reflected the light. Her lipstick also shimmered as if in response. She was very quiet, giving the floor to Lewis, who boomed on about how quiet and rural it was where he lived but how quick the journey to work, how he couldn't stand to live in London now. I couldn't believe it, that people actually went out to other people's houses, drank their drink, and dared to say things that boring – worse, that it was happening to me. You took Deborah over to the sofa and talked to her in your gentle voice (I couldn't hear what you were saying), and when Claire and Will arrived you made sure she was safe and included before you went into the kitchen to check on the dinner. I began to think that perhaps it would be all right. I began to relax. I was careful not to monopolise Lewis too obviously, my idea of putting him next to you at the top of the table so that you could charm him seemed a good one. Opposite, Claire chatted on in her inoffensive and only slightly irritating cheerful way while you were busy. I did the wine and you did the food. I'd longed for a separate dining room, but you made the table so pretty and kept the kitchen end so tidy that it didn't feel too middle-class. I wouldn't say there was a roar of conversation but it was a very respectable hum. I think you and Deborah were talking about paint colours. I was hungrier than I'd expected to be, and concentrated on my plate for a little too long to keep an eye on things, but when I looked up and down the table at you, I noticed that your first course was untouched. You were looking straight at me, your colour deepening, your hands in your lap.

'What's the matter, darling?' I said, as jovially as I could, and smiling. 'Is there something wrong?' You swallowed, seemed to be holding back tears.

'Oh, no,' you said, and shook your head. There was a quick pause as Deborah and Claire looked from one to the other of us. Lewis and Will – discussing property prices – hadn't noticed. You picked up your knife and fork and began to cut up your food into very tiny pieces, as if for a sick child. You put a piece in your mouth and swallowed it, but that was all you could manage, the rest remained untouched. Then you put down your knife and fork and put your hands around the stem of your glass, which you didn't drink from. There was nothing more I could do or say without anyone else noticing – you were right at the other end of the table, and I'd have had to raise my voice again. I was just praying you'd get hold of yourself but I couldn't look. I knew you weren't talking to Lewis, but Will was keeping him occupied. Deborah and Claire were all right. It was peculiar; four people talking while you and I sat at opposite ends of the table in silence. We all knew you hadn't eaten a thing and were agog to see what would happen when we got to the chicken. There was a ludicrous feeling of suspense while I carved it and you handed the plates and vegetables. I can't go on describing this. You know as well as I do that you didn't eat another bite. You recovered your composure enough to smile and talk, you did everything else I could have hoped for – more – to make the evening a success, but it was pointless. Our guests were miserable. They saw you weren't eating, they couldn't ask why. It was vile.

At pudding, Lewis said, 'What about a little bite, for me?' and the awful thing about it was that all his brashness, the bragging I so disliked about him, fell away. His eyes were kind, humble almost. And you looked at him with a thankful gentleness.

'You're very sweet, but I'm afraid I can't,' you said. You spoke the words lightly, as if you hadn't embarrassed us all, made the dinner an ordeal.

And he said, 'Whatever you think best.' It would have helped if you hadn't looked so slender. I looked at you and saw as if down a telescope that your cheek was no longer rounded, your hands looked big at the end of your arms. It was a terrible shock, as if I hadn't looked at you properly for a long time.

I stood up, hoping that coffee and brandy in the sitting room would take our minds off the food and your hunger strike, but as soon as I did, everyone said how late it was and they really must go.

'No,' you said – appealing to Lewis. 'Don't – don't go.' And you blushed again, and Deborah said, 'You sound like a prisoner.' The words tumbled out, I knew she hadn't meant to say them, and you laughed a strained sound and said, 'No, no – I mean it.' Lightly, sweetly, 'Do stay.' They stayed and drank coffee and brandy and you talked to Deborah and I talked to Will and Claire, and Lewis sat and looked at you from across the room and didn't take his eyes off your face. Everybody left loudly protesting that they'd had a wonderful time. It was eleven fifteen. When the door shut on them, you leaned back against it, and closed your eyes. I stood and looked at you, but it was as if I were invisible. You behaved as if you were alone.

'Do you want me to hate you?' I said.

'What do you mean?' You opened your eyes and gave me your child-look.

'Susannah, are you mad? Why didn't you eat?'

'I don't know. I couldn't. It would have been bad.' You were so direct. You didn't apologise, merely explained. I couldn't believe it, the effrontery. Usually, you apologised.

'They'll think I mistreat you – that you're –'

You were still leaning against the door, and you sighed, 'I couldn't eat. There's nothing more I can say about it.'

'Did you think about what they might think?'

'Yes – but I couldn't eat.'

'It didn't make any difference to you what they thought? Are you ill?'

You lifted your chin in an imitation of pride. 'No. I'm pregnant.'

It was one of the most horrifying moments of my life. You, standing, leaning, fully visible, making no attempt to hide, looking out at me with your pale, empty eyes, not caring that you'd humiliated me, ignoring the way you'd humiliated me, stolen my life, perverted my hopes, trampled on my plans – the shock – the idea of an embryo, an embryo, without my consent. Everything I'd believed about you, your innocence, your honesty, was shattered when you said those words – I can analyse it now, but then it was just the unexpected impact of your trickery, your determined lying, your premeditated secrecy. I'd thought you were my girl, but your mind had been twisting away from me all that time, holding its own course, and you didn't care, you relished it, surprising me, implacable. All I could say was, 'You're pregnant –' my words coming out like a nausea, like I was vomiting. 'How could you be? We hardly –'

'I don't know.' You shook your head, smiling. I don't think you meant to smile. You could have, but mockery was never your style.

'Haven't you been –?'

'No.'

'Why not?'

'Because I want a baby.' Your eyes and voice were perfectly steady as you said that.

'What do you mean, "I want a baby"? "*I* want a baby" – what is that? You're *my* wife. It's up to me.'

'No.'

'No?'

'I want something of my own.'

Defiance is not a word that had ever come into my head about you. You'd shown yourself capable of refusing certain things, but until that night, not cruelty, not defiance, not the unflinching defiance of the spoilt bitch you were. I felt my heart could have stopped from fright. But then I felt the rage come. I caught you by the hair with a marvellous giddy feeling and banged your head against the door. The release of it – the joy! Then I hit you – slapped you – you remember. I said, 'Why have you made me do this? Why?' After the rage came the tears. I cried and you cried, and it was a sorry business. But even in my pain I couldn't hit you in the stomach, I still loved you so, and I wouldn't harm the baby you wanted. I wouldn't harm my son. What I remember after that is making love to you on the floor of the hall, and shuddering, laying my head on your milky breast, asking, 'Susannah, why are you destroying me?' You turned your head away from me and wept.

After that, I couldn't trust you. I couldn't trust you to represent me, not to anyone – to be the person you'd always promised so convincingly to be. And the eating, that was the dawn of a whole new battle. I wonder if you ever understood the full horror of what it was like for me to see my wife

pregnant and starving herself. I wonder if you ever understood that what you did was wrong. I couldn't get it into your
head. 'Pregnant women must eat. Ask Claire, ask your
mother, ask my mother, they'll all tell you. A pregnant
woman must eat.' In the first weeks, it was, 'I know, I'll try.'
For the sake of my own sanity I decided you had morning
sickness, although you never complained of feeling sick. You
never complained about anything, refused to describe how
you felt. It made me too angry, anyway, to ask you in a
concerned way, as if you had a legitimate complaint. It was
pure stubbornness, just like Mummy's. I simply couldn't
understand why. I'd given you everything. At first I thought
it best to carry on as normal, you cooking dinner every night.
But I always ended up pleading with you as you pushed the
food around your plate. 'I had a big lunch,' you'd say, or,
'Perhaps I'll have something before I go to bed.' You drank a
lot of water to fill up your stomach. Then I tried ignoring it,
thinking that if I didn't pay any attention you'd weary of the
game. And you must have eaten something, sometime, or
you'd have shrivelled up and died. Of course you must have
eaten, just never in front of me. It was me you were punishing,
but I've yet to discover what for. Within two months you'd
begun to resemble a different creature from my girl-woman, a
large-eyed, luminous-eyed wood-spirit, a creature of allegory
from a lost painting of a lost world. You were a lost girl. But I
couldn't pity you because you weren't my girl any more.
You'd changed your shape. You were wounded, diseased. It
was as if you were being devoured. But I didn't fail you, no
matter how loathsome you became, however much you
revolted me, I never forgot my promises to you ('in sickness
and in health', and all those other rotten spells). I called you
every day, four times a day, just as usual. Once we'd passed
the ignoring-it stage I'd ask for a list of what you'd eaten. 'A
yogurt,' you'd say. 'Some nuts. A salad.' 'My child's in there!'

I'd shout, lose my temper and shout, 'Why are you doing this to my child?'

Claire took you to the doctor for your four-month check. You'd refused to go until then. The doctor told you that because you were so weak, anaemic, she'd have to prescribe supplements. She and Claire tried to frighten you by threatening to hospitalise you. You should have known I'd never have allowed that to happen in a million years, but you were stupid with misery.

I came home once to find you sitting in the dark. You'd lit the fire and were staring into the flames. I remember thinking how peculiar it was to stare into the flames of a gas log fire. It was an unauthentic action. I remember thinking those words. I stood there looking at you crouching on the floor with your limbs such a graceful painful line and I said, 'Sweetheart? Precious girl? Are you still with me?' You looked at me in the dimness and I knelt beside you and took your hands. Your face was smeared with tears, your eyes blurred by them. I didn't feel angry as usual, even when you flinched at my touch. I felt something approaching tenderness, almost sorry for you. 'I've thought of something,' I said. You put your head on one side in dumb enquiry, like a bird. 'Will you let me send for Mummy?' Your slight frown contorted your features, they'd grown so naked and large. 'It might be Mummy who can help.'

You shook your head. You said, very quiet, 'Not in my home. I don't want her in my home.'

I bit the inside of my mouth to push back the anger. I counted to ten. 'Then let me take you to hers. We'll go together, and I'll leave you to talk. Please, Susannah.' I squeezed your hand. 'Please.'

I had to bundle you up warm for the journey. You were always cold in those days. Your clothes were too big for you. I tried to tease you, 'You're my shrinking bride,' I said. You didn't listen to me very much or notice what was going on. I was exhausted because you'd insisted on packing our clothes as you'd always done, so I'd had to check everything because you weren't capable. I knew I couldn't tell you that, but I wanted to. I was so angry. I could have stood in the middle of the road and shouted, 'My wife's as useless as a baby. My wife's a useless thing.' On the journey you sipped water. I'd never seen you drink from a bottle before.

Mummy greeted us with open arms, every fire burning. It's a funny little cottage because it's in the middle of the country but somehow manages to have no views. One could have been anywhere, staying there, which I loved about it. We could have been anywhere in the world – or in the northern hemisphere, at least. The sitting room has tiny high recessed windows with little square panes, one side looking on to the lane and high hedge, the other the garden wall and trees at the edge of the woods. Woods are a real wilderness, and we could feel them all around us whether we set foot in them or not. Upstairs the three bedrooms were so close we could hear one another cough. Ours was separated from hers by a staircase and painted a chilly pink. It looked on to the trees. You stood in it and said, 'I don't remember this room like this.' And I said, 'That must be because it's winter.'

Mummy believes in getting right down to things. We sat in the sitting room and the fire smoked and she sipped her tonic water and smoked her beloved Gauloise. I had a large whisky and you had fizzy water. She said, 'My dear, there are some things one has to force oneself to do because they're good for one,' and tapped her glass and smiled. I felt the hint was much too subtle and was lost on you. After all, you were not clever. When you said nothing she tried a sterner approach, 'Susannah, I'm sorry for you. You're a lovely girl. But this has got to stop.' You didn't say a word to her, you wouldn't even look at her, but down at your ring. God, it made me angry, the disrespect. But Mummy was undeterred. 'Dear girl, tomorrow we'll send Alex away and it will be easier – we'll have a heart-to-heart. We've all suffered from sicknesses of the soul. Alex has helped me with mine. Let me help you with yours. It's what a family's for. After we've put the world to rights we'll both feel better, and you can give me some advice about my garden.' As far as I could see she was wasting her breath. Then she asked me all about the latest dramas at work – and I told her everything and all about our life, without a word of criticism or a detail that might put you in a bad light, loyally pretending everything was as it should be and you were a proper wife. We didn't talk about the baby. She and I laughed in the kitchen together, behind the closed door, while you stayed by the fire. I cooked a good dinner for us all, some of which you actually ate. I was hoping and praying the atmosphere might revive you.

I'll never know what Mummy said to you the next morning, as I ran painfully through the woods, my lungs hurting, and I don't want to know. I've never asked her and I've never asked you. Some things are best left as they are. But I do know it worked, and that I have her to thank for the life of my son. She must have frightened you, the way I frightened her, frightened you with the reality of what you were doing to yourself, to us all. I know you must have been suffering very deeply, but I'll never know why, I'll never discover what from. For me it became much tougher because I lost a part of you both. Once more I'd lost my mother to another person, only this time it was to you, my wife. After that morning the long conversations, the little intimacies, cards and presents with which she wooed you, where she had never bothered with me, troubled and distressed me. But they worked. Every morning her call was to you not me, every afternoon she'd ring to catch up on your day. You were still solitary, but no longer alone. You seemed content to pass the remaining months of your pregnancy with some semblance of normality. She encouraged you to occupy yourself, to plan your day. She encouraged you about your garden, but tried to put you off the idea of fussing with anyone else's. Where I had no patience she was incredibly kind. She tried to make you content with your lot which, after all, was the only thing either of us ever asked of you. On the phone to me she simply told me not to worry, adding, 'Now we are three.' I was glad that through Mummy I would always know what you were feeling. But it made me sad that it would never be you and I, babes in the wood, again. Such phases in life always seem more precious when they're past. Mummy's intervention gave me hope, but at the same time it was the end of you and me, the endless possibilities you'd begun by representing to me. I see that now. Now it's clear to me. Now I mourn you, and I can hardly bear to go on. Wherever you are now, pity me.

Mummy always used to describe you as laid back, because you were so cool, so dispassionate, so reticent about your feelings. We know now that laid back was the last thing you were, paralysed would be a better word. I wish I could understand. Sometimes, I long to. At others, I'm glad you're gone because you can't make me feel guilty any more. I think you looked upon it as your vocation, to make me feel guilty. If you did, you succeeded. But still, you began to eat again. Without joy, without appetite, but you ate. In time, you began to look like any other pregnant woman: disgusting. At first, bloated, just a little fat, thickened. Then, as you ate, it came to be beyond fat, surpassed it, and it was as if you were deformed, with bulging stomach and enormous breasts (where they'd always been so tiny, a young girl's breasts on the slender body of a boy). I couldn't bear it. I couldn't bear to look at you. You were very good, keeping yourself covered up. Before, your modesty and consideration had meant I'd rarely seen you without your clothes, but pregnant, you tried even harder to keep yourself covered, and I was grateful. I remember one Sunday afternoon, May, but very hot. You had another month to go and were still just about up to doing some work in the garden. (No one had warned me that living with a pregnant woman is like living with someone disabled.) I discouraged it, but you insisted. You were weeding. I was bored, tired of adjusting the umbrella to keep myself in the shade. You were wearing a huge gingham shirt, and khaki trousers, and kneeling in front of the flowerbed. I studied your bulk from behind with particular fascination and loathing. You must have sensed this, and you turned your sweating face towards me and said, 'What is it?' Such a challenge, Susannah, you should have known by then, was foolish.

'Nothing.'

You got to your feet, breathing heavily and wiping your forehead on your sleeve. 'I'm so hot.'

'Keep still then.'

'I can't. I have to keep the garden neat. It'll look terrible enough when the baby's born.'

'It's a pity you don't feel that way about the house.'

You seemed to reel back slightly at this, swaying on your feet, and I was almost alarmed. 'I'm all right,' you said. 'But you know what I'd love? I'd love an ice-cream. Wouldn't that be fun? To go and buy some ice-cream?' You so rarely had such ideas, I didn't know what to say.

'You can't go out like that.' I hoped that would put you off.

Your eyes narrowed. 'I'll change,' you said slowly, sensing conflict.

'No, I mean, like that. In your condition.'

'During the week I do,' you said. 'I go shopping.'

I hated you for making me spell it out. 'I'm not going out with you looking like that.'

'Oh.' You were still panting slightly – very undignified. Your eyes filled with tears.

'Not again,' I said. 'Please. Not tears again. Look, I'll go and get you some ice-cream. No scenes.'

'No scenes,' you repeated, blinking at me in the white light. 'No scenes.' I couldn't bear your defeated, self-pitying gaze. It made me angry.

'I don't know why you care so much about this garden,' I said. 'It's all stone. No grass. No water. Just terrace and bricks. It's a sun-trap – no breeze.'

'Why are you angry now?' you said, struggling, frowning.

'Because we should have a better garden – grass, space, on a hill – not in this hot place – it should be better – I work hard enough.' It felt strange to air my grievances to you then. I always took such care to keep them to myself for fear of reprisals.

'I didn't know you felt like that, darling,' you said, more tears in your eyes. 'I'm sorry.' You began to advance towards me like a great unstoppable bear. You reached out as if to take my hand. You had an expression of pity, of concern, you filled my vision with your pink freckled face.

'No,' I said. 'Don't. You mustn't touch me. I'll go and get you the ice-cream.'

Letting myself out into the afternoon, only keys and change in my pocket, walking down the street unencumbered, I had a sudden feeling of singing freedom. I remember thinking I shouldn't feel trapped in my own house, and wondering why you should try to corner me, you who were always so self-contained and self-possessed. I felt embarrassed by you. I'd never expected that to ever happen. But then I hadn't expected any of the trouble you'd brought me. When I got back you were sitting under the umbrella gazing straight ahead at the half-weeded flowerbed. You turned your head towards me with no attempt to hide your emotion. It was as if – disgustingly – you'd taken off all your clothes.

I tried to restore the situation. 'Chocolate or strawberry?'

'What?' you said.

I was holding the tubs in my hands. 'For God's sake,

Susannah!' I shouldn't have sworn at you. But if you had refused the ice-cream it would have been the last straw.

You knew that. With a sigh you said, 'Chocolate.' I went back into the kitchen, fetched you a spoon and a napkin and a glass of iced water to go with it. I carried the whole ensemble out to you on a silver wedding-present tray, the first thing I could find. Your face, body, everything about you, looked hot and dirty and weary. I couldn't bear it. I couldn't bear even to sit with you. I put the tray down on the table beside you and stood waiting to be thanked. It took you a while to realise this. Then you said, 'Thank you,' and I said, 'You're welcome,' and I went upstairs to call Mummy. I really was sick and tired of you by then.

Soon after the ice-cream day I got my promotion. Lewis had me moved from his desk, from Bond Sales to Securitisation. Like a bolt from the blue, he met me at the tiny slice of Formica known as my work station, told me to gather up my things and move upstairs. More money, everything. All I could think was: at last we can move. We can have a decent house with floors of empty rooms, with windows we never look out of, even a bigger garden for you. That was all I could think of: elegance and space, holidays, freedom. I tried to shake Lewis's hand, but he was in a hurry. I tried to say goodbye to the team, but around me their places were deserted, the phones un-manned. It was like a dream. With one bound I was free.

My new office was shared with only three. Three unobjec-tionable people stood up to shake my hand. A meeting was scheduled for lunchtime. I had a wooden desk of my own. I had a circle of space around it reserved just for me. The trading floor, my torture chamber, had vanished. I had a view, admittedly only on to the façade of the opposite building; a hundred windows faced mine. But it was a start. My hands were sweating dialling our number. I had words and sentences planned: 'I'm speaking to you from my new office. Go to the estate agent's, put the house on the market, buy a bottle of champagne.' You'd be so proud you might even behave yourself better. As I plotted and planned the phone rang and rang and rang again. It could have been anything. You could have gone out without putting the machine on, you could have been in the garden, in the bath. But I knew from the sound of the ring that it was trouble. Give me credit for that at least. I have a talent for sensing disaster.

I found you, where else but lying on the floor – the bedroom this time. In the ambulance they had to restrain me from slapping your cheeks too hard, but I was angry and only trying to wake you up. I don't remember very much more. The pictures are surrounded by darkness. Emergency Caesarean, that's a phrase implying clean surgery with shiny knives. But it's blood and more blood. I wanted you to wake up and feel the pain the way I was feeling it. You were spared the sights and sounds of it all, the unbelievable horror. The birth of our son wasn't like a birth. It was like a death: the death of hope, the death of our marriage, my death, the death of the future. At the time we couldn't know it, we couldn't know anything. You had extraordinary power for such an unremarkable girl.

When you opened your eyes and stirred and I gave you our son, you said, 'I'm sorry,' and I tried to tell you it was all right, you hadn't failed me, but I couldn't because it wouldn't have been true. Two hours later the room was like a florist's or a film star's, and I'd become your personal assistant, your press agent. You, reclining against the pillows, sewn up, bandaged up, smiling into the faces of a sea of visitors and me saying, 'Don't tire her,' 'Time's up,' 'Yes, doesn't he look like his mother?' 'Thankfully, perfectly healthy,' and laughing and laughing and laughing. I laughed a lot. Mummy said after-wards it was my handsome yet bashful humorous self and I really should give it a rest. She's the only person who's ever been immune to my charm. She was a tremendous help then: sitting beside you while I was at work, reading to you, the things I'd done for her all those terrible times. She repays, Mummy, always. She never forgets a debt. Your parents made only a brief appearance, as did Claire and Will. (Your allies have always lacked staying power.) You were there for ages, I forget how long. Your room cost a bloody fortune, that I do remember. Mummy had to move out of the house when you came home. She'd been keeping the baby's room warm for him. Because you'd been unable to carry my son to full term, you hadn't had a chance to choose the wallpaper for his room, so we decorated it while Mummy was staying, as a surprise. Needless to say you weren't sufficiently grateful. Some things don't change – you've never acknowledged what others do for you, expecting things as your right. I wish you'd let her stay on, but you were uncharitable about that too, practically packing her off the next day, sighing wearily to make sure you got your own way. Talk about manipulative. Those first months were hell. All that screaming in the middle of the night, the baby crying, you crying. I tried to explain to you what Mummy had taught me about routines, but you ignored me, picking him up whenever he made a sound. You were his slave.

We knew that the most important thing was to keep you eating while you were breast-feeding (something you insisted on, although it's quite unnecessary). Mummy and I were prepared to go to any lengths for the boy to be healthy. I accepted that you were unable to be a real wife to me. (Frankly, rather a relief.) I did all the shopping myself and cooked you dinner every night. At Mummy's suggestion I found a mother's help for you to keep you company during the day. I stopped complaining entirely about your laziness and lack of organisation. I'd have been satisfied if you'd stayed in bed all day, as long as you ate, and fed the baby regularly, so he could have the right start in life. 'The right start in life' were words always in my head, those, and Mummy's other favourite phrase, 'The first six months are the worst.' My father had shown his true colours after the first six months. I knew if you and I could get through them we might stand a chance. I made so few demands on you because I really wanted it to work. I wasn't always at home, thoughtful enough to keep myself out of the way and bide my time.

To be fair to you, you tried to be a good mother. You ate up. I knew you were eating because you remained quite repulsively bloated. As before the birth, you kept yourself covered up, but you did not always spare me the sight of a leaking swollen nipple, and the smell of your sour dried milk. I'd come home from work and you'd be sitting in what you pretentiously described as 'Barnaby's bedroom', in that hideous mahogany chair which was one of your loathsome heirlooms. You'd call out, 'Alex, is that you? We're upstairs.' ('We', as if the baby were a person.) He'd be asleep at the breast. And I'd stand in the doorway like a child and you'd look up and smile a sleepy smile, almost contented, self-satisfied, as if you'd done something good and clever simply by putting your toughened nipple in his soggy mouth. 'How was your day?' you'd say, vaguely shifting your position, and I'd murmur some old bollocks and you'd say, 'Oh?' or 'Really?' and I could tell you hadn't heard.

'Isn't he beautiful?' He wasn't beautiful. He had repulsive spots – 'baby acne', you called it, as if this were a charming idea, a notion to be cherished and oohed and aahed about.

'I can't see him.'

'He's fallen asleep – I don't want to move him.'

'Show him to me another time – when you're decent.'

'I'll be putting him down soon. Last chance.' You'd smile with a hint of a tease.

Once I remember saying. 'Why is the expression for disposing of an unwanted animal the same as for putting a baby to sleep?' (Of course, 'put to sleep' is another euphemism, but I didn't want to labour the point.)

Slowly, as stupidly as a sleepwalker, you said, 'I don't know.' (It's a known fact that motherhood kills brain cells.)

You kept taking photographs of him. I'd say, 'There's no point. He hasn't any expressions,' and you'd look at me puzzled and say, 'What makes you think that?'

Leaving the charmed zone of Barnaby's bedroom, never to be Mummy's room again, to the sound of empty tinkling and the slow revolve of a gaudy mobile, you'd say, 'Sssh.' You made me feel too loud, altogether too big for my own house. I even had to go into the garden to smoke a cigarette and talk on the phone.

What was peculiar about it was that you seemed so imperturbable, armoured, absent. I felt I knew exactly what the expression 'wrapped up in the baby' meant. You were like conspirators. Dutifully, you filled your plate, you filled your stomach, happily you woke in the night and went to him. You'd have midnight conversations with him. You thought I couldn't hear them. You thought I was asleep. 'Sweetheart,' you'd say. (What had he done to deserve my term of endearment?) 'Comfortable? Good. Tomorrow we'll go to the park if it doesn't rain. Mummy's going to take you for a nice long walk.' (Whenever you said 'Mummy' I'd get confused, thinking you meant mine.) You'd even sing in a murmuring tuneless voice, a humble sound, words utterly without originality. But then there was never anything original about you. I never uttered a word of protest, sensing that for the first time you wouldn't care at all what I thought.

We stumbled through the first six months until you

(unilaterally) decided to wean the little blighter. Not before time, I might add. He was about half your size by then and already eating something repulsive called baby rice. You said weaning was a good idea because then I too could give him his bottle and it would help me to – what's the dreaded word? – bond. Now I don't want you getting the impression I didn't love my son. You know perfectly well that he was more precious to me than any other person on earth – it's just that there's not much *to* love in a baby. The rewards come later, along with the inevitable and continual frustrations. But that's another story. With the weaning, the nightmare returned. He rejected the bottle. He rejected the breast (can't say I blame him), he didn't want either, he wanted both – it was a great big bore. Mummy said, 'Be patient,' Mummy said, 'It's a phase.' You wept and carried on so, as if he were starving you instead of the other way round. But eventually it was accomplished. He was weaned. Again I had to watch you like a hawk, in case you stopped eating, but I needn't have worried. You kept right on guzzling, all through Christmas. The only festive thing about that season was my bonus. I took you out to dinner to celebrate it. 'That much?' you said. 'Good.' I think you smiled. Hardly abundant praise. You were so separate and far away and I didn't know what to do to make it better. I was trapped. Your vagueness had defeated me.

I'd left work early, battling home through traffic at six o'clock. The house was dark but it didn't feel empty. How does one always know? You were upstairs packing, the baby kicking its legs inanely on the floor beside you.

'What are you doing?' I said, as if I'd been deprived of my power and had absolutely no say in the matter. If I hadn't been in such a state I'd have realised that you weren't really leaving me. If you'd wanted to leave you'd have been gone before I got home. (In my opinion no decision taken after eleven in the morning can ever be fully acted on in the same day.) You didn't meet my eye or stop what you were doing. I knew it was an extraordinary crisis for you to abandon your exquisite manners. Your packing consisted of a lot of folding and blind marching about but not much else. Only one bedside light shone. The blinds were open. I pulled them down and drew the curtains to give myself time. Then I said again, 'What are you doing, Susannah?'

You stopped and looked at me, the bed stretching between us. You said, 'You promised to be faithful. It's the only thing I've ever asked.' You pulled the letter out of your pocket and waved it at me like a flag. Your face was unmarked by tears or sorrow, your voice clear and high. I'd never seen you angry before but I wondered if this was what it was like. Your eyes were unreadable. You kept waving the letter. 'Take it, for God's sake,' you said. I snatched it out of your hand. It read: 'I've been fucking your husband. I thought one of us should tell you.' It was typed, signed and there was a telephone number. The malicious bitch was obviously not playing it safe. The thing was that I could have lied, bluffed, counter-attacked. The evidence was by no means conclusive. But when I saw this poisonous thing, when I realised that this woman I had indeed been fucking – undeniably the best word for it – had been so cruel to you, I felt a misery so great – I can't find a word to describe it, even now. What kind of woman could write such a letter? For what kind of woman had I lied to you? I couldn't remember why I'd done it. I couldn't remember anything. I couldn't speak. I felt so helpless – I think I hung my head. The baby, you, me, in a tiny room, were all looking into separate space. Why had I caused that? Why had I made that happen? I'd done it so I could come and come quickly and not have to feel disgusted by you, only with myself.

The silence was interrupted by a terrible hooting and

carrying on in the road. Two cars were at a stand-off because in my haste I'd double-parked. That's London for you.

'I have to go down and move the car,' I said, looking at you. I looked at your mouth not your eyes. I could see you were shaking and in shock. 'I've got to go.' You didn't answer me so I went. I took your keys from the hall table and locked the front door so you couldn't escape while I was parking the car. I needn't have bothered. When I came back you had locked yourself in the bathroom with the baby. I could hear you sobbing to the sound of running water. 'Are you all right?' I called under the door. I put my eye to the key-hole but could see nothing. I could have murdered whoever invented doors. 'I'm worried about you. Are you all right?'

'Go away,' you said, not very convincingly.

'I'll do no such thing. You're my wife.' Still nothing. Trained in these situations, I tried to restore normality. 'I'm going to make you a cup of tea.' I went down the stairs again, this time turning on all the lights. I lit the fire as well. The evening was damp and cold for the city. From the kitchen I could hear you sobbing. 'Don't upset the baby,' I called. 'Don't damage my child.'

'No,' you said, and cried all the more. You started to really wail. There was no sound at all from Barnaby.

I made the tea and carried it carefully up the stairs, resuming my siege position on the landing. 'He doesn't seem at all upset,' I said, trying to sound warm and humorous, sensible, reassure you, be practical, a friend, trying to cheer you up. Silence. 'She's just a stupid old tart,' I said. You laughed. I'll always remember that, it was such a shock. You hardly ever laughed in all the time I knew you.

'Go away,' you said again, but your voice was softer, less defeated, or more defeated – I don't know.

'You're the only one for me, Susannah,' I said. 'For ever and always. You're my precious sweetheart, my treasure.'

'No,' you said. 'Don't.'

'What do you want me to do?' I asked. You knew I'd have done anything. More silence. Were you listening? I couldn't tell. 'If it hadn't been for the baby –' I left a pause. There wasn't even the sound of water. I didn't know if you were in the bath, or sitting on the loo stifling sobs – I couldn't stand it. 'Please, Susannah,' I said, 'open the door. I made you tea, and it'll get cold.' Because you were brought up in obedience, because of your generosity I think more than all your other virtues, you opened the door. I gave you the cup of tea. For a second I thought you would throw it back in my face. For a second I think you wanted to, but only for a second. The baby was lying on the floor of the bathroom, still kicking. Oblivious. 'Could you really leave me? After all those years I waited for you? I love you so much. You just shut me out.'

'Is that true?' You sounded mournful, undecided.

'Of course it's true. The baby –'

'He's *our* baby.'

'More yours than mine.'

'But I want you to –'

'It's *you* I want.' I took your hand and kissed it, kissed the wedding ring.

'I don't know what to do with this cup of tea,' you said, and smiled. That smile lifted my heart.

'Sit down and drink it. Then have a bath.' I put my hand on the top of your head, brushing your hair with my hand.

'What about Barnaby?'

'I'll take him. What's he meant to be doing now?'

'Bottle and bed.'

'Bottle and bed,' I repeated, confused.

'Downstairs,' you said gently. 'The bottles are ready, you only have to measure out the formula – five spoons – the kettle's boiled, just make sure it's not too hot. You remember. And dim the lights a little.'

'He's not pooey, is he?'

'I've changed his nappy.' You passed me the boy.

'Forgive me,' I said.

'Yes,' you said, closing the door. 'But not another word.'

'She's hidden her head in the sand,' said Mummy. But of course that wasn't the end of it. There were to be plenty more words. The longer I live the more I believe words between people are useless, immaterial. All that evening I burned to know if you had called the stupid bitch, if she'd tortured you with details – but I came to understand you'd done no such thing. You have no courage, no courage for details. If we could have made love that night – if – but I couldn't force myself on you, didn't want to. You turned away from me on to your side and I didn't dare touch you. My throat was so tight I could hardly breathe. Was yours? There were no sounds between us, no touching. I slept very deeply. I don't know if you slept at all. You'd said you often passed sleepless nights between feeds so it was possible (though women are apt to exaggerate once they get a notion in their heads). I dreamed about her, my bit on the side, my mistress, or Suzie the Floozie as she will henceforward be known. By strange coincidence you had almost the same name. She had an unpleasant taste; in spite of that, or perhaps because of it, I always – sickeningly – wanted more. That was the beginning of constant and overwhelming dreams about her.

Unspoken contracts began with that evening. I had to be home in time for Barnaby's bottle: my daily act of worship – sorry, bonding. In return, if I went outside to make a call you'd never ask me about it. I can tell you now I rarely called the Floozie from home, but you weren't to know that. There was to be no touching in bed – that I knew was important to you. We avoided touching at all, in fact. It was simpler that way, cleaner. We both behaved as if the Floozie were an aberration that had passed – but you never asked me to confirm that, and I never did. It was because we both knew you were too pure for me to lie to you. You were afraid of the words. But I can tell you now I punished her for daring to write to you. Sweetheart, it never crossed my mind at any time voluntarily to say goodbye to my pink and gold girl, beribboned girl – even though she had become only a memory to us both. I still don't undertand why you stood in her place – a shadow-eyed woman, why I couldn't keep my gold-blonde girl. It's not at all clear. I was in hell because I couldn't give her up, she was my one drug, my one excitement, the one selfishness I allowed myself in what had become a drab and constricted existence. I was going through fire for you – I'd have done anything but walk away. I have my own honour. Don't ever argue with that. Allow me that at least. Despite the truce you blocked me, punished me with your misery. At times I thought it might have been better if you had left me that February day.

That time was a very low point. Swallowing was hard. The three unobjectionable men, gradually losing their unobjection-able status anyway, were absolute hell. At my desk I scratched doodles with biros and stabbed paper with the nib of my fountain pen. I've broken many nibs in that way. I'm never sure if it's worth it for the satisfaction. I smoked too much, drank too much coffee, clutched my stomach in what you used to call my 'Napoleon' pose. I bit my nails and they bled. I cursed you in silence, baffled as to why you still chose to take so many – so-called – unconscious actions to wound me.

It was a long cold winter. The 'immaculate conception', as we'd learned to call him, smiling, avoiding one another's eyes, grew like a fiend. He was like a physical symbol of what divided us. First he only stood between us, then tottered, trotted, walked. But, God – those endless ailments! It was as if you gave them to him to make sure I'd come home on time. Mummy looked after you. She put in the time, for me really, the hours on the telephone, hours of gossip, chat, advice. 'We're good friends, Susannah and I,' she'd say. 'Good friends.' She kept telling you to be patient. 'This, too, shall pass,' she told you. 'I make her repeat it after me.' That was clever of her, you liked the Bible, it comforted you. You waited a year. The next winter I broke it off, decided we should have interests: hobbies. In March I took you skiing and all you did was cry for him, and I for her – my Floozie (the one whose legs were open and whose mouth was thankfully shut). But that's another story.

We took an horrendously early flight back from skiing so we'd have time to go straight down to your parents to collect the boy. I'd begged you to let us at least touch base at home first, but oh, no – you were set on immediate and close contact with the M25. In the car looking at the tedium of the English countryside from the gash that was the road, you had a golden face but white eyes, the skiing-goggle tan. Mummy and I would have laughed about it, but you and I couldn't. You have no sense of humour. I was in a bad mood about having to see your mother, I'll admit that, so despite rousing opera highlights we were glum. Cars are terrible places to be sometimes. There's no escape from the other person's moods – yours enveloped me, your longing to see the boy, your contained impatience. I could have shaken you for that control. I think these were our actual words:

'Not too cold.' Profound observation from you.

'Leaves have come on the trees. One forgets how green England is.' Me politely showing willing.

'So many cars, all with one person in them. If only car-sharing –'

'Don't be ridiculous, Susannah. An Englishman's car is his castle, you know that.'

'There's not enough space in the world, it worries me.'

'That's a classic, coming from a landowner's daughter.' Frustrated silence. I was waiting for you to say, 'It's not my fault Daddy has land,' but you refrained.

'He'll have grown.' Admirable change of subject on your part, I must say.

'Undoubtedly.'

'I hope he's been happy.'

'He'll have been happy, Mother-hen.'

'Mummy's first grandchild.' Unfailingly, you stated the obvious. 'She might not have understood –' Unbearable unfinished sentence again.

'But Helena's with him. He's her job.' Buried exasperation from me.

'Yes. I know.'

'Well, then?'

'Nothing.'

'Nothing, what?'

'Nothing.' More miles went by.

'What does your watch say?' Magnificent question, darling, worthy of an eight-year-old.

'Same as yours I imagine.' You were lucky I dignified it with a reply.

Arrival: mullioned windows shimmered, intermittent sun shining through fast-moving clouds. You practically leaped out of the car before I'd parked it, and ran up the steps. I sighed, squared my shoulders, tried not to be afraid, shivering in that perpetual wind. I remember thinking: She's only an old fat dragon. Imagine her in pink tights. Minimise, minimise the enemy like you do at work. She's never made a scrap of effort with me not one scrap. Your voice quivered in that echoing dusty hall.

'Barnaby? Mummy?' The hall table was covered in bowls of bluebells from the woods, past their best and stinking.

Then, at last, came the patter of tiny feet, the sound of voices. Your mother called, 'Susannah? Is that you?' as if she were blind (I've never existed for her at all), and she carried the boy down the stairs as you ran to grab him from her arms and cover the squirming astonished child with kisses. I don't care what you said afterwards, I'm sure he had no idea who you were. They don't have memories at that age, that's what Mummy's always told me. The dragon smiled as you clasped him and he pointed at you, in what you used to call his Leonardo da Vinci point. There was nothing in the least sublime about it, so you embarrassed yourself yet again with that observation. He patted you on your rather sunken cheek and poked you in the eye.

'There, there,' said the ogre that is your mother, and as one you turned to face me, stiffening, straightening, coming down the stairs. You get your height from your father, she has no height at all but she has your reserve, a colder reserve, though. She always seemed stronger. 'And how were the mountains?' she said, raising her eyebrows, as if the Alps were an exhibition or a play I was required to encapsulate in one amusing sentence.

'Cold,' I said, to thwart her.

'Snow good?'

'Reasonable.'

'I'm glad. How did Susannah get on?'

'She'll improve.'

'It's difficult, Mummy,' you said, far too apologetically I thought. I hated seeing you kow-tow to her. Barnaby got hold of a piece of your hair and yanked it. He put his thumb in his mouth. Behind it we could see a glimmer of a smile.

'The best part of a holiday is coming home,' smiled the monster. 'That's what I always say.'

'Which is why we should get going,' I said, looking at you straight. You both looked bemused, which was exceptionally irritating.

'It's a long drive back to London,' said the old hag. 'There's lunch here. I'm not sure if Barnaby's even packed.' When neither of us answered she got the hint. 'I'll go and find Helena.' Off she went, clomping up the stairs: tiny feet, gigantic body. I wished she'd slip. I had far too many ungranted wishes that day. We avoided lunch by a whisker. Of course you didn't take my side, so it was bloody difficult to get away. I felt angry – you'd got the boy, wasn't that enough?

You put him in my arms while you packed the car. 'It's safer,' you said. 'I don't want him tripping up while we're not looking. Gravel and flagstones aren't baby-friendly.' I hated the way you were always trying to explain things to me as if I were a cretin. He didn't try to struggle. He gazed solemnly into my eyes, resting his hands on my cheeks. He didn't flinch. I kissed his brow and told him I was glad to see him. I think he understood.

That fragile silence was disrupted as soon as we were safely up the drive.

'You could slow down,' you said.

'Now it's my driving you don't like.'

'I haven't criticised you.' Miss Prim, you turned in your seat to check for the millionth time that the boy was properly strapped in.

'Not in words. You could have supported me when I said we had to go.'

Silence, infuriating; then the wounded-victim voice, low, husky. 'I wanted to have lunch with my mother.'

'Sorry – separate negotiation needed for that one, sweetie. That bloody –'

'Ssssh. *Pas devant l'enfant.*'

'He's not even two, for fuck's sake!' I shouted, I admit. But you pushed so hard, always, without appearing to. Your strategies were so deep. 'He doesn't understand.'

'He understands everything.'

'If you start crying I'm going to stop the car. I'm sick of your scenes.'

'No crying,' you said, turning your face away to look out of the window and weep. I think you were addicted to tears. There should be treatment centres for it: 'My name is Susannah and I'm a plangent dependant.' This thought made me laugh. I laughed, you cried – what was Barnaby to make of the world? I often wondered that. It must be a myth that the mother's the best parent. You've never given me any evidence to support it, though I must be fair to you and say again that you tried your best.

By now, rage was building. I tried to restore normality. 'Is there any food in the house?'

'I have no idea.' Gulps from you.

'Helpful answer.' Rather than attempt further discussions I stopped at the supermarket and stocked up with easy stuff: fresh pasta and pesto, bread, cheese, fruit, enough for a good lunch. God only knew where supper was going to come from, but I was damned if I was going to think about that too. I was exhausted.

Back to the tiny stale house, tinier and staler after the mountains. You went straight into the garden – your habit – leaving me to do lunch. I could see you from the kitchen window, minutely inspecting each winter plant in the most extraordinary detail (they looked like sticks to me). You put Barnaby down and he held your hand, upright but swaying beside you. You ignored him totally, but he just about kept up. There wasn't much walking. Hardly a tour of the acres.

'I must stake the roses before the warm weather,' you said, coming into the kitchen, Barnaby on your hip.

'Must you?' I said. I was still sick with anger.

You pretended to ignore me. 'I'm just going upstairs to wash my face and change his nappy. Are you all right with the lunch?'

'Perfectly.' God, I was angry. You took ages up there. Your plate was cold when you came down and I'd nearly finished mine.

'Why didn't you call me?' you said, employing your mild, wronged sound.

'For God's sake, Susannah, you know how long pasta takes.' More wounded-doe eyes. 'How long does it take?'

'Ten minutes.' You put Barnaby down and he tottered off purposefully.

'Not fresh pasta, you idiot.'

'I didn't realise.'

' "I didn't realise," ' I mimicked.

'Please stop this,' you said, pleading. 'Please.'

I got up to put my plate in the dishwasher, move away from you. '*You* want *me* to stop! *You*'re the *one* –' It was such a splutter. I couldn't control myself, and the oily plate in my hand was too tempting. I threw it over your head and it hit the kitchen wall. You shrieked in fear. 'I'm not throwing it at you,' I explained. 'I'm just letting off steam.' You were awfully stupid. 'Now eat your lunch.' You were shivering.

'It's cold.'

'Eat it,' I said. 'Don't you dare start that starving again, don't you *dare*!' You tried to get out of your chair but I was too quick for you. I put my hands on your shoulders and pushed you back down.

'Don't touch,' you said, sounding frightened.

'I'm not going to hurt you.' I hated having to explain all the time. 'I just want you to eat your lunch.'

'Barnaby –'

'I'll see to him.' I followed the child into the hall where he was sitting in quiet contemplation of the radiator, which was safely off. I closed the sitting-room door and closed the stair-gate. 'He's safe,' I called. 'Perfectly happy.' When you didn't answer I went back into the kitchen. You sat, head bowed, head in your hands I think, plate untouched. I sat down beside you and pulled you on to my knee. You didn't resist. You felt so relaxed you were actually heavier. Your hands were still across your eyes, blocking me out. 'Bring your hands down.' You obeyed. (After all, it was in the wedding ceremony and you're an old-fashioned girl.) With one hand securing you round your waist, I picked up the fork with the pasta on it. 'Mmm, lovely pasta,' I said, as I'd heard you say to him, introducing solids. 'Yum-mee.' Your eyes were still closed. You held yourself absolutely still, no struggling. 'Open wide for me, darling.'

'I don't want –' Tears were streaming. I rammed the fork into your mouth. You spat out the food. I rammed again. You swallowed. Suffice to say that I got that lunch down you, but really, Susannah, what a way to come home! As soon as we'd finished, the touching was over. You were off my lap and out of the room, flying up the stairs to 'Barnaby's bedroom' where I heard a torrent of tears, but thankfully no sick. You were down again very quickly, calling from the hall in your coolest politest voice. 'I'm just popping out to the garden centre. I'll take Barnaby.'

'Fine,' I called back. I must say I was thankful to have brought you to your senses.

I wish I could say that that was the last time I had to force-feed you but we both know it became something of a ritual. What else was I to do? You didn't eat breakfast, you didn't eat lunch, I came home from work and from the moment I came in the door my mind was on getting you to eat your dinner. Darling, I was trying to keep you alive. I didn't want to shame you by telling your family or the dreaded Claire how worried I was about you – though Mummy knew perfectly well – I wanted to keep it between ourselves until you were back on track. You were punishing me for the affair, it doesn't take a trained professional to work that out, and in a way you had every right, but it wasn't me that was pining away, it was you. And the ridiculous thing was that there was no need to pine. I was right beside you. I know I have to face this head-on and write down how long it all went on, your cruel cruel punishment. It's no time for self-delusion. His second birthday came and went and the Fourth of July approached. He was walking properly, talking only a little, and I think you were house-hunting at last. You really were incredibly lazy about that. We could have moved months before, but at least some effort was being made, I'll give you that. We'd even planned our summer holiday, or rather I'd planned it, renting that villa in Umbria. You'd wanted to go to the South of France – hoping to soften me up with memories – but I'd had to put my foot down and refuse point blank. No one should be forced to revisit their childhood. I tried to look forward to the break, but the Floozie was back and she wanted me to go away with her for a week as well, and I didn't know how it was to be managed while you were still in such a sensitive state. It was preying on my mind. The thought of lying to you was unbearable, the thought of telling you the truth, worse. Those nightly sessions were beginning to take it out of me, but more importantly, they didn't seem to be working for you. You were skin and bone. I was ashamed of you. We hardly ever went anywhere. We could just as easily be on the side of a hill somewhere for all the use we made of living in London. It was a disaster.

So to the Fourth of July. Such is the colonisation of our little island by the Americans, one could hardly escape it and, especially as my bank was an American one, I was fair game. We'd had loads of special bulletins and drearily festive faxes, tedious celebrations disguised as group evaluation meetings, and to add insult to injury the American office was closed on the actual day so I couldn't get anything done. It was a Friday and most of my fellow worker-bees had taken a long weekend. We were in no position to do the same because of your disgusting state, but at least it meant that the traffic on the Embankment wasn't too bad. I remember thinking about the new car I would get that summer and wondering if you'd object if I went for a sports model, or if you'd think it a rejection of our marriage if I didn't provide you with a family car. The thought of your stricken face irritated me, but I banished it because the afternoon was fresh and I felt surprisingly young. I made the car whiz through traffic and took a couple of risks overtaking, which made me whoop with joy. My happiness wasn't conscious. So often I had to count my blessings in those days and close my eyes to my burdens (you, Mummy, *her*) to coax a feeling of well-being. Either that or plenty of champagne. But on that drive the mood came over me of singing, feeling that behind the window of every house, flat and office there were other people who might possibly be friends rather than enemies, that I was part of something which wasn't necessarily hostile, that I could almost feel in tune with. Fat chance.

You were lying on the floor of the kitchen (AGAIN) and you didn't appear to be breathing. You had obviously fallen. Barnaby was standing solemnly beside you. I had no idea how long he'd been there, but he looked dimmed-out – away with the fairies. I'll never forgive you for letting him see you like that. Everything was like a still photograph: you diagonal on the black-and-white tiled floor (thank God it wasn't the hard terracotta you'd wanted or you might have cracked your head open), Barnaby a white waxwork beside you, me in the doorway. The sun streamed in from the window and the glass door to the garden, which was closed. It was hot and stuffy. I ran to you, knelt, put my ear to your heart. That you were breathing came as a shock. You were right underneath the wall telephone, perhaps you'd meant to call me. I didn't want to touch the boy. I felt afraid of him, but after a while I scooped him up and held him on my hip as you always did. He stared. I murmured at him for a while and he began to see me. That was after they'd taken you away. I called Mummy and then I called your parents. Fatal.

If you could have spoken to them, I know you would have stopped it, all of it, everything that happened. I wanted you to wake up so you could tell them how much you loved me and how it wasn't my fault, explain to them about our marriage vows and what they meant, tell them to leave me in peace. But I couldn't even see you alone, let alone try to wake you up. Your father was in London on business that day, so when I called the dragon she got hold of him and he went to the hospital straight away. She said she didn't want Barnaby at the hospital, so my instructions were to stay with him in the house, and because I couldn't think at all, I agreed, believing it was only for the time being. For me it was only a question of waiting for my mummy. The evening became cloudy and rain fell. I turned on all the lights on the ground floor and opened all the windows and the back door. The rain fell in at the windows and cooled us down. I sat with Barnaby on my knee. We felt bereaved. Time passed. When the bell rang, I thought it was her. I don't think any child could have been more relieved at the idea of seeing its mother than I was at that moment. But of course it wasn't my mother, it was yours. She looked like a chalky-faced toad. The first thing she did was grab Barnaby without a word, without a gesture or greeting.

'What are you doing?'

'Granny's taking you to stay with her,' she said to Barnaby, who wasn't really listening. Then, 'What have you done to him?'

'Nothing. I've done nothing wrong. Come in.' I wasn't going to leave her standing on the doorstep. After all, she was your mother. She said no, and it was only then that I began to understand that she was about to kidnap our son. You have to understand, Susannah, that it wasn't ever what I wanted. I was in shock. All my usual strength was gone.

'I have to go.' She was walking away, fast. She'd turned her back on me, and I was running after her.

'But what about Susannah?' I was actually begging. I still can't believe it.

'Call the hospital,' she said. 'Find out for yourself.' She's so fat she was already out of breath. Do you see what I had to deal with? The extent of her lunacy? You were still unconscious, as I was to discover later, and she didn't even tell me that, not one word. In the end I stopped running and stood and watched her take him away. It wasn't what I wanted. I didn't understand what was happening. After that – you know that theory we all brood over as children: if you can't see someone how do you know they're still there? That's what it was like. I was all alone in the house and I didn't know if I was still there. Until Mummy came and took my hand.

In the morning I called the hospital, I was afraid to call your mother. The nurses said there'd been no change: you were unconscious and they didn't know why. The doctor advised total peace and seclusion. They would be running tests. I can't believe they actually sided with your mother against me, but that's what it came down to. 'No visitors,' said the faceless one, when I finally got him on the phone. Later he became the one with the red hair and beard, you probably don't remember him. 'No visitors,' was all anybody said, over and over again. The week after that the tests began: leukaemia, MS, heart disease, you name it, you had it. They should have asked me. I would have told them it was a broken heart and that I was the only person who could mend it for you. By then I was in agony. Only Mummy kept me sane. She helped me: things like having to give the mother's help notice because I didn't know when my wife and child would be back. Did they think once of the humiliation? Did they, fuck. I was still your husband, still his father, still me. You would never have denied that. I know you.

In the end they were left with severe malnutrition and possible kidney failure. You weighed seven stone. Two weeks had passed. I'd recovered outward composure. Mummy never left me and I was a bit better. Our holiday was still booked. I had visions of smuggling you out of the hospital and taking you away to recover under a real sky. It wasn't as difficult as I'd feared it would be to get in to see you. It wasn't as if you were a Mafia gunshot victim and had armed guards posted outside your door. No one in the hospital had any idea what I looked like. I knew if I could find a young enough nurse I could rely on my charm. And I was in luck – happening on just the right one. She was hot and tired and awfully relieved to see such a handsome husband almost engulfed by an enormous bunch of white roses with glossy London leaves begging in a cracked voice to see his young wife. I explained that no one understood the true situation. I wasn't about to lie. We stood outside your room, the last at the end of the private ward. She knocked, explaining to me she had to ask your permission first, that it was your right. Persuading her was the hard part. Persuading you, I knew would be easy. She closed the door behind her but I could still just catch the sound of your beloved voice, low and musical, but very very quiet. Mummy said afterwards I must have imagined it through the door because you were still so ill, but I knew it was yours. No wishing could have made you real – no wishing in the world. The silly cow tiptoed out. She had a lot of freckles and moles. Why do nurses, pretty or plain, always seem to have so many? It must be a genetic thing. Slowly she explained that knowing I was there had 'flustered' you, and that I could only go in if I promised only a short visit and no upsetting you.

'But does she want me?' I was suddenly frantic.

'She understands you're here, and she's agreed to see you, yes,' said the ninny in a pinny.

'Bless you,' I said, and looked at her as if I wanted to touch her. (I did, but not in the way she hoped.) She blushed.

'I'll be just down the hall at the nurses' station,' she said. 'There's a bell by her bed.' I could have screamed waiting for her to finish.

'Thank you.' I knew she wouldn't go away until I went in, so I concentrated with all my might on opening the door slowly, looking down at the knob: no bursting in, no sudden movements. It was a box of a room, the wall opposite me a covered window, your bed parallel with it, one of those horrid televisions ogling you from the high corner. You were lying down flat, which I hadn't expected. At least you weren't wired up to anything, which is my worst. I can't bear that. You turned your dear head towards me, your eyes looked dull. I laid the flowers beside you on the orange blanket and knelt down at the bed, burying my face in the stiff sheet. I couldn't look at you. I felt so ashamed. I wanted to cry but I knew I absolutely mustn't. Mummy had made me promise. I felt your bony hand on my head, a light pressure, and your voice said, 'Hello, darling.' When I looked up our faces were close together and you filled my vision. It was heaven.

'I'm so sorry,' I said. 'I love you so.'

'Sssh.' I was moved to kiss you on the mouth. The kiss was full of tenderness and the salt of our tears. 'You can get up,' you whispered, and your smile trembled.

I sat on the flowers. I'm sure you smiled. I extricated myself from them and showed them to you. 'Your favourites,' I reminded you. 'Roses.'

'I wish you'd brought some from the garden. But I suppose they're over by now.' You spoke hoarsely, it wasn't your normal voice.

I stifled my irritation. Those roses had cost a lot of money, plus I couldn't bear to tell you I hadn't even looked in the garden. 'Next time,' I said. I held your hand. 'Are you getting better?' I asked. You didn't look better. You looked ghastly.

'I think so,' you struggled, with the old frown. 'I don't know.'

'Yes, you are.' I tried to encourage you. 'You're awake now. You weren't awake for a long time.' You listened very carefully, intently, as if there were only my voice in your world. 'You don't have much of a view.' I tried to be jovial, looking round: it was all net curtains and subdued light.

'Nothing much to see.' You were losing concentration.

'When you're better I'll take you away.' There was no reaction, as if you were still thinking about what the words meant. 'Do you want to sit up? Shall I get you something?' It made me nervous, your blankness, nervous.

'No,' you said. 'No.' I knew you were suffering and I didn't know what to do.

'Are you in pain? Does it hurt?' And I put my hand over your heart, the way I used to do with Mummy. I was trying to ease your suffering, but I could see you flush and begin to sweat. I could feel your heart beating faster and the sweat on your face and on the hand I was holding. I let it go. You were looking at me like a frightened animal. 'Now, Susannah. Calm down. Breathe.'

'I love you,' you said.

'And I love you, always.' I tried to coax you and make you smile with the words but they seemed to hurt you more. You were almost panting. I felt claustrophobic. 'I must go,' I explained. 'You're getting tired.'

'I've missed you,' you said. 'But please go.'

I think your mother must have been deranged with worry about you, the only kind explanation for why she rang me up that night screaming, 'I'm not going to let you kill my child.'

This time I screamed back, 'She's my wife and there's nothing you can do about that.' Mummy loved it when I said that. The worst thing was that I hadn't managed to say any of the things I'd planned to say to you. I could see you weren't well enough for Italy, but I'd still wanted to tell you all about it, that I was still there, planning for you, for us. At that point I couldn't think about the boy. It was much too painful. I'd even stopped asking to speak to him, there didn't seem much point. Your ogre-mother kept screaming, 'Relapse,' rather like the boy who cried wolf if you ask me. I was afraid they were going to move you to another hospital after that. In any event I was spared that anxiety, because you couldn't be moved. There was no improvement. There was nothing left, no more I could have done. I knew I was played out, at least for the time being. So I decided the only sensible option would be to go to Italy with Suzie the Floozie – there was no use wasting the villa, it was paid for. I still maintain that holidaying with one's mistress when one's wife is severely ill in hospital and one's son has been forcibly taken away is hardly a picnic, but even Mummy wasn't especially sympathetic to my plight, so I won't say any more about it. All things considered, I needed a break. I didn't get one.

When I came back from Italy I put the house on the market: too many bad memories. We needed a fresh start. As you know, I can get things done in a hurry if I need to. Mummy helped me find a better, bigger house on a hill near the common. Still a small garden but you can't have everything. There were four bedrooms; room for more children, room for Mummy. I was excited for the first time in ages. Your family had agreed to keep me informed if I promised not to try to see you again, and I began to content myself with that. After all, I'd waited for you before, and at least this time I knew you were reasonably safe and I had no competition. My fear was that they were poisoning your mind against me, but there was absolutely nothing I could do. Mummy moved into the new house with me and helped me with the architect and builders. I don't know what I'd have done without her.

At the end of September you called me. You actually dialled my number and spoke. 'Alex?'

'Sweetheart.'

'Say it again. Say sweetheart again.'

'Sweet heart. Where are you?'

'I'm at home.'

'How can you be at home? You don't know where we live.'

'No, darling, I'm at home – the country – Mummy's.' In the silence I bit my tongue. Old habits die hard. 'Don't be angry.'

'I'm not angry.' I almost choked on the big fat lie. 'How could I be angry?'

'I wanted to see Barnaby, and we felt –'

'I understand,' I said. 'When?'

'Yesterday.'

'No. When can I see you?'

You took a quick breath. 'Whenever you like.' You said this lightly, as if it didn't matter.

'Tonight.'

'What about work? It's a long drive.' You were nervous and couldn't conceal it.

'All right then, Saturday.'

'Saturday.' You broke up the word into soft syllables. Something stopped me from asking you if you'd be packed and ready. I just said goodbye.

The garden of the new house was overgrown and I'd left it like that in an attempt to romance you with its wilderness. It had the advantage of being square anad relatively private. A tired pink rose was still in bloom on the back wall. It was straggling and looked pretty ropy to me, and probably had every disease imaginable, but I decided it was the thought that counted. I cut stems with kitchen scissors and nearly shredded my hands on the thorns. I'm quite vain about my hands. I tied the bunch with one of your velvet ribbons I'd kept by the bed to remind me of you. Raffia was beginning to be fashionable but it still looked like bits of string or the remains of a seventies' Chianti bottle to me, and you know me, darling, I give of my best. I decided not to bring a present for the boy. I didn't want your mother telling you I was trying to buy him. I sang along to Frank Sinatra, shouted along to 'That's Life' all the way down in the car to keep my courage up, but that long driveway is a bugger, the ugly old house coming closer and closer like something in a nightmare, no visible hill for miles around. I felt the way I used to when I first went there, that I ought to pay to get in and would only be allowed in certain rooms.

I tried to cheer myself up by playing your mother's favourite clichés in my head: 'So much less populated than the Home Counties, so unspoiled. There it's like living in Surbiton.' I'd always ached to shout back, 'Haven't you worked out why you stupid old cow? East Anglia is dismal and brutal – that's why no one wants to live there. It's like going back to the Dark Ages.' In imagined rows my opponent always crumbles like plaster and disappears. Arriving was horribly silent. You could all have been put to sleep for a hundred years. I scrunched the car on the gravel in a glorious skid when I parked. In my elated terror I swallowed a sick-swallow. It never occured to me to say to you, 'Enough, Susannah, you've made me suffer enough,' to just turn and walk away. It was all done because I loved you so much and you were my wife.

Barnaby answered the door.

'Say hello to your father,' you said. You were standing behind him, prompting him, I hadn't noticed in the darkness.

139

It was so dark in there. The child looked as if he'd been struck dumb, but eventually managed the word. I'd forgotten the sound of his voice, his eyes, that he was real and months had passed for him as they had for me. You'd had your hair cut quite short. It was sensible and didn't suit you. When you saw me looking you put your hand up to touch the exposed part at the back of your neck.

'Too much trouble when I was ill,' you said, afraid to smile. I should have shouted, 'Boo!'

'Come outside.' I couldn't bear that hall yawning behind you. 'I've got something to show you.' It was so much better outside, the September sun making everything softer. You came out just a few paces behind me, followed by the boy, who looked rather uncertain. You turned and picked him up. 'There's Daddy,' you said to him, pointing. 'That's your daddy.' He looked at me – studied me, more precisely. It was bizarre.

'He's very quiet, isn't he?' I could hear myself shouting falsely.

'Like his mother,' you replied.

You came to the car and I rummaged for the roses. 'They're from your new garden,' I said, employing all my charm. You took the flowers but I couldn't tell what you were thinking. Child in one arm, flowers in the other, my tall pale girl. You looked older, plainer, more of a mouse.

'They're lovely,' you said. I felt as if I were looking down on us from the top of a tower, tiny figures in the flat landscape.

'When are you coming home?'

'It's difficult. Let's go inside.' When I hesitated, you said, 'Don't fuss, there's no one here but us. Have a drink.' The studied carelessness of our courtship had returned. I wanted to say no, let's go anywhere, the village pub, anything, but I didn't want to frighten you away. I didn't want my will to obstruct you. I had to remember to indulge you, give you the illusion you were free. 'We can sit in the garden,' you coaxed. 'No need to stay in the house.' We tramped through the passage – you could have ridden a horse through it, probably two – and out through the garden room. You left the flowers on the hall table – not a good sign. Lunch was served on the terrace with Barnaby exploring the borders. The walled garden was saturated with sun but the air was autumn-cool. You ate everything, methodically, carefully. I had no appetite but forced myself to eat, make conversation, play the suitor all over again. It was a job interview. I'm good at job interviews.

After lunch we drank lukewarm coffee while you told me how rested you felt and I tried to figure out how to get you out of there. 'I have to keep looking after myself. Taking it easy.' Almost a sly look from under lashes undarkened by mascara.

'I'm sure. Your health must come first.'

'He likes it here,' you said, smiling after the boy. 'He likes the peace.'

'What about other children?'

'That's harder.'

'He'll need –' I searched for the word. 'Interaction.' You didn't laugh at me. You weren't perceptive enough to know I'd chosen the word at random, dragged it out of the ether, desperate for the acceptable expression.

'Yes, he will.' You looked vague again. We both pretended to be comfortable, pretended to be relaxed. I wanted to say: 'Look – are you my wife, or aren't you? Is this my family, or isn't it?' I could have turned the table over. But romantic impetuosity wasn't what you craved, I knew that much.

'Think, Susannah. Think of Claire and Will. Claire's pregnant. You'll have a baby friend. There's the new garden to do, the common to play on.' You appeared neither confused nor moved, but turned your head away.

'Yes – flower,' you called to him, enunciating the word. 'Pretty flower.' He held it out to you and then toddled away. 'I

141

have to keep an eye on him,' you said. 'Everything still ends up in his mouth.' I laughed. You looked at me.

'I want to make love to you again,' I said. It was the only way of getting your attention. I had to come up with something big.

'Don't,' you said. 'Alex, don't.' But you were thrilled: thrilled is the only word I can use. 'What about *her*?' you said, reaching for the ring on your finger, drooping, but drooping invitingly. 'I can't come back if you're still seeing her. I was wrong to think I could live with it. I can't.' (Wow, Susannah, you had the courage to make a statement.)

'It's over and done with, I've made sure of that.' (This was true: old Suzie had begun to gab about when I would leave my wife and marry her, putting paid to any suspicion that she might have had a brain in her head.) 'It wasn't even an it.' The cliché was all I could manage but I hoped it would do the trick.

You looked up, suddenly direct. 'I know about the holiday – you took her away on our holiday. Your mother told me.' If you were trying to provoke me, you succeeded. You succeeded very well because you had one of the best weapons, surprise. I was very angry with Mummy, for meddling, going behind my back, and with you, that you should dare to try to negotiate with me about the Floozie when she had nothing at all to do with us. It was you. 'Some men take a holiday with their wives and one with their mistresses every year,' I wanted to say. 'Some wives count themselves lucky they're not divorced when they lose their looks the way you have. Some wives mind their own business and fuck their husbands every once in a while and eat up their greens – they don't scare them half to death by nearly dying on them.'

'What can I say?' I said. 'It's over now. I promise.' I was longing for a brandy, I could almost taste it I wanted it so much. Thank fuck there was wine left. I sipped. I did not gulp because you were watching me from under those coy bland lashes. 'There's nothing more I can say, apart from that you have my heart and I'm sorry. Think about it. We'll talk on the phone. When you're ready, come home.' I had to leave then because the pain was too much.

As soon as I was out of sight of the house I stopped the car and threw up, wretchedly hoping you hadn't given me your illness too.

I won't go into detail about the row I had with Mummy. She was certainly very sorry by the end of it, you can count on that, and it was more than her conscience that was smarting. I was so angry I fired the architect and builders the same day. She called it a flounce, but I was miserable. I felt I'd lost sight of my goal, could no longer picture how I wanted the house to look with you, me and him in it. I'd already had the floor-boards stripped and varnished in every room. It looked revolting – like something out of MTV – I couldn't imagine what I'd been thinking. It was a fucking mess. I thought it would jinx your return to go any further with it, anyway, so we lived in draughty splendour – Mummy's words – marble bathrooms, naked windows and three pieces of furniture. I worried about winter and splinters and chilblains. I couldn't concentrate at work. My ulcers burned my guts. I was close to a breakdown over you, golden girl. You can put that down on your dance card, at least.

One of those autumn days that could almost be spring: the same light, the same excitement, but different smells and colder breath in your lungs, we'd been blackberrying in the woods behind the cottage and had only just got back to London. I was making pastry in the kitchen for the blackberry and apple pie and she was having a rest upstairs. I'd just had a bath and was contented in a towelling dressing-gown – the one you'd given me the Christmas before. My feet were damp and picking up dust from that fucking floor. I was just calling up to ask her if she wanted a cup of tea or a drink when there was a knock and

I could see you standing there through the frosted glass, your shape and the boy's, soft and indistinct. I felt guilty straight away: shocked and guilty because I was happy and not even thinking about you. I couldn't take it in that this was the moment, this was it at last, you'd come home. I just stood at the foot of the stairs, turning to notice my footprints on the floor. You never surprise anyone, never do anything on a whim. You must have planned it, planned it without telling me. I was amazed. I didn't know if you could see me on the other side of the door or if the light meant I was all part of the shadow. I was clammy, damp and cold, undressed and quaking. You didn't knock again but shifted your weight. I took a deep breath and opened the door. You smiled and looked almost pretty, almost like my young wife should. The boy pointed at me and emitted a puzzled sound.

'Come in,' I said.

Mummy called down, 'Darling, I'll have a tonic water and bitters if you're making drinks.'

For some reason I couldn't look at you. 'Susannah's here,' I shouted. 'She's home.' My voice sounded false and bright and it cracked. 'Come in, sweetheart. Do you like it? Do you like the house?'

'It feels quite big.' You looked at the ceiling, its coving, the empty light socket, then at me, then up the stairs.

I didn't know what to do. 'Would you like to come down to the kitchen? It's a basement kitchen but I've put in a big door to the garden, and a skylight. It's not dark. Or you can get to the garden from the other end of the drawing room, there's a Victorian balcony, wrought-iron, and stairs to the garden.' I was gabbling.

'What's the matter?' you said. 'Why haven't you kissed us hello?' Your voice was almost sharp, another first.

I moved to kiss you but you took a step back. 'If I'd known you were coming I'd have welcomed you properly.'

'Not like this?'

'Not exactly, no.' You had on a very pretty grey knitted coat. I'd never seen it before. For some reason I started calculating how much of it was cashmere, where you'd got it from, and how much it had cost. The boy looked incredibly clean. 'Where are your bags? In the car? Do you want me to get them?'

'No.' This firm, decisive.

'I'll be down in a minute,' Mummy called.

Quick as a flash you deposited the boy at my feet, saying, 'Stay with Daddy, Mummy'll be back in a minute,' and you ran up the stairs so fast I could hardly take it in. I thought you must be desperate for the loo, but I forgot to tell you I'd had one put in under the stairs.

I dropped to my knees beside Barnaby and tried to talk to him, but he was closed. 'Would you like some juice?' I tried enunciating slowly, but he gave no sign that he'd heard. I felt paralysed. I heard a low guttural sound – yours. Without thinking, I ran up the stairs after you. On the half-landing the back bedroom door was open, the room empty, sash window closed, dusk creeping. Next flight, our big bay-windowed room, naked except for bed and fire, Mummy sitting up in rumpled sheets, undressed and smoking a cigarette. You'd got beyond the doorway but hadn't approached the bed. As I came in you shrieked again, doubling up, your hands over the soft low part of your belly. (I'd seen it bruised before.)

'Susannah, have you gone completely mad?' I said. Mummy, motionless, spoke not a word, nor did she seem about to. I put my hands on your shoulders and you straightened up.

'That's our bed,' you said. 'She's in our bed.' You were frantic, so was I.

'No, she's not, silly. I threw our bed away. This is new. New house, new bed.'

'But this is our room.' That wide-eyed bloody shrieking again.

'How do you know that? You've never been in this house in your life before. Our bedroom's on the top floor, with ensuite bathroom, you idiot.'

'The master bedroom is always on the first floor,' you howled, like some demented estate agent.

'Are you quite mad?' I said. 'Will you *shut up*!'

'She's –' You pointed at Mummy.

'Having a rest. She's having a rest. You know how easily tired she is.' Mummy's smeared mouth muttered some confirmation. I had you by the wrists now because you were beginning to make me angry.

You shook me off, in gawky movement bolting out of the room and up the stairs to the top floor, your heels clattering. (That's one of the problems with wooden floors.) In the room you screamed like a banshee. 'The bed's made!' You screamed and screamed. 'The bed's empty!'

I don't remember running after you but I remember screaming back, facing you four square. 'That's because my fucking wife chooses to live in the fucking country with her fucking mother!' I took a good long swipe at you, bashing you across the face. It was such a relief and you crumpled, buckling at the knees, so I kicked you in the ribs, once, twice, three times, then stopped to get my breath.

'You've been with her,' you said, 'all this time.'

You kept right on screaming it, so I kicked you one last time, though my heart had gone out of it. I said, 'No,' again and again, but it had ceased to matter. I no longer cared if you believed me. I didn't care about anything. When we'd got our breath I took your hand and pulled you to your feet. You were gasping and bleeding. 'I'll drive you to the hospital,' I said – in crisis-mode, matter-of-fact. You wouldn't meet my eye. 'Just let me get my trousers and some shoes.' They were downstairs in Mummy's room. I didn't have any clothes in the wall of immaculate cupboards I'd had built up there and I didn't want you to see that. 'Wait downstairs.' Obedient, quiet, you stumbled out of the room, not running any more. I heard you pass Mummy's room, and when you had, I crept after you. Mummy was still bolt upright in bed, her hands over her face in terrible shock, but I didn't have time to comfort her. Every time you walked into my life you caused this disarray. And yet I never learned. I was ransacking the room for clothes when I heard the front door bang and knew at once that you'd taken him and got away.

I was desperate, thinking you'd crash the car on the way back and it would all be my fault. I decided not to follow you because I didn't want to risk you seeing me and driving faster, putting yourself and my son in any kind of danger. What I did do was swallow my pride and call your mother to warn her that we'd had a row and you were on your way back, quite distraught. I wanted her to be prepared to help you immediately. I even put up with her insults and the time they wasted when you might have been trying to call her from the road. I wanted to make it absolutely clear to her that you needed her help and that she must be calm and strong. I couldn't bear to think beyond that moment, of myself rather than you. I couldn't bear to think that this could mean you might not ever be coming back. Sweet heart.

A Letter to Kitty

Beguiled to the very heart of loss.
SHAKESPEARE, *Antony and Cleopatra*

Kitty. Everyone calls you Kitty because you look just like a cat: not the comfortable cosy striped kind with loose tummy that has housed a dozen litters, but the young hard agile green-eyed kind, the special over-bred over-pampered kind: Siamese or Burmese, the ones with kinks in their tails and growls in their throats. I've never liked cats. Give me a dog's unconditional love any day. You were quite fascinating in your physicality: the sturdy slender legs of a Narnian animal, a fawn, a slight bony upper body with almost sharp hips but the belly and breasts of a real woman, the arms and shoulders of a girl. And your little sharp shapely head with its cheekbones and thoughtful forehead, eyes that always moved to take in everything, a head so proudly set on its shoulders I was surprised I didn't see your ears flatten when you heard something you didn't like. Kitty, the tip of your nose almost twitched when I kissed it. With your short dark hair and soft scrubbed skin, you were so young, so young and so old, and only when I plunged into you could I take the fierce look out of your eyes, make them focus on me and only me, make them tender. Seventeen is very young to be the object of so much desire and be indifferent to it.

I can't write to you without telling you how much I hate you hate you, though if you were here I'd beg your forgiveness on my knees and bury my head in you. I'd kiss you until I was empty and you were full. I don't know if you are the love of my life or the fuck of my life. Sex is in the head, as you once told me, and I'll never climb inside your head again. That's what causes me pain. This must seem a great big joke to you. I must

151

be such a joke. But I can't imagine you laughing at me, Kitty: it would be so much easier if I could. (It's just that you've always been so kind, such a soft touch, unable to resist a television appeal for a child's hunger in a faraway famine, phoning up and donating money and hating yourself because it wasn't enough. That it was my money was never the thing that disturbed you.) Would you tease me to death even now, would you? Finish what you started? Or perhaps – unbearable idea – you no longer care. You're the worst of my three women, the lowest, but the most brilliant, the most talented, the most exquisite. There's no competition. You've no type. You're unique.

In the tradition of these God-awful letters I have to tell the story bit by bit and promise not to rant and rave, so I'll try to calm myself by imagining you sitting still long enough to read all these words. Impossible, but I'll picture you now how I first saw you and try to keep you like that, at least for a while. It was only just after all that business with Susannah and I was so desperate I was reading my horoscope in the paper every day. It said something about new horizons (don't they all?) so when the call came from my old school asking me to give a career talk I said yes. If I'd been married and settled like other people my age I'd have refused point blank to give up a Saturday afternoon in November to drive to the leafless country, but that's not how things were. It's just not. I didn't go so far as preparing what I'd actually say, though. God forbid I should make things that easy for myself.

The whole place looked smaller, which was rather horrible, like bad magic. Endless avenues of trees had become short driveways, long slopes mere landscaping. It felt so unreal I wondered whether the world would keep shrinking at the same rate, so if I came back in another ten years I might not fit inside the doorways. I wasn't sleeping at all well then, so it was a feeling of strained and constant fatigue, and then sudden terror when I saw the podium and a sea of faces lit by stained-

glass shafts in unexpected glamour. I'd somehow thought I'd
be in the library or somewhere where I'd feel safe and more
contained. There must have been two hundred people and I
had a vision of toppling over into the pit: it's ridiculous
because I'm used to presentations at work, and the key is
participation, so I stood there swallowing and clearing my
throat, thinking if I could just waffle briefly for even two
minutes I could throw it open for questions almost immediately. Scanning the faces of the uncomprehending children was
a mistake. One must never look at an audience individually,
one must simply appear to encompass the group with a roving
humorous, knowledgeable glance. I was in trouble. No words
had passed my lips. There was a feeling of embarrassment but –
properly disciplined – no one fidgeted. I took a deep breath
and reaching the back of the hall with my frantic gaze saw one
of my old English masters looking at me with his guarded
curious smile and somehow I found the courage. For no reason
I can remember or explain, I grasped a quotation from the
Bible: ' "Though I speak with the tongues of men and of
angels, and have not charity . . . I am nothing." ' It was an
inaccurate quote, as you later reminded me, but it did the trick.
Thanks to the microphone my voice resounded around the
hall. 'Of course, that's rubbish,' I went on, and everyone
laughed. 'Charity, or love, as the word has become simplified
to mean, doesn't stop you from being nothing: money does.
I'm in the business of making money and it's exceptionally
enjoyable. I'll tell you what it's like.' And off I went
pretending to be in control, pretending to be likeable, feeling
less and less naked as the words went on and the laughter grew.
I spoke for fifteen minutes and then I took questions. As any
actor will tell you, fifteen minutes is a long time in show-
business. And I'd forgotten there'd be girls, we didn't have
them in my day. They asked most of the questions. One came
from an insipid blonde next to you, who reminded me of my

wife, but you said nothing, you just sat and stared at me, glowing in the dark like some secret nuclear reactor. I only glanced at you and you made no sign you'd noticed but equally you never stopped watching me. And there it was: love, lust, at first sight, for me at least. Or, 'two pathologies collide', which I believe is the expression you prefer.

There was tea in green cups and saucers and disgusting yet comforting greasy cakes afterwards, a general hubbub and milling. You'd disappeared. I decided it was just as well. I talked to the old fellow, which depressed me. I thought he was disappointed in me despite my evident success. Not surprising, as I had hardly been intent on instilling the correct values in his young flock. I hate the lighting in schools, all institutions, but schools especially. The windows were blacked out and we were left with fake chandeliers.

You were waiting for me by the car, parked in full view of the not unimposing building. Little sturdy cat-thing. You said, 'You were rather disappointing.'

I thanked you, and when you smiled, unperturbed, I added, 'You're at the challenging stage. You'll grow out of it.' But you only laughed. I wished it hadn't made my heart beat faster and forced me to fumble for my keys but, sadly, it had.

'And you missed out the important part in your quote about charity.' You didn't smile, but paused and taking a light breath, said, 'It "beareth all things, believeth all things, hopeth all things, endureth all things".' I never thought I'd take comfort in anything from the Bible, but when you said those words, breathing out the syllables, I could have cried. You were an actress already. I couldn't reply. 'I'm sorry if I've offended you,' you said gently. But you weren't at all. Right from the start you were utterly selfish and totally irresponsible. I asked you how you knew the Bible so well, and you said, 'I read a lot – voraciously.' This time teasing, this time nothing in your eyes. I could see there was to be no clinging to dogma in your dipping world. Games – always games with you. It made me feel sad because I was already half in love with you. It didn't seem fair.

'Young lady,' I said, marshalling my best Jilly Cooper scorn, 'you'd better go inside. You'll get cold out here.'

'Take me with you. At least to the gates.'

'All right.' You climbed in. You had me stunned as a mouse.

'I'm Kitty,' you said, prettily.

'Pleased to hear it,' I replied, trying to think of a way out of it, even as I carried you off with me. 'And what are you going to be when you grow up, Kitty?' I put your name in inverted commas in an attempt to make you feel foolish and small. It didn't work.

That was when you said, 'I know what I'm *not*–'

'You're not going to be like me. Understood.'

'I might be an actress. I don't know.' You didn't try to look at me, but concentrated on the darkening sky and the road ahead, the hedgerows untidy with dying. 'I'm coming to London the weekend after next. Can I call you?'

'Why on earth would you want to do that?'

'Why "on earth" do you think?' You were innocent enough to want to give the impression of being easy, I'll say that for you at least. It made me decide you must be a virgin, or at least a virgin of the heart, if there is such a phrase. I felt less foolish and more in control.

'Now, sweetie –'

'Don't call me that, it's disgusting.'

'Darling –'

'I'm not your darling.'

'Now, Kitty, you don't really want to do that.' But of course you did, and I gave you my number under seeming-protest but actually with a growing feeling of triumph and unbecoming glee. I'd decided that if I deflowered you quickly I could forget about you and so exorcise my embryonic obsession. (Foolishly, I believed I was beginning to know myself.) You got out at the school gates, making no attempt to say or do anything memorable as a parting shot. You had more confidence than that, more confidence than any woman I'd ever been with. Off you went on your sturdy little legs, looking almost as if you'd been grown out of the ground, given life with one breath of the Creator. I'm sure that's some classical myth but I can't for the life of me remember which one. On the journey home I counted the days.

I'd sent Mummy home (in a rage) after Susannah's departure, so I shared the draughty house only with my wedding china and boxes of memorabilia stacked unartistically in the back bedroom. I'd intended it to be Barnaby's but, under the circumstances, believed it never would be. I hated that house. But then I've hated every house I've ever been in that didn't belong either to the future or the past. It wasn't bad: it was newly ripped up and plastered over – it was a blank canvas. I just didn't have the heart for it. I'd put out photographs of Susannah and the boy, even Mummy, for company, but I could hardly bear to look at them. As for the garden – it was a wilderness and had begun to smell of cat.

You called on the Saturday morning at twelve-ish, very considerate of you. I was in bed with the papers and a hangover, which wasn't too bad because I'd eaten a good breakfast in anticipation. You were dead on time by my calculations.

'Alex?'

'Kitty.'

'It's me all right.' You laughed. 'What-you doing?' You elided the first two words lazily, charmingly.

'This and that. Thinking about you.' I asked you where you were staying. It was with some aunt in Hampstead: ghastly place and most inconvenient for Clapham. I didn't say that. 'Where are your parents, little girl?'

'I don't have any.' You laughed into the pause. 'That's not entirely true. I'm not exactly an orphan. I've an ancient mother who lives in Wales – I was a late child.' You sounded as if you were trying much too hard to be detached and amused about giving me this information. 'I don't see much of her. She makes me crazy.' Alarm bells went off in my mind but I said nothing. I didn't like it, though. A child not devoted to its mother is deeply flawed, if you ask me.

'Crazy, how?'

'Crazy with rage, mostly.' You didn't seem to care about telling me this. In your long silence I felt abandoned, as if I were no longer the object of your call. I hated that.

'No sob stories before six,' I said. 'House rules.'

'I'm not in your house.' You sounded bad-tempered, adolescent, unattractive, and you didn't care. Most women try to impress me, all the time.

'Shall we start again? How about dinner tonight?' I'd put on my best voice without deciding to.

'I don't know, I think I'm busy.' You really did sound as if you'd lost interest, but totally. It was disconcerting being wrong-footed when you sense it's not even part of a strategy.

'Maybe lunch tomorrow,' I said brightly, artificially.

'Don't call us, we'll call you.' You put the phone down. I was fucking angry then. *And* I had an erection.

I didn't see you that weekend, you must have changed your mind. The next time you called was about two weeks later, another Saturday. I got your number out of you, and that made me feel much more secure. You even parted with your last name, Morrow. I just couldn't get you to commit to a date for the seduction. It wasn't as if you had plans – you said you were spending your time reading and staring into the fire, your aunt worked all through the weekend. You were cooking for her, though, which I decided was a good sign.

'I read recipe books in the bath,' you said. 'For escape. Not the new ones, the old ones. Portraits of vanished ways of life, you know – romantic. At the minute it's Elizabeth David and the South of France.'

'There's nothing at all romantic about the South of France.'

'You seem awfully young for the world-weary line.' (I should have said, 'That makes two of us.') 'How long are you going to keep it up?'

'Just let me see you, and we'll find out.'

'Maybe the next time I come up,' you said. Every hour of that weekend I was on the phone, trying to tempt you, to make a definite date for next time. I got ballet tickets, opera tickets, I boasted about how rich I was, I didn't boast about how rich I was, I offered to drive you places, have my secretary type your essays, I was humble, I was sweet. Nothing worked, but I couldn't hate you for it. It was just the way you were. You didn't know your own mind.

It was a new Saturday, and on Sunday you had to go back to school.

'We can have dinner tonight if you like,' you said.

'I'll pick you up.'

'No – I'll meet you.'

You were very keen on Soho where I felt very out of place. All those gays. You seemed to like it, though – I chose a staid pale green restaurant with air-conditioning and businessmen. 'We'll have coffee somewhere else,' I said, at your disappointed look. 'We'll have fun.' You smiled then, unsure. You wore a lot of black eye makeup and a crimson lipstick. I love makeup on a woman and Susannah would never wear any. You wore a little black dress, you looked a bit grubby, but in a good way. Your nails were bitten. 'Like mine,' I said, and you smiled. It was a fantastic smile.

'There are an awful lot of Japanese in here,' you said, in the loudest stage whisper I've ever heard in my life. It made me laugh. You could really make me laugh. It was your delivery, I suppose.

'Will you be offended if I order for you?'

'No. I'd love it.' You spoke with great clarity, definite and passionate. The waiters fussed too much to begin with, but after champagne and light and delicious things to eat, it got better. You looked small opposite me, as if you needed a cushion. It made me feel protective. I felt delirious, pushing down hysteria, swallowing irrelevant mouthfuls that had neither taste nor smell. I kept looking at your mouth. I just wanted to get inside your mouth. That and to stop visibly trembling. We drank pudding wine. 'I love pudding wine,' you said. I think I might have even said, 'Do you? That's nice.' I couldn't work out what to say to make myself desirable, spouting some idiotic words about my work having some kind of grace in it, and that winning – closing the deal – was a form of art. (I believed it at the time.)

You said, 'It sounds as if you work too hard,' and I had to bite the inside of my mouth to stop myself from explaining that you knew nothing about anything because you weren't yet in the world.

'There are compromises one can be forced to make,' I think I said, and you added, 'The key is not to have to make them, ever,' and I almost believed you. 'I'm going to do exactly what I want, always.'

'Do you want to come home with me?'

'Yes.' I was so frightened then. I've never been so frightened in my life.

You complained that the house was cold.

'I like it like that. It feels more real.'

'Don't these floorboards give you splinters?'

'Yes.' We stood in the living room. There was the armchair, the television, and the picture of Susannah on the mantelpiece.

'Who's that?'

'My wife. I told you I was married.'

'But she's a girl.'

'She was then.' It had been taken on the roof of my flat. She'd been standing looking at the view and had turned round to look at the camera, without smiling (smiling is overrated in today's world), so very young, so very sweet, so very trusting. The picture caught all that, and a softness in the light that suited her. She was so gentle then. I liked to remember her like that, before she got spoiled. You looked at that photograph for an awfully long time as I stood there studying your back.

'Come downstairs. The kitchen's a bit cosier.'

You turned to me – I think tearful, almost – I didn't imagine it. I wanted to kiss you very much then but I just couldn't do it. I only stood and looked at you and you approached and took me by the hand. 'Is this better?' you said. Your hand was rough and uncared-for.

'Yes. Much better.'

We went into the kitchen and I opened a bottle of champagne. First you sat opposite me and then you climbed on to my knee, sat across my lap, and nestled your head on my chest, so enquiring, so comforting, listening to my heart. 'It sounds pretty healthy to me.' Then you sat up straight, holding my jacket by the lapels and staring me in the face as nakedly as an animal or a child. 'Do you still love her?'

'I don't know.'

'Do you believe me when I tell you it will be all right?'

'Not quite.' (I didn't want to disappoint you.)

'Not quite – but almost?' There was no smile. You were fierce in your conviction. I was almost afraid of you. 'Don't quail, Alex.' You said my name softly as if it were a promise.

'All I've ever wanted was a happy family.' I went to pieces then and sobbed, quite unexpectedly, forgetting about thinking of how to keep you, sobbed and hung my head. You clasped me against you, which was uncomfortable because of the way you were sitting.

After I'd cried for a while you let me go. 'Now listen to me,' you said, like some sort of nanny, which was very endearing. 'If you marry the wrong woman she's bound to make you unhappy. Anyone will tell you that.' (Why must all you women compete with one another? It's always your first and strongest urge. In our case it helped me out no end.)

'It's not that simple.'

'That's what you get for marrying a blonde. I bet she always made you feel like a criminal. She looks so correct. You're not correct, are you?'

'No.'

'There you are, then. Neither am I.' You got off my knee, pulled me by the hand towards the immaculate unused kitchen sink and turned on the tap, splashing my face with water. 'Go on. Wash your face. Then we'll go to bed.' I felt unexpectedly quiet, meek. You kept hold of my hand and led me up the stairs.

I couldn't get it up that night. You were so kind about it. We'd got into bed quite calmly, like children, and when I couldn't, it didn't matter at all. Our sleep was the consummation – I think you said that. In the morning you got up and walked out. You wouldn't even let me make you a cup of coffee. I felt like a prostitute.

The rest of that term was like a nightmare of darkness to me. You'd gone back to school without a word. And what kind of situation was that? You were a schoolgirl and I couldn't live without you. It was already out of hand. The winter turned very cold and raw, hurtling towards the shortest day. I kept calling the school and pretending to be your cousin. It was stupid. You sounded distracted. 'I'm working hard,' you said. 'I've got A levels,' as if that explained everything. 'What about exeat weekends?' 'I'm going to see my mum.' You were irritated, angered. 'Wait till the holidays. Just wait.' You shouted at me as if I were an enemy, 'Just *wait*!' I should have stormed down, broken into your dormitory and had you up against the wall. I fantasised about it. But it really wasn't my style. Besides, I had a lot of other things on my plate. Susannah's family were making it very difficult for me to see the boy and throwing around all sorts of wild claims – as if it were my fault, what had happened to Susannah. Solicitors began wrangling. It was driving me mad. Mummy was whingeing about me paying for central heating at the cottage, but I didn't know what kind of money I was going to have even in six months' time. And at work, the atmosphere in my office was thick with rumour and bad feeling. I couldn't trust my colleagues. I couldn't trust anyone. Despite your treatment of me, I saw you as my one friend, clinging to the memory of your determined little face. I used to look at myself in the mirror and say, 'It'll come right, it'll come right, it'll come right,' over and over again. This either made me laugh or cry. (I think because of the word 'come.') It wasn't a good time.

Eventually I found out what day you broke up (not difficult once I'd thought of it). It was a Thursday, and as an act of optimism I filled the house with incredibly expensive red hothouse roses, 'Just *wait*!' echoing around my ashamed head. I couldn't decide whether their musical-comedy technicolour beauty made it look worse or better, but I did know that women love flowers. It's just a rule. I decided not to pursue you, a gamble that paid off. I came home from work and you were sitting on the doorstep. Your hair had grown – it was floppy and unsophisticated and made you look even younger, your fringe in your eyes.

'Bankers work stupid hours,' you said. 'I'm freezing.'

I grabbed you and covered you with kisses. 'You're too contrary. You should have let me know when you were coming.'

You laughed. Beside you on the steps was a small suitcase. I picked it up and took you by the hand. 'I thought I'd stay for a while,' you murmured. 'I can't wait to get you into bed.'

The trouble with happiness is that it's incredibly banal. I don't know how to describe how I felt, how we felt. You touched the flowers and kissed their petals. You thanked me. I lit a fire and closed the shutters I'd had fitted in anticipation. We smoked cigarettes, drank champagne. You shivered, quiet, not concentrating on me fully, thinking your own thoughts.

'I think I'll have a bath,' you said. Knowing you were upstairs washing and changing made everything better. I didn't have to see you or talk to you, touch you or even imagine you – I just knew you were there and it was enough. Enough has always been an elusive state for me. I sang getting the chicken ready for roasting, smearing it with butter and piling on the herbs, I actually sang. When you came down you said, 'There's so much stainless steel in here I feel messy for breathing.' But you were helpful, peeling the potatoes and carrots, such a helpful little girl. We did everything together. Our love-making wasn't very accomplished, but it was passionate. All intentions were good. I still had to go to work the next day, but it didn't feel the same, not lonely any more. When I woke you at half past five, you said, 'Sleep. It's night-time.'

'No. I have to go to work.'

'Ssshh.'

'I'll see you later. I love you.'

'Yes yes,' you said, screwing up your face, asleep. 'Just *go*.' Cross cat.

'Why do moments of happiness always fill me up with useless tears?' You said this once after we made love. Right at the very beginning. 'Aren't there enough in the bad times?'

'You ask too many questions.' The truth is I don't think I

ever answered any of your questions satisfactorily, although you answered plenty of mine. As a child you'd travelled with your parents, while they were still in love. Your father was a journalist who wrote about places until they were spoiled for him. Your mother called herself a feminist and an academic, which meant she wasn't big on cooking and cleaning, making a home. Like I had, years before, you'd been plonked into school once they no longer had a use for you, feared you'd lost whatever chance their giving you life had given you, forgetting that they'd been the ones who had destroyed it. Perhaps I'm unfair. Telling a story from any point of view means you're unfair to someone. This is your story, after all, and it requires my generosity. You deserve it. I feel disconcertingly wise when I write to you. (You're the only person who has ever given me a glimpse of being wise. For that I thank you, fear you.) You adored your father. What you had with him, I could only guess at: what I knew was it couldn't have left much for your mother.

'How did he die?' I asked you, when your face was soaked with tears, remembering.

'He didn't die. That would have been too simple. He abandoned me. My father abandoned me.'

'And your mother?'

'It must have been both.'

'Where is he now?'

'I have absolutely no idea.' If you lied I felt you were entitled to lie and I let it go. I had an odd respect for you, Kitty. I imagined him still travelling somewhere, moving on, your mother taking root in some prosaic part of Wales.

'Abandonment. Abandon. Abandoner.' You said the words slowly, in your rhythmic way. 'It must be an English word with French roots.'

'I like the clever way that sounds.'

'You take me too seriously. I made it up.'

In your throat – is that where it lived? Behind your eyes? In your soul? You were one of the few people I've met who I could safely say had a soul.

'"His delights were dolphin-like,"' you said, over and over, lying in my sun-dappled bed and bicycling your legs in the air. 'Exercises. I'm just exercising my mouth. Actresses have to do that you know. Try it.'

'"His delights were dolphin-like, his delights were dolphin-like."' It was no good, I made a mess of it, but you didn't mind. We gazed at the ceiling, our hands behind our heads, as if it were a substitute for the sky.

'I long for the sound of the sea,' you said. 'To live another life.'

'You did live by the sea once.'

'But then I dreamed of crossing it, getting somewhere else.'

'Never satisfied.' I loved you, so I didn't throw that in your face. Instead I played along. Living another life was one of my favourite games. 'Hot country or cold country?'

'Both. We'd winter in the sun – like they did in the last century.'

'And between the wars.'

'Is this a history lesson?'

'Of course not.' Musing pauses.

'South of France?' you asked carelessly.

'No.' You should have known that. You could have been after a reaction, I don't know.

'Italy?'

'Possibly. The tropics?'

'Never again.' (You'd lived there as a child.)

'The world's shrinking,' I said. You were undeterred, laughing.

'There's a corner of it somewhere for us.'

'Let's summarise.' I always liked the semblance of order. 'We're agreed on white sand.'

'A stone house.'

'Or a wooden house.'

'Plenty of fruit – bare feet.'

'Idleness.' I think we both contemplated the idea of idleness and found it wanting. I didn't know why I'd said it.

'That's winters,' you said. 'How about springs?'

'Spring in a European city. Paris. Rome. Somewhere civilised. We'd live in cafés, restaurants with white tablecloths.'

'Or no tablecloths at all.'

'I'm not sure about that.' (Loss of luxury has never appealed to me.) 'We'd be very cultured.'

'Well read. We'd give a lot of salons.'

'Now you're really being fanciful. I'd prefer anonymity, I think.'

'You said we could imagine anything we liked.'

'So I did.' A pause while I kissed and tasted you.

'We've still got to do summers and autumns,' you said. It was hard to satisfy you. You could never get enough fantasy.

'How about summer in the mountains?'

'I hate the mountains.'

'Thunderface.' It had closed into a little ball. I stroked it, stroked your cross soft face, made you smile again.

'We could have an English summer, just for a change.'

'We could. But no crowds – there'd never be crowds in our world. I hate crowds.'

'Autumn somewhere brightly coloured. America.' Saying the word made you smile. 'But just the good bits – the westerns, the rivers and the deserts. Or Boston and Maine. Henry James.'

'We'd be incredibly busy.'

'Mmm.' Gales of laughter from soft-eyed you, followed by

more, abrupt silence. 'We've only done the places, but not the people we'd be,' you said, drawing up your knees.

'We'll do the people another day.'

'An Other Day.' You dropped the sounds with your voice. An awfulness came over me then – of silence and lacking. We were played out, exhausted. Did we quarrel then, or separate, or just turn over – spent – and fall asleep?

In your childhood abroad, you told me, being able to get things was a luxury: fresh eggs, fruit, fish. There was always a chance that the supply could end, suddenly finish, and that made you feel relieved – that there was a connection between the land you lived in and on and the food you ate. It had been the same for me and Mummy, which was why I loved the supermarket, but when I took you there (once we'd started to get out of bed long enough to shop), you said it was an array of plunder of the natural world, the last word in colonialism, in wealth, in domination of the globe. It sickened you, the choice. (Personally, I have no problem with capitalism.) You'd walk up and down the aisles, pointing angrily and shouting, 'Look, there's everything you didn't know you could dream of wanting. It's a disgrace.' At the time I thought all this fury had shaken you, weakened you, Kitty – undermined you, and I was worried for you – but I was a fool. It had only made you stronger.

Christmas was dismal: Mummy in one of her worst moods, sulking because I wouldn't let her meet you. I went down to visit the boy on Boxing Day and he didn't recognise me. I wanted to hit him. You'd have understood that. You understood everything. I took you to some place in South America for the New Year, just a cheap week, because you wanted a change. It was not ideal. It was hot and it was poor and it was dirty. But you set your mind and decided it was all good, that the whole of it was good, no room for doubt. I felt then that you chose to be simple: chose to be clean and see things only one way – the easy way. 'Isn't it beautiful?' you'd say. 'Look at the light on the water – the gleam on the horizon, the colours in the sky.' You wouldn't say: 'See how the water is polluted – look at the floating scum, the bubbles. Did you know that the fishermen can't fill their nets – there are no longer limitless fish in the sea?' You saw these things, but you refused to name them. Yours was an incredible strength of will.

We were less connected to our lives, and we could talk. We sat on our balcony, looking at the sea.

'What do you think of, Kitty, when I say the word Provence?'

'Colour and light. My father took me when I was thirteen and –'

'Where?'

'Nice, Antibes – other little places.'

'What about the hills?'

'We went to St Paul de Vence. The museum was –'

'Surrounded by swimming-pools.'

'What's your point?' You were irritated by then. I liked that about you – the courage to have a short fuse.

'The point is that the place where I lived was nearly two hours from the sea. It was woods and hills, trees and crags.'

'The views must have been amazing.'

'When it rained and the wind was blowing we couldn't see anything. And it was very cold.'

'What did you do?'

'That's not important. I'm just trying to explain that there was no romance. I wasn't living in a Cézanne.'

'Now that's a good game,' you said. 'But I'd choose Matisse. I'd live in those rooms overlooking the sea.' You won then because you were so incorrigible, so determined to make me live and be happy.

I tried one last time. 'I know so much more about life than you do.'

'No, you don't. You just think you do.' And you kissed me, sipping at me like a humming-bird.

I wanted to take you back to school but you'd only let me drop you at the gates.

'If I come to London at Easter, you'll have to put up with me working. I'll be a vile teenager, I might even smell.'

'That's fine. Just keep giving me blow-jobs and I'll be happy.' You laughed. I wanted to beg you, 'Laugh again, Kitty, laugh again.' You were in a play that term and I wanted to come and see it.

'You can't, you'll feel like a dirty old man.' There was no arguing with you. I didn't want to cross you in case you changed your mind and I never saw you again. I drove back to the house, got into our bed, curled up in a ball and howled.

In the next vision I have of you you're wearing jeans and a dark blue T-shirt and you'd put on weight. I wanted to cry with relief when I heard you clomping down the stairs, the April light behind you, and then seeing your face, very white and pale.

'You look awful,' you said.

You were much more withdrawn, listless, preoccupied. I got hold of you and you stood, tired in my arms, as if I were an obligation. I took you out to dinner because we somehow needed something to do. I couldn't think of what to say, so I tried to be practical. 'I know you'll be busy revising this holidays – I thought you could work in the back bedroom, among the boxes.'

'No need to move them for me.'

'Of course not.' I'd wanted to fill the room with hand-painted Renaissance frescos and glorious furniture, festoon it

169

with cloth of gold for your return, but had had to content myself with a bog-standard blond-wood Habitat desk so as not to frighten you away. The sacrifice had been very hard.

'You've been thoughtful,' you said. 'Thank you.'

'There's no need. I'm just so glad you're home.'

You looked up – sharp, quizzing me – as if you were my boss. 'We've never said anything about home.' It made me blush and feel close to useless tears.

'Of course not. No more mention of the H word.' I could have cried with relief when you hung your few things beside mine in the cupboard, put your dark blue glass bottles in my bathroom, your work books, pens and pencils in your study. I didn't even dare tell you I'd given it that name.

The truth is you were so preoccupied with work, so self-absorbed, it began to drive me crazy. The machine was always on, I couldn't get you on the phone. I went through a phase of thinking you weren't working at all, I suspected you of having an affair. I'd come home and let myself in quickly, trying to surprise you in the act. 'Got to go – Bye!' I'd often hear – and you slamming down the phone before calling airily, 'Hi.' You could get a lot of syllables out of that word. 'Who was that?' 'Just a friend.' That clinched it. Eventually I asked, trembling, if you were being unfaithful and you laughed, saying, 'You are joking, aren't you?' and when I said no, you said, 'Think about it, Alex. I don't have time.' Your answer was practical enough to satisfy me. But everything was different. You stopped cooking, playing music, even talking to me, you were no companion at all. You didn't even come out of your study to greet me when I came home in the evening, leaving me to knock on the door like a salesman. You'd look up from the page and not see me. 'But I told you what it would be like,' you'd say. 'I've got exams, A levels. They're important.'

Losing my temper once, I goaded you. 'If you're going to be an actress why does it matter if you get As? Why care?'

Your mouth dropped open, simulating surprise. 'Because I have to be the best at everything I do. I want to come first, I want three As. Surely you, of all people, can understand that.'

'For God's sake, Kitty – you're only a girl.' (You have to understand I was wild with frustration.)

'What are you talking about?' Your voice was low and cold. 'What do you mean, I'm only a girl?' I knew I was in serious trouble then. Serious.

'I didn't mean anything – I just miss you.' You had a habit of biting your lips and your mouth used to get dry and scabby. It didn't make me want to kiss it any the less.

'You amaze me,' you said. 'You've got no patience, no perspective. You're incredibly insensitive. I mean –' You said these words in astonishment, as if the truth of them was only just dawning on you. Frankly, I think you overdid it – there wasn't going to be any applause. I'd begun to have shooting pains in my nervous ulcerated stomach. My whole body was in some kind of rebellion at the harshness of the change in you, your words, and the injustice of their coming from you, Kitty, Kitty.

'What do you mean?' I stammered, stuttered. 'What are you saying?'

You got up, stretched, sighed, rubbed your eyes. 'Sorry. terrible temper,' you said. 'I shouldn't have shouted. I'm not easy – and you're so good to me – I'm very lucky. Not every girl has a gorgeous sexy rich banker to look after her.' There was something false in your apology, in your teasing. But I wanted to believe you and accept it, so I did. You nestled, purred up to me, your ear against my heart, and I felt as if the touching should dissolve all the anger you'd hurled at me and the terror I'd felt, but it didn't. It made me tremble, but not because I wanted to make love, because I wanted to cry. You drew back, taking my hands and kissing the wrists over my pounding tender pale veins. 'Let's go to bed,' you said.

Things in the bedroom had been very low-key since your return, and I know I should have jumped at the chance. 'I'd rather have a gin and tonic, if you don't mind,' I said.

You looked up at me then and your eyes were sharp, glinting. 'I feel as if I can feel your feelings and it scares me.'

'Why?' I did my best mocking smile.

'Because you can be so cruel.' I didn't lose my temper, but just dropped your hands and turned away – one in a whole string of empty victories.

Mummy was still on at me about meeting 'the new love of my life,' but I wouldn't let her. I couldn't tell her you were only seventeen and doing your A levels, so I said your job was very demanding at the minute and all social life banned. 'But I'm your mother,' she said. 'It's not the same.' I didn't like it, I didn't like the way things felt. And I couldn't neglect her, so I had to keep going away to visit her at the weekends. And that made me miserable. Preoccupied and self-obsessed as you were, at last, you noticed. 'You'd better let me meet her,' you said.

'The thing about Mummy is – she lives vicariously. If I let you meet her we'll never hear the end of it.'

'Do you want me to be part of your life or don't you? You're always saying you'd wish I'd make more of a commitment.' You fluttered your eyelashes like the ingénue you were.

'We mustn't fool ourselves, my darling. You're only seventeen.'

'Eighteen in October.'

'It's April.'

'So? Don't change the subject.'

'Are you determined about this?'

'Yes.'

'I'll arrange it, then. But on your head be it.'

True to form, Mummy surprised me by having absolutely no scruples about your age. 'Your happiness is all that matters,' she said. I thought of warning her to behave herself when she met you but had no idea where to start. 'Why don't you think she'll like me? And does it matter?' she'd have said. 'It's up to me to approve of her.' I could have said, 'She's a rival. She's young, she's beautiful – she's enchantingly charming and off-the-scale clever. She's talented, she's –' But something told me she'd have said, 'Moody little bitch then, is she?' so I held my tongue.

We decided the meeting should be in London on neutral ground.

'Dinner somewhere swanky,' said Mummy on the phone. 'I never get out nowadays.'

'All right, but you can't stay the night.'

'Don't worry, I have my pride. But you're paying for a car to take me home.' I chose the Connaught. In for a penny in for a pound.

I had to get there straight from the office with no time to change. Seven o'clock: Mummy and I waited in the lobby, then in the bar. We're both very punctual. It was important that you shouldn't be late.

'Don't worry, darling,' she said, playing with the ice in her glass. 'They'll hold the table. Stop watching the door.' I knew that she was disappointed you were keeping her waiting, but she was too polite to say so, giving you every chance. Every minute that passed lowered you in her opinion and I knew it. I wondered if she wanted a drink. I was glad of mine. When at last you came into the room, looking around for us, almost frantically, I thought, I could hardly stand up I was shaking so much. I've never seen you so nervous. You looked beautiful, but you looked all wrong. I hadn't thought of approving your dress beforehand, and as I moved towards you to kiss you (attempting to seem at ease), and introduce you I was quickly trying to remember if I'd ever seen it before. I shouldn't have been so careless. It was new, and it wasn't an expensive dress, obviously bought for the occasion – always a mistake. None of that would have mattered if it hadn't been so vulgar. It was black, embossed and shiny, and it was short, with a tulip skirt that fell open as you sat down and crossed your legs, and a cross-over neckline that seemed to gape at the slightest move-ment. Your black lacy bra (one of my favourites) was clearly visible. It wasn't the kind of thing you usually wore, you usually had better taste. All this could have been overcome if you'd known how to carry it off. But you didn't – you were much too young. You had presence and beauty, but no height and no grace, and it was too revealing, every move you made as you sat and sipped your glass of champagne was awkwardly seductive: when it fell open you didn't seem to notice. I knew that Mummy felt instantly sorry for me, and was as embar-rassed as I was. She doesn't respect women who show off their looks in so obvious and sexy a way. The Connaught isn't a hotel where everyone dresses flamboyantly, God forbid. Also, I couldn't work out why you were trying to prove that you were sexy. It was a mistake.

I was irritated and I wanted to snap at you, at least whisper at you not to lean forward, but I couldn't catch your eye. When I did, your blushing and embarrassment only made me more impatient. It was so out of character. Where was my lovely, playful Kitty, the girl who could have enchanted Mummy as she enchanted me? Did you really think I wanted to introduce you to my mother so she could get a good look at your breasts and the black tops of your stockings? I found I couldn't turn to either of you and start a conversation: I wanted to deflect, diffuse the situation, use my charm, find my best manner, but I felt paralysed, distant, nauseous. Your eyes were serious, but you were punctuating your speech with ridiculous girlish giggles which I'd never seen before. I couldn't do anything. I longed for the drinks to be over so we could move on to our table. Once we sat down to eat I felt I might be able to control the evening better. And at least your legs and appalling high heels would be out of sight. Worse, Mummy was beginning to get quite gregarious, seeming almost to be enjoying herself looking at your legs, almost titillated, flirtatious, like she used to be when she was drinking. That was all wrong. Couldn't you see, couldn't you realise that if you were to be a serious prospect you couldn't play with Mummy as if she were prey? My heart was beating, moving upwards in my throat, and I swallowed, tryng to push it back down.

Dinner passed in a blur of pretences. Mummy pretended to find you charming and intelligent and beautiful. I pretended I didn't think you ridiculous. You, gulping down the wine, unsuspecting, leaned towards me affectionately across the table, your eyes shining with inappropriate sentiment, and tried to take my hand. I nearly died. I've always hated public demonstrations of affection ('PDA', Susannah and I used to call them). I realised you wanted to flaunt me in front of her, get the edge. I couldn't say anything because the shame would have only been doubled if I tried to stall you, admitted I was anything but spellbound by you. Your confidence grew and grew, you were quite tipsy (drunk), beginning to float on a wave of useless drowning emotion, and I felt cheated and afraid. My classy piece of goods had turned to trash.

As soon as was decently possible, I paid the bill and got you out of there. 'No after-dinner drinks?' you said. Mummy made some joke about new lovers dying to get back to bed. I knew that this meant you'd been irrevocably degraded in her eyes to the level of an affair – to your shame, a public affair – when I'd hoped for a calm sure chaste acceptance of you as part of our family. By making this joke, Mummy had signalled that you couldn't be taken seriously, you were dismissed. And the pain of it was that you had absolutely no notion about what had just happened.

I couldn't speak to you in the taxi. I couldn't think of one word, and you seemed content with silence, holding my hand in both yours.

'I'm dying to get out of these high heels,' you said, pulling off your earrings and putting them in my pocket. I still couldn't reply. I just wanted sleep – oblivion – not to have to acknowledge this disaster until the next day when I had the strength.

Back at the house I quickly retreated to the bathroom, while you called to me, chattering about your impressions of my mother.

'Looks her age.' How you dared I still don't know. I couldn't answer you. You were an irritant, a stranger encroaching, and all I wanted to do was sleep. You were sensitive, I could never deny you that, and by then you knew something was wrong. 'What have I done to upset you?' I was undressing in silence with my back to you.

'I don't want to talk to you and I want to go to sleep.' The room felt airless, the tops of the trees outside unmoving against the pink sky.

'Please tell me what I've done wrong. You were so strange to me this evening.'

I couldn't be bothered to keep quiet any longer. 'You insult my mother by being late, embarrass us both by wearing that revolting dress, show me up by flirting outrageously – and then you dare to ask me . . . !'

'Don't be unfair – I – you're being so weird.'

'I'm being myself. Why do you want to be with me anyway if you think I'm so unfair to you?' I knew I'd shocked you then because you shut up for a minute.

'What do you mean? How have I insulted her?'

'What do I mean? At the risk of repeating myself, I mean that you arrived to meet my mother fifteen minutes late, a long time for me to distract her from your appalling rudeness, and that from the moment you did arrive, you behaved like a –'

'Like a what?' You were angry. I couldn't believe it, but your cheeks were red and you were angry. My exhaustion left me in a rush, and from my bowels I felt my rage sound through me. 'She wasn't exactly nice to me – and you didn't –'

'Like a disgusting, dirty little bitch. You can't forget about it, can you? That you're sexy, that you're "in love"?' I mimicked your soft-voiced mooning over those words and saw you take a step backwards. 'You may be the best fuck I've had in a long time, but you want to make sure everyone else knows it too. Especially my mother. It's – what makes you think you're right for me, for that expensive hotel, for my life? You haven't the first idea how to behave.'

'What is it with you and her? She's –'

'Nothing you can do is going to take me away from my mother. So don't even try.'

'What?'

'We've been through too much together.' I felt calm, saying that.

'What are you talking about?' you spluttered, incoherent, colour red and raw in the face, like a shop girl. 'How can you speak to me like that? Are you mad? What can you think of me? I must be crazy, crazy in love – but you!' You bellowed at me like a slut, shouting and crying at the same time.

'Be quiet,' I said to you, cold cold cold. 'You'll wake up the street. They'll hear.'

'Good. I want them to hear! I want everyone to hear! I'm not staying in this house with you and your insults.' You skidded out of the room and thudded down the stairs in your slippery stockings. You'd have to come back, of course, you were just having fun being a drama queen. I couldn't feel anything at all by then. I'd been very hot and very angry, and now I was cold, and the exhaustion was on me again, back on top of me again. I went back into the bathroom and slowly brushed my teeth, took out my contact lenses, threw my clothes in a heap on the floor and got into bed. In the dark, for a moment I couldn't remember where I was – then realised I had to leave the door ajar for you so you wouldn't wake me when you came back. I didn't want to sleep in the same bed with you at all, but knew that if I curled up very tightly on my side and put a pillow against my back, if I were lucky I wouldn't have to touch you even in my sleep. I began to think about ski slopes, sliding down mountains with snow on them, alone and at great speed.

I was woken by the sound of sobbing, unmuffled, uncontrolled gulping and choking. You were sitting up in bed behind and above me.

'Alex? Alex? What's just happened? Why has it just happened? What's the matter? Speak to me. Do you still love me?'

'Stop crying and go to sleep.'

'But I can't if I think you really have bad thoughts about me. I'm sorry if I did anything wrong. I didn't mean to be rude to your mother. Do you still love me?'

I hate pleading and crying. All women – even you – indulge themselves with it and it's disgusting. Why do you all take it for granted that your feelings are so much more important than mine? 'I can't love you when you're like this.' I tried to explain and be patient. On and on you sobbed. 'Stop crying. It's very late now. Stop crying. Stop making this scene. I want to go to sleep.' After a while I thought you were at least trying to cry more quietly. But your attempt wasn't very successful. 'Stop crying.' It was my turn to plead. I put my hands over my ears and buried my head under the pillows. If you didn't try to touch me and didn't talk any more I could go to sleep to the sound of your tears.

In the morning I went to work without waking you, or

wanting to see if you were awake. You called me in the office, croaking at me, sorry for yourself. (Though you were the one lucky enough to sleep late and make self-indulgent phone calls.)

'Is it over? Perhaps I should go.' (No, 'How are you and have you had any breakfast?' – of course.)

'It's up to you. Though I must say I didn't think you'd turn out to be such a coward. Your publicity was so good. You know – young, perceptive, challenging woman. I'm disappointed.'

'Why are you doing this?' you said, again.

'I've had enough of this conversation, your accusations. If you think I'm so – impossible, you can leave. All I can say is I've never lied to you.'

There was a pause where I heard you breathing, then you said, ''Bye darling.' I felt hollow when you put the phone down, consoling myself with the irrelevant observation that things could be worse.

Mummy called. 'Bit of a flibbertigibbet, isn't she?'

'Don't rub it in.'

'Fun for now, I suppose.'

'Yes.'

You were still there when I got home. Up in your study working. I'd managed to forget it all by then, erase it. I hoped you had too. I only bring it up now because I'm looking for clues.

'Blooming with health and good looks,' I think you said as I came in. You weren't, you were weary and looked bleached out. 'Forgive and forget?'

'Forgive and forget.' After that there was no mention of another meeting, hardly any mention of Mummy at all, though you began to be much more wary about referring to her. I continued visiting her by myself. The fact is you didn't seem to mind my absences.

Only a few spring days later I came home to the sound of

noisy sobbing echoing down the still-uncarpeted stairs. From the hall I could see your door was open – unusual – I climbed up to your study very slowly because I didn't really want to see. You were on the floor surrounded by paper, the window tight shut. All the boxes were open. More accurately, you were on your knees: not a bad position in different circumstances, but your head was down, forehead resting on the floor as if in some kind of prayer. Your eyes were closed and you were breathing with difficulty. I was appalled. The room was in such confusion. I bent to touch you rather tentatively, but you took no notice.

'What's the matter?' I thought of patting you but decided not to touch. You lifted your head, and I sat down beside you. I hate sitting on the floor. You looked hideous, to put it mildly.

'I've read her letters,' you said. How the blood must have drained from my face.

'Whose letters?'

'Susannah's letters,' you said, as if I were an imbecile, while I swallowed the temptation to laugh. This was a considerable relief.

'Oh, Susannah.' Susannah seemed very far away in time, distant. Nothing to say about Susannah.

'She loved you so much – they're all pleas.'

I knew you wanted me to say something so I said, 'Yes.' I was wondering how bad the scene was going to be and if it would be a long time before I could have a bath. I was very tired. 'It looks like a bomb's gone off in here,' I said, 'such a mess,' in an attempt to jolly you out of it, but you weren't to be jollied.

'Aren't you angry? Angry that I opened the boxes?'

'I suppose it was inevitable eventually,' I said. 'They're here after all. Freud would say I probably wanted you to. But then he's always struck me as having had a very contrary view of human nature.'

You grabbed my sleeve. 'But I did it on purpose. I didn't do it by mistake.'

'I know.' I looked around, unwilling. There were files, lawyers' letters, gardening catalogues and plans for Susannah's business (rather hopefully entitled Forever Flowers), budgets, planting schemes. There was our wedding list, endless receipts from Peter Jones, maps used for holidays, wallpaper samples, washing-machine guarantees, staples, light-bulbs, even hair ribbons, envelopes with shopping lists written on them in her simple round handwriting. You name it, it was in those boxes. I'd had a firm in to pack up everything from the last house. There had been no time to throw anything away. You were watching me and shivering with tears. 'Why don't you go and wash your face?' I said, trying to sound kind and disguise my exhaustion.

'It's your marriage. I've opened up your marriage and scattered it on the floor.'

I don't mind telling you your flair for the dramatic was really beginning to get me down by then.

'I know.'

'I'm sorry.'

'It's all right. I'm rather flattered.' (This was true.)

'I intruded.'

'You were entitled. You wanted to know.' This didn't seem enough for you, so I went on. 'She suffered, so did I. We were very unhappy for a very long time. It's nothing to be proud of, or jealous about for that matter.' (I hoped you were jealous.) 'I'm glad she's gone. You've made me be glad.'

My words proved useless. You just went on. 'I don't think I understood before – how deeply you both felt – fifteen years.' You looked at me again then, were concentrating on me at last, instead of the boring old blonde, which was something. With any luck the tide was turning.

I stood up. 'Look – there's no point in dwelling on Susannah,' I said. 'Absolutely no point at all. I've told you

before. I lost her, and what happened to her – it was a tragedy.'
I pulled you to your feet, using only one hand. I was too
rough. I hadn't meant to be.

'That hurt.' You were frowning, rubbing your arm.

'I'm sorry. Long day.' You kept on searching my face in that
irritating manner you had. I felt very angry very suddenly.

'Alex – what happened to her? Did you –?'

My head felt black with rage. 'I did nothing worse to her
than the things she did to me.' I felt that if I heard another
word from you I'd absolutely have to hit you. And I knew that
you sensed that too, knew it deep down in your animal soul.

'Your face has changed,' you said. 'It's different.' It was
terrible, it was a terrible moment. You didn't shrink away from
me the way she used to, you solid little defiant thing. But you
knew you'd sailed too close to the wind and I could feel you
wanted me to get out of the room – you were afraid of me. It
was desperate. The effort to control myself was gargantuan,
but I made it. I made it for you. Not that you deserved it, not
that you were grateful: another woman pushing me, pushing
and pushing, no sense of dignity, no sense of restraint. I
couldn't understand it: you – the opposite of Susannah, with
your spirit and your bravery and your attack, behaving just
like her, whimpering crying and weak – grieving for someone
you didn't even know, who has nothing to do with you,
someone who was by rights your enemy and *my* ghost.

That was a turning-point. After that you'd close the door
and threaten to lock yourself in if I disturbed you. It was like
living with an angry baby bear. It stopped amusing me quickly,
though, and just hurt like a bruise instead.

The night before you left, on my way up to bed, on impulse
I went into your study. The light was on under the door and
you were still working. I stood behind you, leaning against
your chair, over you, resting my cheek against yours. The mess
was still everywhere, you'd made no atttempt to clear it up.

You wriggled. 'You gave me a fright.'

'Don't be silly. You knew I was there.' Together we examined the page. You'd written, 'Sometimes when he is not Antony, he lacks that great property that should go with Antony.' That was it: the rest of the page was blank. 'What does that mean? Is it a riddle?'

'You think I made it up?'

'Wouldn't put it past you.'

'It's Shakespeare, silly – my tragedy exam.'

'How can you have a tragedy exam?'

'Trust me, I do.'

'Tell me.'

'It's loss of self – our hero's being destroyed, but he knows, they know, we know, that he's better than the person he's become.'

'Aren't we all?'

'Look – did I invite you in here, anyway?' You turned to look at me, your face all screwed up – like a cat dropped in water.

'I missed you – you didn't used to mind.'

'I'm working. Do you understand what that means? *I am working!*'

'All right.' I backed away, hands in the air in cowboy-film surrender, trying to tease you. 'You don't have to be such a bitch about it.'

'*Salope.*'

'That too. Don't quarrel with me, Kitty, I love you so much.'

'Too much. You love me too much.' You'd stopped looking at me by then and were staring at the page.

'There's no such thing as too much love.'

'A good exit line,' you said, turning, and smiling a crooked smile.

The remaining time before you went back to school for the summer you conducted yourself as if you were in mourning and I an insensitive intruder on your grief. 'It takes time to get over these things,' you said. Though I wasn't sure what it was you were trying to get over. 'Have you lost faith in me?' I asked once, but you didn't answer me. I tried not to make demands. In those last days you abandoned your work and went out for hours at a time without explanation. It unnerved me, the break in our routines, the debris of your discoveries scattered on the floor, your study unoccupied.

After you went away I went in there to tidy it all up: hurl it back into oblivion more like. It was terribly painful, which I hadn't expected it to be. Your presence in the room outweighed Susannah's, but only just. There were textbooks piled up – forgotten? discarded? – notes in purple ink (pretentious, if you ask me), blotches and splotches that were intense: 'Comedy is tragedy plus time,' was one of them. What kind of nonsense is that? And other cribs about Shakespeare's tragic energy, I remember them particularly because they sounded so good but had to have meant nothing: 'Tragedy: the infinite imprisoned in the finite', and 'The impetus of tragedy is *sacrificial*.' Then, in capital letters on a strip of paper many times folded, I found the words, 'BE A CHILD O' THE TIME.' I felt they must have had some importance to you because it was hidden away in the desk drawer amongst postcards and cinema tickets (you often went to the movies by yourself), but it meant nothing to me, nothing whatsoever. I realised you hadn't even told me the dates of these precious exams so that I could send you good-luck cards on the appropriate days. That kind of thoughtfulness couldn't help but make a difference, I'd decided, and now, once again, it was out of my hands. I didn't think you were coming back – that is, if I thought at all. Things were that bad between us.

It was a very pretty June that year, my wedding anniversary marked by a fresh pale gold day. I wangled business meetings at Wimbledon: a mistake because my intense involvement in the outcome of the matches was considered highly *de rigueur*, and I couldn't control my feelings at all. It seemed that everything was about winning and losing. Mummy wanted to come up and spend some time but I put her off. 'You're pining for some girl, aren't you?' she said. 'When am I ever not?' I replied, ashamed of myself for allowing her to see my bitterness. I began to take diving lessons. Being close to death has a way of concentrating the mind.

You didn't come when I called, but I called anyway, stood in the garden and called, 'Here, Kitty Kitty, pretty Kitty, pretty pretty Kitty.' When it happened I thought I'd surprised burglars. Loud music was bursting from the house, and I knew that was a trick they used to disguise the noise of what they're doing. I wasn't afraid, only angry, letting myself in and shouting at the top of my voice, 'Who's there?'

'A friend,' you sang out from the top of the stairs, then ran helter-skelter down into my arms. In a blink I saw your joyfulness had returned. You looked exquisitely pretty.

'Ravishing.'

'Ravishing is now my favourite word,' you said. We kissed and kissed, you laughing in my mouth.

'Let me look at you.' It was a pretty loose print dress, short with a flirty skirt. I'd forgotten how young you were. 'A sight for sore eyes.'

'Do you ever run out of clichés?'

'But, Kitty, you don't look as if you've just finished exams.'

'I went down to visit my mum for a few days – fresh country air.' If you'd been a cat you'd have arched your back as you said that. You'd already made the house alive again, opened all the windows at the back, strewn the living room with plastic bags; your sunglasses were face down on my new dining table, your makeup bag and a fat paperback next to them. 'I can read trashy books now it's all over,' you said.

'You left some others,' I began. 'Upstairs. I didn't know –'

But you weren't interested, giving no energy to the idea of them. 'You should have thrown them away.'

'I was clearing up – I wasn't sure –'

'I don't want to go in there any more. That was a bad time. Let's not go in there again, either of us, ever. Promise me. Promise me, or I won't sleep with you!'

'Now, Kitty –'

'Promise!'

'I promise, if it makes you happy.'

'You make me happy – *you*.' You moved away to turn the music down, showing me your solid little back.

We sat on the tiny balcony drinking Pimm's and surveying the wilderness of the garden.

'I must get some proper chairs,' I said.

'Look how perfect the other gardens are,' you said, 'and ours is so –'

'Neglected?'

'So untamed.' We laughed, self-satisfied, at the idea, suddenly smug as only lovers can be.

'I wish you'd come home sooner.'

You raised your eyebrows, sharp. 'If wishes were horses –'

'What's that supposed to mean?'

Avoiding my look, 'Whatever you fucking well like.'

'What an extraordinary thing to say.'

Turning your head away, 'I don't think so.'

'Why are you so angry?'

'I don't know.' It was as if you were provoking me, because you made no attempt to apologise.

'Let's not spoil the mood.'

'Of course not. On no account must the mood be spoiled.' You shrugged, and half smiled, a rather European gesture. It wasn't spoiled, only punctured for a little while. Mummy was right, you were a moody little cow.

Once you were back I wanted to capture you and take you away. I told you you could name the place, but you were vague about it. Plus, the situation at work meant I wouldn't be free until the middle of August anyway, which got me down. 'That's only next month,' you said. 'Only three weeks.' But it was too long to wait. I knew it was too long.

When I look back, it's amazing how much you accomplished in those three weeks. What was the first thing? I have to get this right. The first thing was your indulging me (uncharacteristically) by agreeing to go to an exhibition with me. 'If you so want us to look at paintings together, that's what we'll do,' you said, rolling over in bed with a secret smile. I knew that smile, your pleasure smile. 'But you must let me choose the exhibition, or I won't come.'

'All right.'

'Provençal landscapes at the Tate.'

'Sounds like a big wank to me.'

'Shut up.' Shut up I did, but you knew how I felt about the South of France, I didn't have to remind you that I never spoke about it, had no intention of ever going there again, etc., etc., but I didn't want to make a row. If you were testing me, I had to rise to the occasion and be malleable. Putty in your hands, more like.

'Don't go all stormy on me,' you said. 'It'll be good for you to see the beauty of it.' That was rather oblique, if not fey, of you, I thought, but I said nothing.

I booked tickets, queuing has never been for me, and took the morning off from my prison of an office. I made you get up early, because I wanted us to arrive for the first session and get in before the coach parties.

'You should relax,' you said. 'Other people have a right to see the paintings too.'

'Not stupid, uneducated people. Not people who go because they happen to be in London, or because their three-day break includes tickets, or because *Time Out* says so or because they want some culture before lunch and shopping. Art is an élitist thing. It belongs to the chosen few. Always has done, always will do.' All this I spat out in the car on the windy Embankment.

'Heil, Hitler,' you said, and looked out of the window in one of your amused yet preoccupied gestures.

'I'm sorry, Kitty.' The apology seemed to pain you unnecessarily. I didn't understand why at the time, resisting the urge to pull over and grope you. You wore a gingham shirt and tight black skirt, a retro look, vaguely reminiscent of my young mother at her glamorous best.

I always forget how cold galleries are. I was freezing when we got in there. The first room was too annoying to stay in, everyone bunched up with their exhibition guides clutched in their hands, peering at the words and attempting to match them to the pictures, which is hardly the point. You'd scooted off as soon as we got in. I could hear those machines in people's ears, that tinny sound, and then a real voice, that of an old woman leaning on her cane, shouting deafly at the young man beside her, 'They grow up so fast, it seems a shame to miss it. Still. Does she have any help?' I had to get out of there. In the second room the people were fewer, better dispersed, more intent. I took in blurred visions of bleached landscapes, exaggerated colours (why *do* people rave about those two-toned Cézannes?). It was all just about OK. The Van Gogh room was quite insane.

'Of course, his life had nothing to do with his art,' announced one American to another. 'Pull the other one,' I wanted to say. The flocks of birds frightened me – and as for the perspectives – the less said about those the better. I moved on, wondering where you were, and why, if you were such an art fan, you weren't examining everything more closely. I wanted to be with you. That was the whole point of the morning, after all.

At last I spotted you at the other end of room three, big and beige and drenched in hideous mustard-coloured ambient light. (I believe that's what they call it.) It was like drowning in sick. I imagined the painters spinning in their graves and suppressed a laugh. You looked very small, sturdy as ever, your stomach sticking out. You were gnawing your thumb, contemplating something or other. I felt corkscrews in my heart. You were a perfect vision, my one true thing. You were so glossy. I couldn't remember where the phrase one true thing came from. I didn't care. Walking over to you was fantastic, as if I had a loud-hailer and were calling, 'This girl's mine!' but I didn't need that. I just needed to know it for myself, as a certainty. You didn't acknowledge me when I stood next to you, so intense was your concentration; that was part of what I loved about you. So I looked at the painting too. First there was a feeling of blue and then a feeling of white. It was a small canvas, the little white tree standing out so firm and structured and joyful. The hot blue sky around it was very warm – it wasn't heat-of-the-day sky. Could it have been noon sky, or mid-afternoon sky? I don't know. It wasn't happy tra-la-la blue and white like Monet, because the skeleton of the trunk and the branches were so dark. I could tell the blackness would remain when the leaves and blossom had gone, endure in a way that was reassuring and frightening. And there were powerful hot red colours and yellows around the depths, the base of the trunk – I can't say it reminded me of my young life, it *was* my young life. I'd seen so many of those trees in bloom like that. What was it? The archetype. It was the archetypal tree. Tears streamed down my face. I put my hand out and moved to touch the picture and you grabbed my arm, roughly you grabbed my arm.

'You can't do that,' you hissed. I wanted to take up the picture and hug it, I wanted it to be mine for always – mine to destroy if I wanted. It was something that belonged to me. 'What's the matter?' you said. 'Why are you crying?' You were very hard. You had no feeling for me. 'Why are you crying – why?' It was your stage whisper – harsh. 'Stop. Stop crying. Alex, stop. Stop crying. Stop crying now.' I think I was close to fainting. I think that must be what fainting feels like. You shook me. Did you slap my cheek? I don't know, but somehow you stung me awake and you dragged me out of that gallery as if I were a two-year-old having a tantrum. We stood on the pavement and it was windy and rustling. 'You really are a complete fool. I only went to the bloody thing for you.'

'Please don't be mean to me,' I said, putting my hands over my ears. 'I don't feel well.'

You walked a circle away from me, coming back with a softer voice. 'No. No, of course not. I'm sorry. I'm so sorry.' I think you were sorry, but I'll never know for sure. Certainly there was no touching, just nose-blowing and general snivel-ling.

'I have to go to work now. Mustn't be late. Forgive me.'

You shrugged. '*Pas du tout.*' Your accent was superb.

I came home that night expecting more of a scene, deeper trouble: but you seemed to have forgotten. Blasé, you were in the garden playing with a skipping-rope. I have no idea why.

'I didn't know I even had a skipping rope,' I said, from the balcony, shielding my eyes from the low sun, squinting at you.

'You don't. I bought it this afternoon. It's great fun.' You weren't very good at it, breathless and untidy, but you wouldn't stop. 'Join in. Let's skip together.'

'I'm too tired.'

'You're so old and boring,' you taunted. 'Old and boring. Boring and old. I'm going out without you tonight.'

'Good,' I said. And, sweetie, I meant it. One thing I'd learned from my marriage is that trying to hold on to someone never works. My tactic puzzled you. I think you thought you'd destroyed me that morning and now the job required finishing touches only. You were wrong.

What was the next mad thing you did? Following the general trend towards infantilism came your baby-and-child obsession. In one hot Monday, you made what I called your Barnaby shrine, which consisted of all the photographs I had of the boy, combined with others you must have dug up and stolen from your day with the boxes. This corner was part of the living room, at the back, near the door to the garden. I think your strategy was to choose a place I'd be unable to avoid: every time I went outside I'd have to pass it. Being far too simple-minded you failed to anticipate that I would take avoiding action by going out through the kitchen door only. I didn't want to have the boy in my face hour on hour. I'd got used to the one or two photographs I'd chosen to keep on display: I didn't see them any more. You knew that. This was a new torture. I chose not to mention the shrine (an apt description, as you'll recall there were also flowers and candles), because I didn't want to get angry with you. Then the nagging started.

'How old is Barnaby now?'

'Just three.'

'Don't you miss him?'

'I try not to.'

'I want to talk about him, let's talk about him.' You, climbing all over me in bed, lifting my closed eyelids and shouting, 'Wake up!'

'I will not wake up. I'm asleep.'

You pulled my ears and tweaked my hair. 'I want to see him, let's both go, let's go together, let's go and see him together, oh, do let's, do!'

'Don't use that expression.'

'Why not?'

'It was Susannah's.'

You cried, 'Her name on your lips – the inscrutable, masterful lips!' You clutched your heart and rolled your eyes in mock palpitations.

'Leave it, Kitty, Leave it alone.'

'His master's voice!' Laughter, high and uncontained. Not your pretty, lovely laugh.

'Stop it. And stop squirming.'

Obedient silence, sleep beckoning, then, 'If you really loved me, you'd let me meet your child.'

'There's no point in it. You'd only harm him.'

'And how would I do that?' You reached over me and put on the beside light, straddling my chest, your hands on my neck. 'How? How?'

'Do you want to strangle me?'

'Sometimes.' You kissed me, moving your hands from my throat to my shoulders. 'Let me see him, let me, let me, let me, *let me.*'

Even now it's hard to communicate how exhausted I was, how exhausted you'd made me. I tried the calm, sensible approach. 'Give me one good reason why you should meet him.'

You squashed my nose with your forefinger, lowering your head like a bird of prey. 'Because I want a child.'

'My dear girl, you *are* a child. Since when are we having children? I can't even be sure you'll be here from one day to another. Furthermore, the reason has to be about him, not about you, you selfish little bitch. Even I love him enough to stay away from him.' You burst out crying then and there. I took a blanket and went to sleep on the sofa.

But it began to plague me; the idea took hold that I hadn't seen my son since Christmas and it was well into July. I felt ashamed. I knew I should go, call the old battleaxe and arrange a visit, a quick visit, something, anything. But I couldn't. 'I'll come with you. I'm good with children,' you'd say. 'You'll see.' You went on and on. You wouldn't leave me alone. You were like a plague of Furies, whispering, shouting, giggling, poking. 'Brother Alex, I'm going to call you that – we're really only brother and sister now, aren't we? Is that why Susannah left you? Is it? Give me a kiss, kiss me, kiss me. Give me a kiss.' I didn't throw you out because cunningly you spaced out these attacks between racks of rosemary sweet lamb, roasted vegetables and organic strawberry fool, between baths to-gether, between ironing my favourite linen shirt for an hour using the sweat from your brow instead of starch, between sorting my socks into perfect pairs. You interpersed each advance, each attack, with every sweet little unselfconscious loving act a woman could ever perform for a man, a child for her father, a mother for her son. And you didn't ask anything of me in bed. You just gave and gave. Awash with one-sided sexual favours, I think that's how our love-life could by then be described. I'd lost interest in pleasing you but not in your interest in me. Besides all that, I knew you had nowhere to go. Your unexplained absences, however, were always a relief.

The combination of my guilt and your pleading made me act against my better judgement. I called the old she-dragon, pleaded, threatened and cajoled. I promised my mother would be there to chaperone me. 'Please. Just for the afternoon.'

Susannah's father dropped him off at the house.

'My mother's on her way,' I said, but he didn't seem to care that it was only me, standing far away from the front door and avoiding looking me in the eye.

'I'll be back at five,' he said, scampered into the car and drove away.

Barnaby looked like the photographs of me as a child, but more colourless: the same large thick-fringed eyes, but pale like Susannah's. He was too pale altogether, God knows what rabbit food they fed him, there were smudges under his eyes. His golden hair with its long golden fringe was cut into a pudding basin – a bit too effeminate for my taste. He was a boy-child, after all. He stood on my doorsteps in his corduroy trousers and little navy jumper with a bear on it, he stood as straight as any statue. I'd made you wait in the garden so it was just him and me.

'Aren't you hot in that jumper?'

'I've got a shirt on underneath.' He had a delicate, unfamiliar, piping voice, little white teeth, a milky white face.

'Do you know who I am?'

'You're my daddy.'

'Yes, I am. I'm your daddy and I've missed you very much.' There wasn't much he could say to that, to be fair to him, it was foolish of me to say it. I wanted to pick him up, but didn't dare. 'Come in. We can play in the garden.' On the steep stairs down to the kitchen, squashed together, he put his arm up to take my hand, clasping one of my fingers in automatic trust. The stairs were a bit of an obstacle to him, I think. You'd laid out biscuits and cake, bread and butter and jam on the white tiles of the counter, too high for him to reach or see. 'Would you like some orange squash?' I was conscious of peering down at him from my great height.

'No, thank you.'

'Let's go outside then.' More steps, only two, up this time, into the garden. A tangle with a space cleared by us the day before, rough-mown by me, a rug, sitting on it, you. 'Barnaby, this is Kitty.'

You didn't stand up to approach him, bad manners, I thought. But your smile did him good because he said, 'Hello,' quite confidently.

'I'm glad to see you, Barnaby. I've got some blocks here and I'm trying to make a tower, but it isn't very good,' you said.

The little fellow let go of my hand, approaching you with care. 'I'll help you,' he said. 'I'm good at helping,' and kneeling down on the rug began to build the brightly coloured brick tower with great unsmiling concentration. I tried to catch your eye and failed. I felt invisible to you both, after a short time, retreating up the wrought-iron stairs to sit on the balcony looking down on you. The afternoon was warm, a bit of a glare, but not bad. You worked, together, and you murmured at him, inaudibly, confidingly, and he laughed. I don't know how you resisted grabbing him, cuddling him, tickling him – I would have wanted to, but you seemed unnecessarily polite to him. After a while he took off his jumper. You helped him, folding it for him like a servant. You fetched him some orange squash.

'Come down and have some with us, Alex,' you called. I could think of no reason to say no, so I said yes. Sitting on the rug, the uncut grass high around us, felt like an adventure.

'Where are your flowers?' he asked.

'We don't have any.'

'I'll help you grow some if you like. I know how.'

'That's good,' you said. 'I'll remember. Thank you.' After the orange squash I didn't know what to do with him next. 'Which do you like best?' you said. 'Jigsaws or books?'

'Never give a child a choice,' I said. 'It's a rule.' His eyes went from one to the other of us. 'Show Kitty your forehead. We always used to do this, do you remember?'

'No.'

'Lift up your hair.' The child obeyed. 'See how like mine his forehead is – broad.'

'Very pretty,' you said. 'It's a lovely forehead.' You sounded idiotic, praising him like that. He looked so like his mother, so like me, it began to hurt a bit, the joy of rediscovery wearing off, and no connection made.

'Do you remember me, Barnaby?' He looked at you first as if you should prompt him, which was aggravating.

'It doesn't matter if you don't,' you said, letting him off the hook.

'Of course it does. I'm his father.'

'Seven months is too long for a little boy to –' The child kept looking from one face to the other. I didn't like the familiar feeling that gave me.

'Who am I? Barnaby, who am I?'

'You're my daddy.'

'There. That's all that matters,' you said, interrupting too loudly in a Mary Poppins voice. 'It's getting hot out here. We'll go in and have tea, and I'll read you a story, and then Grandpa will come and pick you up.' You lifted the little boy – my little boy – on to your hip, no permission asked or given. He seemed aggravatingly content, and off you went into the kitchen where I could hear you laugh together after a while. After the sounds of some clattering I sat down on the rug, lying on my stomach, shielded from you by the long grass. I didn't want to go in, nor did you come out to invite me. I tried to tell myself that it didn't matter that I couldn't talk to Barnaby, my own child, that my stomach hurt, that I was angry and didn't know why. I felt drowsy, forced myself to feel sleepy, trying to tell myself it was pleasant, the faraway drone of people's lawn-mowers, traffic, the odd plane, your voice quieter as you read the story, answered the occasional question from the boy. I must have fallen asleep because I woke to the stupid sound of my father-in-law's voice.

'I'm Kitty,' I heard you say. I pelted up the iron stairs. 'Alex's friend.'

'How do you do?' He was very polite, didn't try to knock your block off and say, 'Who said you could have my grandson?' the way I would have done. I kissed Barnaby goodbye, he was carried away placid and imperturbable as a little king, clutching a daisy you'd found for him, untidy, but not unhappy as far as I could see. I closed the door.

A LETTER TO KITTY

'See, I'm good with children,' you said.

'He used to gurgle when he laughed, really laughed that is, up and down some invisible scale.' I don't know why I suddenly confided in you like that. I'd meant to freeze you.

'We didn't get him to the real laughing stage. Maybe next time we could go to the park with a ball, get him running – that'll make him laugh.' But we both knew there wouldn't be a next time. The three of us couldn't make a family with all the wishing in the world. Better to leave the child be.

It was a kind side to yourself you showed me that day, I won't deny it. My son liked you, so you can't be all bad.

I began to feel very unhappy indeed.

'What's going to happen to us, after the summer? What will happen to us next?' I couldn't bear it, not asking you, stopping myself, any longer.

'But, Alex, you always have a plan.' You were reading in the evening garden (or wilderness) and I was lying at your feet, grass dampness seeping through the blanket, my eyes closed.

'I'm asking –'

'Will you be quiet? I'm reading.' You were so irritable, always. I couldn't get to you, get close to you at all.

'What are you reading?'

'A book.'

'Don't try to make me angry – I'm not in the mood.'

'That's unusual.' I rolled over on to my stomach and tried to become absorbed in the intricate wildlife among the roots of the grass. I couldn't find any. I stared at your bare foot instead. One was tucked under you, the other resting on the ground. You could hold the same position for an hour. I can never do that, I always fidget. You'd painted your toenails, but they needed doing again, they were growing out and didn't look their best. You'd forgotten about them. I stroked your instep and you nearly jumped a mile in the air.

'For fuck's sake, Alex!'

'I was just stroking –'

'You could have warned me. I thought –'

'It's perfectly obvious what you thought. Why don't you just talk to me?' You put down your book with a sigh, beside you, on its front, spine stretched. 'You shouldn't treat books like that.'

'I know.' You smiled at me. (Smile again, Kitty, smile again.) In the chill of the evening your skin was beginning to tighten, your arms becoming prickly. At your throat you wore a velvet ribbon with a heart suspended on it.

'Who gave you that?'

'My father. I told you.'

'I'd like to give you something.' You frowned and looked over my head, as if to the windows of the house, up a little, at your study, perhaps. 'No need to go in there, now,' I said, following your look.

'What?'

'Your study –'

'No.' You focused your eyes on me again, as if with renewed effort. 'Did you say you wanted to give me something?' You seemed only a little anxious when you asked me.

'I'd like to give you a ring.'

'What would the ring mean?' (It was like being interrogated.)

'That you were mine, of course.'

'Of course. How silly of me.' You leaned towards me as if to kiss me, then drew back, sneezed instead, and stood up. 'I can't think about the future now.' I knew exactly what you meant. We were like butterflies pinned. Neither could I.

'When the weather changes.'

'Yes – that'll be the right time.'

It wasn't as if the immediate future were empty. There was our holiday – you had no interest in that, so I decided to avoid confronting you about it and make it a surprise. Then there would be auditioning for drama school. You had the prospectuses and the applications had been made. There was no need for you to go back to school, to leave me ever again if you didn't want to go, no new term for me to dread.

'We could decorate the house,' I said at dinner – that same evening? – I don't know. White August clouds had settled on my soul.

'You're perfectly right. We could.' At night you turned away from me on your side and I didn't even dare touch your hair.

'Must you go out every night? I don't get to see you during the days – I look forward –'

'Being so plaintive doesn't suit you.' This conversation took place on the phone. 'I have things to do during the day – stuff – I can't just sit here waiting for you to ring me up.'

'I know – but when I get home –'

'I don't want to sit in with you every night and go to bed at quarter to ten because you have to get up in the morning. I want to see my friends.'

'Spotty youths.'

'You make yourself sound old, saying that.'

I brooded over that accusation for at least five hours, then called again. The machine was on. I left this message on my machine in my own house: 'I was wondering, that is thinking, that perhaps you might want to have – people over – not a party exactly – well, a party if you liked, anything you like, really. It's up to you. So think about it. Darling, it's your home too and I don't want to stop you. I love you. See you later – 'Bye.'

When I got home I played that message to myself, resisted wiping it, turned off the machine. There were no other messages, no sign of you. I sat on the balcony, suspended over mine and the other gardens like a diving board or a trapeze, and drank most of a jug of Pimm's, waiting for you. When the light faded I went in and ordered a takeaway. The trouble with being alone in a house that's too big for you is that there's either no sound at all, or the wrong sounds – sounds not of your life but of the life of the building – creaks and groans, sighs, echoes, or cries from the imagination, memories, fears. I couldn't bear it. It seemed to me that I'd spent far too great a proportion of my life alone. I couldn't bear it is an exaggeration, of course, because I did bear it, human beings endure. For some reason very few say to themselves: 'No, this is too much, this has to stop.' I'm talking about suicide now, or that phrase from your tragedy exam, 'self-slaughter', which is far more accurate about one's state of mind.

I ate my takeaway and listened to the radio, which felt friendlier than the television. And then I went to bed. You came in at midnight, playing my message downstairs as you kicked off your shoes, then burping and swaying in the bedroom doorway like a stage drunk trying to draw attention to yourself. I ignored you and went back to sleep. It was hard because after that you went out every night for a week – it could have been longer, I don't know, I haven't kept my diary – and I missed you terribly. But there was nothing I could do.

By Saturday morning you were bleary-eyed, coming down long after I'd got up and was attempting to read the paper in the drawing room.

'It's like living with a teenager, isn't it?' you said, coming in with coffee and a plate of bad-looking toast and sitting down on the floor with them, leaning your back against the fireplace. 'We should get a sofa.'

'Fine by me.' I kept the paper in front of my face.

'You're ignoring me.'

'You've noticed, I'm so touched.'

'It's terribly dark in here – shall I open the shutters?'

'No.'

'Is this about to be a lecture about staying out late? Be-cause –'

'I worry about you, that's all.'

'That's a lie – a sanctimonious lie.' You were instantly more furious than I'd seen you for a very long time. 'You never have a single thought for anyone else. Sometimes I seriously wonder whether I have any existence for you outside your own head.'

'What's that supposed to mean? Or is it another line from a play?'

'What it says. I mean what I say.'

'And I don't?'

'Just forget I said anything, OK?'

'Yes, Kitty Kitty, whatever you say. I'll do whatever you say.' (Sentences with your name in it always had the possibility of becoming songs.) I could never stay angry with you for long. That was your charm for me. Having said that, I think you truly were absolutely and inexplicably furious.

'Moving swiftly on,' your voice held its mocking tone again, 'I'm going to take up your kind offer – have some people over.'

'Good. When?'

'Tonight.' You fumbled around for a cigarette and lit it, blowing smoke everywhere, exuding it from every pore, the way only teenagers can. Half dressed, hair flattened, grubby-faced, what on earth did I see in you? I wanted to tell you you wouldn't always have that blossoming blooming skin, that face with a sheen on it, a shine, a dew. One day you'd wake up and years of smoking would have made your skin grey and lined, your hair brittle, your eyes filmy, and you'd no longer have the power to go out drinking all week and still have the energy or charm required to taunt your neglected lover with a party you knew he didn't want. You were watching me, waiting for me to try and make it difficult, put you in the right by making an unreasonable scene.

'Sounds excellent,' I said. 'I'll give you the money but don't expect me to do any heavy lifting.' You looked disappointed that I'd side-stepped a scene. You so hated to be out-manoeuvred.

Your party planning wasn't at all bad. It reminded me why I loved you in fact, that you showed so much style. You worked like a dog. I mowed what we laughingly referred to as the lawn but you said there was no point in decorating the garden because there was nothing to decorate. You put lanterns out on the balcony and took away our chairs so that people could stand on it and look at the dark garden and imagine something far prettier and more mysterious than what was actually there. You bought a lot of flowers and stuffed them in anything you could find once you'd exhausted my supply of vases (two). You bought mirrors and put candles in front of them. There was hardly any furniture to push out of the way, but you covered it with sheets, 'So you won't worry,' which made the bare rooms look more unreal than ever. You found some good music – old stuff – from my enormous record collection (still boxed up and forgotten in your study). I hadn't seen you go in there since you came back – I never did – but you knew where to find them. That was the extent of your set dressing. You knew the important thing was the food and drink and the rest was all rubbish people put in magazines. (It's very common if everything matches and looks neat and thought-out.) You mixed jugs of martinis ('I know – I'm *so* sophisticated,' you said, pointing your toes in your tight jeans to make me laugh), and the rest was champagne and champagne cocktails for the dedicated few. 'My friends can't possibly live up to this,' you said. You made a tapenade and spread it roughly on fresh crusty bread ('Life's too short to make toast for more than two'), piled Susannah's plates with smoked salmon and quails eggs and a very sweaty Brie, made mountains of overripe peaches and raspberries cut up and mixed with lemon juice, icing sugar and something abandoned and alcoholic you found in the back of one of the cupboards. 'That should keep us going,' you said. I helped you, worked like a Trojan in fact, I was so relieved that we were doing something together and that you were happy about it, drinking too much coffee and not having time for lunch. It was strange to be so busy, too busy to have time to eat, like cheating time by getting the day done faster.

We had fizzy water and messy sandwiches at about six.

'Mustn't start a party on an empty stomach,' I said. 'Fatal.' I ran your bath for you and put rosewater in it. 'What are you going to wear?' I asked from my place on the edge of the bath, monitoring the water temperature. You were rifling through your cupboard, fast.

'Can't you see I'm late now? Must you talk to me?' I didn't answer, feeling myself shrivel as I trailed my hand in the water. You came into the bathroom, kicking off your shoes. 'Ready yet?'

'Yes, ready.' You stared at me furiously, which I knew meant, 'Get out of here while I have my bath.' I longed to see you take off your clothes, but that was obviously no longer one of my privileges. I lay on the bed, sulking, waiting for you to come out, for what seemed like an hour but was probably only fifteen minutes. You emerged in your towel, so big it shrank you.

'Still here?'

'This is my room too.'

You glared, 'I want to get ready.' Out I slunk, like a little boy.

You came down wearing a tight red velvet dress – probably second-hand – that I'd never seen before. You were very made-up, it was almost stage makeup. The dress lifted your adored little bosoms and made them generous and inviting, like presents.

'You look divine.'

'Good.' For a second you answered me from a part of you still well disposed towards me, then shut it fast with a snap. I'd stood up when you came into the room. You began to light the candles, saying over your shoulder, 'What are your plans for this evening?'

'What?'

'You can't stay here with us.' You were sharp, impatient, as if it were obvious, moving from candle to candle, lighting matches, shaking them, concentrated.

'I – Why not?'

Then you turned to face me, allowed me that courtesy. 'Because it's my party and you're not invited.'

'I paid for the damn thing.' It was the only thing I could think of to say, and I knew it made me look pretty bad.

'I'm sorry, darling, it would be too embarrassing for me – I thought you understood that.' You looked very upset, much too upset for the cold Kitty who was delighting in rejecting me and no longer cared.

'Mmm.' I didn't want you to see me cry so I went upstairs to our room, which was strewn with underwear and makeup, crumpled clothes – all the preparations for the little red warrior you'd become, that evening's invention. I didn't know what I was doing up there. It wasn't my bolt-hole, it was yours. I thought of going into Mummy's room, but couldn't face that either, so I came back downstairs. You must have been in the kitchen, so I called out airily from the hall, as airily and proudly as I could, 'I'll be back later then. Have a good time. 'Bye.' I picked up my keys slowly in case you'd changed your mind.

''Bye darling.'

''Bye.'

Not wanting to interrupt anything, I didn't go back to the house until the next morning, about seven. The place was deserted. Disgusting, dishevelled and deserted. It took me hours to clear it all up: the ashtrays, the glasses with cigarette ends in them (why?), the smeared food and paper napkins – you know how you left it. The smell was quite unbelievable. I listened to opera while I did it – that's what I used to do clearing up parties in my Cambridge days. I remembered those days and they didn't seem so bad then as they had at the time. Funny that.

At lunchtime I went to the pub and had their withered but bracing Sunday roast and some very nasty wine. (I forgot that one must never drink wine in pubs – ignore what the colour supplements say.) I couldn't feel or think much because I was very tired and stiff from sleeping in the car the night before. I tried not to think more than I possibly could about where you were, and be too angry or worried. The party had probably moved on somewhere else and you'd followed it: simple as that. You were free after all, a free creature, my free girl. You deserved to have some fun, a good time, without me. You were only seventeen, and didn't mean to hurt me.

In the evening I watched television, expecting the sound of your footsteps and voice any minute. But there was nothing, so I went to bed.

You stayed out all Sunday night which, beyond the shadow of any doubt, was beyond the pale. Little cat-thing, I heard your key in the door around five, which is when I'm waking up if not getting up for work anyway. I had a pounding heart, a pounding in my ears. I heard you pause in the hall and take your shoes off, as if that would have made a difference. You didn't come up the stairs, but went down to the kitchen. Without thinking, I got up and followed you down. I found my dressing-gown but not my pyjamas – you'd taught me to sleep naked. You were standing at the counter waiting for the kettle to boil and looking out at the dawn garden. You were still wearing your red velvet dress. You knew I was behind you but you didn't turn round. I looked at you looking away from me and knew I'd been defeated before the scene began.

'African tribespeople consider turning their backs on one another an act of the greatest cruelty and treachery.'

'Do they?' you said, turning, weary and dull. Your expression was battered, your mascara smudged – a look I loathe – you hadn't repaired your face since you'd done it on Saturday evening, I could tell. That wasn't like you at all.

'Where've you been?'

'Out picking up men, where do you think?'

'Must you be so boring and predictable? I could have thought of that reply myself.'

'I suppose I must.' You didn't even bother to look at me after the first glance, but delivered your sulky teenager's speeches while fiddling with the teaspoon and getting the milk out of my vast fridge. You didn't offer me anything either, also utterly unlike you. 'Shouldn't you be getting ready for work by now?'

'Since when do you give me orders in my own house?'

'There's a first time for everything.' You were facing me now, holding the rose and white china teacup, giving me a look of such venom and loathing it quite literally took my breath away.

'What's got into you?'

'I believe it's you.' You spoke very slowly, in your clipped grown-up's voice. 'And I think it's time you got out.' You raised the cup and sipped, leaning back against the counter. I zeroed in on your mouth, the watery tea that smelled very fragrant, very strong in the empty early room. I had a sudden memory of putting my tongue in your mouth. Puss, I wanted to feel it again, passionately, half discovering, realising, I don't know – that I hadn't done it for such a long time. It seemed the only point in life at that second.

'How could I have been so stupid?' I said aloud, looking at your tired cracked lips and thinking how your breath probably smelled and knowing I didn't care. I let you keep sipping. It was great foreplay, especially as your lashes were lowered and you didn't know what was on my mind. You put the cup down and looked at me again with the same undisguised loathing, the same distaste. When I grabbed you I got your wrists behind your back with one hand, and with the other I was in your hot tight dry soft-hard place. I thought of a rock and a hard place, I don't know why. Easy summer weather, the joy of no tights. Your eyes wide with surprise I sucked at your mouth. You remember everything that happened then, I'm sure.

You were very tired after it all and just wanted to lie still. I had to rush off because I was late for work.

Kitty, you know what happens next but I deserve to be heard – deserve that you should know how it felt and still feels. A message on my machine at home. That was merciful because you knew my work number and could have given it to them but chose not to. Instead, one of those impersonal disaster voices I've come to know so well. Something about my friend Miss Katherine Morrow being admitted as an emergency and would I please contact the hospital. I couldn't think what had happened to you, that familiar feeling of emptiness and disbelief, staring at your sunglasses on the table, lenses down and smeared, wondering why you never chose to look after your things and how I should wash them in Fairy liquid because somebody had once told me – I don't know. Stuff and nonsense. Stuff and nonsense. I couldn't imagine what could have happened to you. Had you been run over? I was on the phone to the hospital and they were making me press star keys and numbers and it was no good at all, so I just got in the car with my mobile, only getting through once I was in the car park where predictably it cut out.

You were on a ward. I couldn't get over that. You weren't in a private room. I told them you'd have to be moved immediately. I wouldn't talk to them at all, insisting they take me to you straight away, so I could see for myself you weren't dead. They led me to your bed, which was just as well because I wouldn't have recognised you. You cried when you saw me, cried out of swollen eyes, but it was like a reflex, the tears, and I cried too because I was so afraid. Your hair was damp and sticking to your neck.

'What happened to you?' I said. 'What happened?' The swellings and bruises were horrific, and your face that looked as if it had been battered.

You said, 'Beaten black and blue,' quite clearly and audibly. The nurse was standing there. I asked her to explain, and that was when she said you'd lost the baby. She wasn't confidential about it. The curtains were pulled but we were still in the middle of the ward.

'The baby was lost as a result of the rape.' She said this more kindly, as she could see I was about to faint with shock. I think she touched me and then went to get water in a plastic cup. Because it was hot summer it was warm and tasted of the plastic it had been cooled in when I finally drank it.

'Kitty, who hurt you? Who raped you? Tell me and I'll kill him.' I bent over you, trying not to shout.

'You did,' you said. I remember that you smiled, but you can't have done. You can't have been that wicked. And it would have hurt you too much. That was when the nurse came back with the water.

'Were you the father?' she said. It was quite grotesque. Hadn't she had better training in crisis management?

'I don't know.' I don't know why I said that. Who else could it have been?

'Yes, yes.' You were impatient. 'It was him.'

'Well, I'll leave you together,' said the nurse. She padded away on her rubber shoes.

'Why are you saying I hurt you?'

Your eyes were very sharp and you half whispered, half hissed – 'Ask Susannah.'

I couldn't get any more out of you after that, there was no point in trying. You just turned your head away. If there'd been a wall you would have faced it. It was too much. I left you, forgetting to harangue the nurses about when you would recover, forgetting to ask for the doctor, check that the police had been informed – the whole thing. You'd known that would happen. You were always one step ahead.

It was evening outside the hospital, quite a gentle summer evening: it mocked me. Birds were tweeting, competing with the traffic, the sky arched and high, painted scudding clouds crossing it slowly. I didn't even think of going home – or back to the house rather. I remember vaguely trying to work out when I'd last had a home, and failing. Thank God the tank was full of petrol because I forgot to check that too. The car knew the way, like Chitty Chitty Bang Bang it made sure I got there safely. I don't remember the journey. Another two hours lost. More of my life's time obliterated by you.

Thank God the boy was in bed – it was night-time when I reached the house – but summer night is incomplete until midnight, and I could see the trees against the sky, leaves' shadows. There were few lights on. Nothing had changed. I was out of breath as if I'd been running. I leaned on the bell. I would have hammered on the door if there'd been a knocker. There should have been. Her mother answered the door. You won't have met Susannah's mother. She's the closest thing to an ogre I'll ever know – but what am I saying? You must have met her. Such is our mutual hatred that when she opened the door at first she didn't say anything, then, 'It's you.'

'Yes.'

'It's late – you can't –'

'I don't want to see him. It's Susannah I want to see.' I felt irritated at her standing guard. She didnt realise how unimportant she was. She didn't see how she was wasting time.

'It's out of the question.'

'Do you want me to beg?'

'No. I want you to leave now, or I'll call the police.'

I tried explaining. 'She'll want to see me, I know.'

'If you still think that . . .' She paused to invent some elaborate insult.

'Tell her I'll come back tomorrow. Tell her it's about Kitty.'

'Out!' she shouted, as if I were one of her poor dogs. I got in the car and drove away.

I stayed at the village B-and-B, washing out my underwear in the basin and leaving it on the window-sill to dry as I used to as a boy. I didn't sleep much. In the morning I borrowed a razor, called the office and said I had flu (a lame excuse) and sat in the car and waited at the end of the drive, waited till ten o'clock. I knew Susannah well enough to know she'd be in the garden on a summer morning. There was no need for me to go through the house to see her. There's a way across the fields that opens on to the gardens, but I didn't take it. It would have been wrong, furtive, dishonest, underhand. Instead I confronted the ogre, once more, at her own door.

'Your child is upstairs, playing. I don't want him to know you're here, so don't shout. Your wife is in the garden.' I followed her along the flagstoned passage, out through the garden room, on to the terrace. No sign of Susannah in the walled garden where I'd once walked with her. We went out through another wrought-iron gate, through a kitchen garden, a rose garden, and on to a lawn I didn't remember where croquet hoops were set out. She was sitting on an old quilt under a tree close enough to the one flowerbed to touch the flowers. Her legs were straight out in front of her, covered by what looked like a baby's shawl, her wheelchair at a discreet distance, her back supported by the end of a little bench and some thoughtfully placed cushions. I had to cross the lawn to get to her, my legs shaking. The ogre had left me at the gate and I was by myself. Her hair was long again as it had been as a girl, and she was wearing a straw hat because of the sun and I couldn't see her face until I knelt down beside her. Because she couldn't stand up to greet me, I felt that was the least I could do. I forgot all about you then, Kitty. I forgot about everything. She didn't smile at me, how could she, but she didn't look down, either. The steadiness in her eyes made me so ashamed I couldn't speak. Her hands were in her lap, idle.

'You're as beautiful as ever,' she said, and I began to cry, feeling my gorge rise in my throat, the sickness. I told her I was sorry.

She left the words in the air, waiting for the tears to subside, and then said, 'Ah. So there is remorse.'

'It was nothing to do with me. I wasn't there –'

She interrupted me and plunged without hesitating into a stream of words. 'When the horse threw me, the day after I ran away from you, and came home.' Her voice was patient, as if I were a child. I wiped my eyes on my sleeve. I wished I had something with which to blow my nose. 'To begin with, I wondered if you'd have said it was nothing to do with you. To begin with, I would have believed you, I'd have seen you, and I would have forgiven you. But you never came.' That calm voice, those calm merciless eyes, the sickness in my throat returning, trying not to look at those straight legs, the ankles loose underneath the shawl like broken branches. The dappled sunlight through the tree made sunlight on her, on her but not on her face, which was white and guarded. 'I'd have said it was an accident, my own recklessness, my own fault riding Mummy's horse when I hadn't ridden for so long, riding that big horse. But not now – now I've had enough time for it all to become clear to me. Shall I tell you how it happened?'

'No.'

'I want to. I want to tell you how it happened.' Her control was absolute. But then it always was. I could have run away, but it didn't occur to me. I just shifted, sat cross-legged, tore the daisies from the grass and ripped and shredded them in my hands. The smell was lovely. A breeze came up over the level ground. 'Pay attention,' she said. 'No fidgeting please.'

'Susannah, must you –'

'Yes. I really must.' In the look that passed between us then, my heart shivered.

'I woke up very early on that morning, after – I'd thought I wouldn't sleep at all but I'd slept like a dead person. When I woke I sat up in bed as if someone had given me an electric shock, and I leaped up in a sort of desperate – I had to see Barnaby, see that he was all right. Mummy had said he could sleep in my old room, she'd given me the spare room at the front of the house, but he had a view of the garden, and my old dolls' house was with him, and the horse stuff – my very few rosettes.'

'You were never a confident rider.'

'No. But I had a kind pony.'

'Thimble.'

'How well you remember.'

'I have known you for fifteen years.'

'Only that?' That was the first time she hesitated, but she concentrated again, quickly she concentrated. 'I stood looking at him sleeping for a while, but it didn't make me feel peaceful – it made me restless, distressed. I hadn't wanted to remember

– you, and I didn't, not consciously – it was other things, like
my wedding dress, which I knew was still there in the
cupboard, and the shoes and the veil, and other things, things
I wanted to get out and look at and knew I shouldn't. Things
from when I was a girl.' When she said that I wanted to say I
couldn't listen any more. 'I knew that that wouldn't help
anyone, and I had Barnaby to think of, but beyond that it was
all confused. I couldn't see how I was going to get through the
minutes – the day. And that was when I had the idea of going
for a ride. It was a bright morning – windy. The riding in the
park is good – there's no need even to cross a road. I wanted to
have a good gallop – not even that – only to be away and not
just with myself. No one was up at the stables. I wasn't even in
proper riding things – I found my old boots in the tack room.
And a hat. Mummy's gelding hadn't even had his feed, and he
was restless, putting his head up when he saw me, rattling his
door with his teeth. But he's quite old, quite gentle. I gave him
some hay while I brushed him off. I was trembling terribly –
I'm sure he sensed it. And I kept saying to myself: "You
mustn't be afraid, you mustn't be afraid." But I was. He's a big
horse. Pretended to shy at the mounting block.' She closed her
eyes then, sighed a little. 'If I'd been sensible. But then I've
been sensible all my life.'

'Timid.'

'Yes. That too. I started walking and trotting him along the
drive towards the front gate. I had no balance, no seat, I hadn't
ridden for years. He was quite amiable, danced and skipped a
little bit, shying at rabbits. They were up feeding. There was
still dew on the grass. When I reached the gate I turned him
right-handed and cantered back across the park, up the slope
towards that little wood. Some ancestor planted it because they
were sick of the flatness. There's another one much further
away. I felt safer in canter because I could sit down and kick
on, fool myself I was riding him instead of just sitting up there

hoping for the best. He snorted in canter and tried to stretch out a bit. He was quite fresh. He felt joy, I didn't. My fingers were sweating. It all felt wrong. Out of his routine – out of mine. I remember thinking: I'll walk through the wood, let him stretch his neck for a bit, then turn for home slowly, walk and trot back across the park, round the gardens into the yard. I was dreading turning for home because we'd only been out half an hour at the most, and I thought he'd pull, try to dash home, want breakfast.' She turned her head away from me then. Blinked. Quivered. 'I forgot to pay attention, planning ahead. On a very long rein. A bird flew up – loud. He shied and jumped sideways. I grabbed at the rein, jabbed him in the mouth, tried to kick him on, he bucked a big nervous buck, threw me, galloped home. If I'd fallen when he'd shied it would have been all right, but I clung on, so when I fell it was on my back. Soft landing. I felt the pain before I passed out.' She paused. My head was in my hands. In another tone she said, 'Are you listening? Still? Still listening?'

'Yes.'

'Look at me.' I looked at her face. It hadn't lost its sweetness. 'Look at my legs.'

'I've seen.' For a fraction of a second I feared she'd move the shawl and make me look, but she didn't.

'There was nothing they could do. Even if they'd found me earlier. I hadn't gone far though, you can see the wood from the house. He galloped straight back. They all were up in the stables by then.' She stopped and seemed to forget about me then, staring into space like a blind person watching something in their mind. Then she shook her head a little and looked at me. 'Would you like to know what's the worst thing? I can't kneel down among my plants. I can't weed, I can't plant unless I sit like this. I can't walk in the garden and cut flowers if I want to, prune the roses on a whim. It has to be planned. I have to be wheeled. I have to supervise.'

'I didn't know –'

'Of course not. Why should you think about me? I'm useless to you now.' She sighed and her voice became calmer. 'I get angry. Sometimes I'm all right, but – Barnaby is patient. I'm occupied. I design my gardens. I read. I've made a life. It's more than you ever gave me.' That was so cruel – Kitty – when she said that.

'You've become excellent at torture.'

'I've learned something from you, then. You recognise that about me at least.' We looked at each other again, in our life together for the last time.

There seemed no more to be said after that. I sat and looked at her hands, quiet in her lap, and returned to ripping at the daisies. She might have cried a little, I don't know.

'It would be crass of me to ask your forgiveness.'

'Yes. It would.' Then presently, 'Have you forgotten why you've come?'

'Kitty.' In a rush, I had a vision of you.

'Your darling, injured Kitty. Your girl.'

'Oh, my God.' Susannah smiled a slight smile.

'When she first got in touch with me, I thought she was a madwoman. Then I remembered I'd been a madwoman once, so I agreed to see her. She cried terribly and spat and swore. She's very like a cat.'

'Yes. It doesn't matter – tell me – When did she –'

'She came in April, right before she went back to school to do her exams. She said she'd found my letters and that they'd moved her – oh, lots of things. That she was afraid of you. When she first saw me she thought you'd beaten me into the chair. I told her there had been beatings. She hadn't guessed about the rapes, of course, and the incest. But that's natural. She was very distressed. She asked me so many questions about you, your mother – I realised you hadn't told her anything about me. I don't know why I was surprised.'

'Kitty wouldn't –'

'When she came back to see me again –'

'When – when was that?'

'About a month ago, or a few weeks – not long ago – she'd done her exams. She was different. She said she'd planned to go away and not see you again, now she knew about you. She wanted to leave you – to forget about it – you – but it was no good. Instead she'd made the decision to go back for you – but it was very hard. "Go back for you, and get you." Those were her exact words. She asked me to help her.'

'What?'

'She's trapping you. And I've agreed – we're doing it together.' In that second I wanted to grab her, grab her and shake her till her teeth rattled. She looked at me, and she knew this, and she wasn't afraid. 'We're going to win,' she said.

On the way back to the house I thought of all the things I could and should have done or said. Any sensible man would have asked all these questions: Get me – how? Get me – what for? Or would have protested my obvious innocence, even laughed and said she was deranged. But you have to understand that here was someone I'd loved – deeply – declaring herself against me, in a way that was total, in a way that in her place I could never have felt, stooped to, let alone expressed. It was the shock on shock that floored me, demoralised me, disarmed me. You'd counted on that, too. The unbelievable unfathomable betrayal – hers – yours, and I was trying to piece it together, make sense of it in my mind. I'd known it was all different, broken, when you'd come back – but I hadn't wanted to see it, I was afraid you didn't love me any more – but this – I couldn't understand why you should both hate me so much, why you should plot against me. It was pitiful really. I see that now. Susannah's injury had driven her right over the edge. And as for you: you're just a wicked little witch. Bad, through and through. I wish they still burned witches. They should do.

When I'd calmed down I called my solicitor and asked him to recommend me a woman lawyer. At that time I was hoping you would go for a settlement that would solve your money worries and pay for drama school. If you wouldn't settle it would look better in court if your so-called rapist had a woman defending him. That was before I realised Susannah would bring charges too, that you intended to establish, 'a pattern of cruelty, rape and physical abuse'. (I quote some document or other.) Believing there was a chance I could control the situation, I managed to think quite calmly on that journey. It was easier if I could concentrate on what could be done to discredit you so I wouldn't have to suffer from your delusions – in terms of practical consequences – more than was absolutely necessary. Or rather from your and Susannah's shared delusions. At the same time I was desperately worried about you, lying in that hospital bed convinced I'd raped you, or knowing I hadn't and wanting to tell the world I had – neither reason made you out to be one of the world's clearer thinkers. And I still loved you so much then.

I knew I had to find out if you'd made any kind of statement and what the extent of your injuries were. At the time I couldn't think about the glorious baby we might have had together or I'd have broken down completely. Vanessa, my admirable lawyer (or so I thought then), kept using the words 'physical evidence', and asking if your injuries could have been self-inflicted – a fall down the stairs, for instance. I refrained from screaming, 'How should I fucking know?' down the phone at her. I needed an ally. I was praying for one. She kept talking about your 'vagina', and 'semen traces' (perhaps that's why these women want these jobs – it wouldn't surprise me), which was absolutely disgusting. She said it would all be on the police report but there was no harm in trying to find out as much as I could for myself now. So my second – unavoidable – visit to the hospital took even greater courage than my first. I couldn't find you in the ward because they'd moved you into the private room I was paying for and I'd forgotten all about all that – as if it had happened years before. I tried to speak to a doctor but they weren't particularly interested in summoning one, as I wasn't next of kin. I explained that I'd been the first one called, the one closest to you. They spoke as if they disliked me, the women, and it dawned on me then that you must have told them your story about my being a rapist. That was very hurtful, but I had to harden myself not to mind. When I asked to see you I was refused point blank. 'I don't want to have to make a scene,' I said, after wheedling and charm had failed. But it was no go. I was left in the dark.

That was also the day I was charged. I can't remember all the things you accused me of, but mental cruelty came up quite a lot (good old mental cruelty, it covers a multitude of sins), as well as physical abuse and rape. There was even an insinuation from your lawyers to mine (impossible to prove, a scare tactic really, and quickly dropped), that I was somehow to blame for Susannah's lamentable paralysis. What connection could there possibly have been to any logical mind between Susannah's accident and our row of the night before? It was all so far-fetched. None of the countless barbaric, random words used to describe my experiences with you both had anything remotely to do with me. Once I'd got over the horror of the words, it became quite laughable. After bail was set I sent for Mummy and she came. At least we were together for a while. She was steadfast through the unimaginable horror.

During all this, my detached wakeful mind kept showing me close-ups, beautiful visions of you, both blurred and clear. At the beginning, on that cold evening, getting into the car with your secret smile, why did you choose me to love you, me to destroy? Had it been a plan from the beginning or was it revenge for how much I loved you? I couldn't decide, and I couldn't decide either if it was your gaiety or your sullenness that had made me worship you the most – your smile, my glimpse of paradise, which held only you and me in its perfect world, or your rages, the banging doors and the tears. I'd wanted to give you safe haven: I'd never asked anything of you, and you'd repaid me with such viciousness. One thing was certain, the memories that tortured me were too perfect to possibly have been mine.

When they fired me from my job, Mummy and I closed the shutters and retreated. I tried to feel the safety she'd once given me as a child, but I only felt more frightened and more alone with her there. We hardly spoke, our life contracting. It was a suffering – I won't describe – I don't want to reproach you. I tried to lick my wounds but they wouldn't close. I had to see you again, I had to ask you why.

Like the little chameleon you are, you'd vanished. I knew you wouldn't have gone to your mother in Wales, but I went there looking anyway, for the show of it, I suppose. I knew where you'd be. You'd be with Susannah.

My dear Kitty,
    You may think you've made an enemy, but it isn't so. The only thing I continue to want out of life is to see you again. (I thought this would appeal to your sense of drama.)
    All my devotion and more,
    Alex

Mummy spat nails when I told her I'd written to you. 'How could you beg her? She's a little whore.' (Mummy was still using her sub-Georgette Heyer vocabulary.)

'You're quite right. But she's *my* little whore and I miss her worse than poison.'

It was good of you to see me. I suspect you were overwhelmingly bored by Susannah's martyr-act by then and longing for some excitement. We've always made plenty of that. Thank heaven for small mercies – the ogre had chosen to be out. Her car was gone and I prayed that it was one of her London day trips and she was busy bossing some stunned shop assistant about in one of her dismal haunts. Barnaby's nanny answered the door. Needless to say there was no sign of him either. I waited for you in the dining room – its redness reminding me of a ghastly dinner I'd had once with Susannah and her parents what must have been aeons before. I stood with my back to the door and looked out at her fatal copse of trees, picturesque, in the distance. For some reason it was teatime and you came in followed by a man with a tray.

'I'll be just outside the door,' he said, as if I were a dangerous animal.

'Who's he?' I said.

'It doesn't matter.' You were slow, gentle, saying this, so I forgot him. But I was so confused by all the coming and going I couldn't take you in. When we were alone my knees went weak and I couldn't speak. You looked smaller than ever. I suppose it was because I'd remembered you so large. You stood, I stood, blushing like a boy.

'It's so good to see you,' I said.

'Apparently.' Your face was all healed apart from a scar in your eyebrow.

'Did I really do that?' I asked, wondering, in a dream.

'Yes, you did.'

'I want to touch you.'

'No.' This almost with venom. Then, 'You'll drink tea.' And

a gesture, a smile, ever so slightly, ever so minutely, flirtatious. You poured it out and handed it to me. I sat at the table – there was nowhere else to sit. You sat, opposite, quite close. You wore black, wool I think. I sipped. You sipped. I was afraid to say anything in case my words made you run away. My hands shook with the cup. You did not lift yours, but stared at my hands.

'It's true then, I did hurt you.'

You looked up. 'It was you.'

'Why didn't you tell me about the –'

'I didn't know.' You interrupted before I could start the syllable which began with B.

'I love you.'

'You're very cruel.' Your expression was clear, open, as if you trusted me and were trying to explain. I tried to stop the anger.

'Are you coming back to me?' I hadn't known what I would say to you, but I hadn't planned it to be that.

'No. Never.'

'Do you want to destroy me?' You frowned your pretty frown. I could have stroked your puckered forehead smooth. 'Don't you love me any more?'

'I have to stop you.' You said this to yourself, as if for the hundredth time.

I felt desperate. 'You've got Susannah's money now – she'll pay for your life – anything you want – she'll protect you – isn't that enough – can't you leave me alone?' I was shouting. You got up in a hurry – spilling tea, a pained expression.

'Stop now or I'll call him. Stop now!' Then more quietly, 'Stop and breathe.' Through the pounding in my ears your voice repeated, 'Stop. Count to ten. Count. Stop and count.' A silence while I tried to do what you wanted, then, 'Don't get angry – please – because I want to say something to you.'

'I miss you – and at night –' But I could see it was useless. 'Please come and sit down again and tell me what you want to say. Please say something to me that I can remember afterwards.'

You didn't move – I wanted to get up and grab you and force you down, but the sorrow was worse than the anger and it won. You said – and see, I do remember – you said, 'I loved you once. And I don't believe how you are is your fault – entirely – or hers.' That was so gentle. Your voice was so lovely. As you said that, you were an angel. 'But you must understand. We *will* stop you.' I cried terribly then. You went away after that and I'd forgotten to ask you why. I don't think I'll ever understand.

That was the last time I ever saw you. I don't count the times in court. But I'm skipping ahead.

I went away. The man pushed me out of the door I think. I was screaming, shouting my head off for you, Susannah, Barnaby. I even asked for my mother, forgetting she wasn't there. You'd really got me into a terrible terrible state.

It's all a bit blank in my memory after that. A great many tears: both hot and cold. I came to notice and record the temperature of my tears.

Mummy never left me – though sometimes I begged and begged her, daring to hope that she would. But I'm confused.

Here, now, in this place, I'm trying to think of what I did to make you happy – give you a good time. Racking my brains in fact. It must have been something. You used to go on about how beautiful I was, which was faintly embarrassing, as I knew perfectly well the best of my looks had passed, they were bequeathed to Susannah, she had photographic evidence. But I gave you my remaining elegance, what you used to call 'the long line of me', and I knew how to be charming in the old-fashioned way, opening doors and ordering for you, deferring to you in public as if I were honoured to have you with me, which I was. I think it was Mummy who once said I was better for public than private consumption. I was good at food and drink too, the pleasures of the table I think they're called: took you to the right places – for food that is – and gave you the right wines to taste. That's no mean present, a delicious lunch with heady, yellow wine, the best fruit, the best of everything. Then bed. And when we were first together I bought you clothes, even underwear, and you said, 'I feel like a mistress,' which, of course, was exactly what you were, but for some reason felt it necessary to deny. Just because times change, it doesn't mean the essentials do. Not for you and me anyway. In another life I'd have married you. I thought often about asking you – you know that. It was just that I wasn't free – and I say that in the most literal sense, also I knew that I was your first love, but it would have been quite wrong of me to expect to be your last. Not that I didn't hope that I was and fantasise. For one thing, that's part of what keeps an affair alive, shared belief in the future, preferably detailed plans for it, and for another, what could have been more exquisite to me than to have and to hold you for ever? Mummy wouldn't have allowed it though. I really don't think she would.

'They take suggestion as a cat laps milk' – that was another one of your favourite quotes. Now I see why. 'I once was blind and now I see, but there's no amazing grace for me.' That's my new doggerel, which actually wasn't hard to invent. It rhymes quite well. But the scansion, as you would point out, is crap. Anyone reading any of this would see that I was never cut out to be a poet, I have no talent for words – dressing things up – but even if I had I wouldn't want to do it: it seems so self-indulgent somehow. Mummy had enough self-indulgence for both of us: I had to make her the money to support the habit. Why I should choose another woman with nothing but the (in your case) vague desire to express herself I don't know. More fool me.

The thing about writing these letters is that the doctor – another woman – seems to think that they'll help: or to use a word from your tragedy exam – what a joke – that there'll be a catharsis. It's a policy, a recommended therapy. I don't want to be critical, but it seems so terribly naïve. I'm meant to write to all three of you, and then I'll feel better. I'm not meant to send the letters, so as an attempt to talk to you, they're doomed. I think I'll try and see if they'll let me send them. You might feel touched, moved, sorry for me. Perhaps you'd come and see me, the letter might make you come and see me and then I'll see you again and the story wouldn't be over, the way it is now, finished and done. There is a chance I could be let out for good behaviour, but between you and me, I think that's just something they say to people to stop them from trying to kill themselves and making a mess. Because conditions make it impossible for one to succeed. I know that now. For a long time I didn't, but I do now.

Kitty Kitty Kitty, come, Kitty. Come, Kitty. Kitty. Come.

And so I turn to the final betrayal. I can't bear to spin it out any longer.

You and Susannah – Snow White and Rose Red, in the flat country with the boy, plotting and hatching and talking talking talking. Mummy and I, the other army, in defensive barricade position in the London house, lawyers working like infantry cavalry and artillery combined, letters and calls flying like arrows between them. Cases being prepared before the last battle joined. It was very tiring: hours of interviews to be recorded, an obsession with dates. Because of bail I couldn't get away, go and lie on some beach somewhere or sit on the top of some mountain – nothing. Just that empty stage set of a house. Mummy was very quiet around that time, very sad, worse than I was often, but that was nothing new. She went off on a lot of errands to do with the cottage, kept herself occupied. The plan was that if I were convicted she would rent it out and come and babysit the London house, or sell it, depending on the length of the sentence, or was it the other way round? That the cottage would be – I'm not sure. That must have been why the errands were for the cottage. Yes, that's it. I do remember now. She was very preoccupied with radiator covers for at least a week – endless glossy leaflets and primitive sighing. Darling Mummy.

She wasn't there that special world-tipping morning, and that too had been planned. It's extraordinary reading about yourself in a newspaper. I'd had some experience of it because there'd been coverage of the case, and it had been insulting and banal but after a bottle of wine the shock had receded, become part of the joke. But this. I had the papers delivered and, after I didn't go to work any more, more than one, to keep me busy. Headline: 'Wife-Rapist's Mother Speaks'. There was a picture of Mummy and me taken in the South of France, at the beach I think it was – one of our rare outings. It was incredibly distorted, blown up, but it caught me first, pointing at the rim of the world, the grey horizon at the end of the flat sea, and her laughing, turning away from me so the camera could catch her face, her knees bent, graceful and gauche as a girl. There was also a big mug-shot of me taken by you, possibly, that very year. I looked suitably grim, and then a brand new colour picture of Mummy looking uncomfortable on the bench outside the cottage, surrounded by things in pots not even flowering and hastily placed. 'Wife-Rapist's Mother Speaks. Mrs Truman, 50: "It has been an unbearably painful decision for me to speak about my own son."' (Or was it 'against', 'against' my own son?) 'But I have to say that quite honestly I've always been afraid of him. Ever since he was a tiny child there has been something not quite right about him.' Then it went on about how much she loved me, I think, and how she'd had no idea for years about my, 'cruel treatment of my wife, Susannah (30)'. They're very particular about people's ages, newspapers. That, if nothing else. 'I knew the marriage wasn't happy, and that she was a gentle girl who found it hard to live up to his expectations of a wife.' (That was the sentence which told me the thing was total – real. Only my mother could spout such twaddle.) I wondered if she'd written it herself or if there'd been a microphone shoved in her face. Either one she would have relished. There were three pages of the stuff. Front page (it must have been a boring, quiet time of year), and a double spread inside. You must have read it: you and Susannah. 'When I married again when Alex was fifteen he was madly jealous. My husband kept assuring me that in time he'd settle down, that he needed a father.' (No mention of my own invisible father.) 'I believed that family life would be a stable influence on my darling boy. How could I have known that within a year my husband Gerald would perish at the hands of my own child?'

I can't go on writing this. She said I killed him: that I was a murderer, that she'd hoped for many years that it had been an accident, but now she could hope no longer. She knew it was me. I think I was still standing on the doorstep when I got to the end. I wasn't even dressed. My own mother. After all my love.

It was the timing of it that was so clever. Even if there'd been a case against me for Gerald's death – which, of course, there wasn't – I couldn't have been tried. It was in another country and too long ago. But the story was there, what was important was the story, which would poison the minds of every prospective juror in the country, spawning other stories, spiralling on to radio and television and, of course, that backwater of filth, the Internet.

'You know he murdered his stepfather?'

'And almost killed that poor crippled wife?'

'He's a maniac.'

'He's crazed.'

'His own mother couldn't keep quiet any longer.'

'He seems so sane, doesn't he?'

'And just imagine – that pretty young girl.'

'Just think.'

I couldn't cry, I couldn't shriek, I couldn't move. I just lay with my eyes open, curled on the floor. The phone started ringing. When I could I pulled it out of the wall, in room after room after room. I dressed: I got in the car and drove away. I was in my car and I was driving but I didn't know exactly why or where I was going. The morning was uselessly bright, it would have been hot, but there was a wind, and at first I didn't know what to do. I drove along by the side of Battersea Park. I wanted to cross the river but I was confused about which bridge I was near. I wanted to be on the Embankment driving as fast as I could, but the city was choked with traffic, other people with Saturday spirits, trips and journeys to embark on, supermarkets and DIY stores to explore – because it was Saturday and their radios told them, 'The weekend starts here.' The car felt heavy to steer. I ceased to care about the road and the rights of way, stopped concentrating, looking at the people and reading the signs and billboards, advertisements aimed at lives so much cleaner than my own. Mummy had told lies about me – I remembered this as I gazed at the façades of the houses in Cheyne Walk and thought my usual thought, that I would like to live in one, but could never decide which was the prettiest and would have the best view. I remember wondering why the brain, which is so complex, still behaved in this rudimentary way, thinking the same thought when presented with the same image. I decided it was stupid, then remembered that I'd decided this before, too, so many times. The traffic had come to a complete stop. I found I was looking at a piece of paper taped to one of the trees – covered in plastic, tattered, flapping slightly in the breeze. It said, 'Lost mongrel Sandy – phone,' and there was a number. Then it said, 'Reward.' What kind of reward could that be, I wondered, and who would find the dog, and who in this city would be bothered? The animal must have been long gone. I wondered how people could have the arrogance to hang out their sufferings to flutter on the weekend breeze, and to suffer so much about an animal – my smothered brain couldn't take it in.

There have been times in my life when time has speeded up but that day it slowed down. Once I'd drifted through London, I couldn't drive fast: not as if I were going anywhere. It would be safe to say that I drifted, drifted down the A2. I looked at the bumpers of the cars in front of me, sometimes at the trees and sky ahead. The clouds were doing that mackerel-sky thing and the sun was setting. The motorway which goes into the sunset (metaphorically speaking, of course), that was the motorway I drifted along, reminding myself to breathe. I knew she'd be waiting. I had no anxiety about that.

You haven't been there – or have you? I'm confused – but there's a crooked door in a crooked wall, a crooked path leading to a crooked house, the bulging wall of a crooked house. She'd heard the car and was standing in the doorway, leaning on her stick. It's very dank, the garden, even in summer, because the cottage blocks the sun. There's a lawn raised up – I can't describe it. I hardly had the strength to walk towards her, I could have crawled like a baby. I had to stifle the urge to fall to my knees and crawl.

'Mummy.'

'Don't call me that. Call me by my name.' It was a bit like those films you're so fond of watching. I half expected her to shoot me full of bullets. The evening was quiet, damp, unremarkable, almost night. Twilight. That's the word. She was very stooped, but doing her best to stand upright. Her powder had gone into her wrinkles, she was wearing too much rouge, and the same thick lipstick she's always worn, the same delicious scent. Her clothes were the shabby clothes she's been in for years. She'd drawn the line at dressing up, but she'd washed her hair and there was white about the throat – an attempt to lighten and flatter her sallow inelastic skin, the shadows all around the eyes.

'I was a great beauty once, you know.'

'You know you always say that.' I could hardly stand.

'Because it's true.'

My mouth was dry. 'You've no need to remind me. I was there.'

'Kiss me.'

'I can't. I can't do that.' But I took her hand. 'Let's go inside.' She settled by the fire and I made her her tonic water and bitters and a whisky for myself.

'You'll need it,' she said, giggling. 'I could do with one.' I sat at her feet because it was better than having to look her in the eye. She rested her hand on my 'tawny head', and sighed, slurping at her drink, the ice tinkling. 'Like the old days,' she said.

'Why did you say those things about me, Mummy?' I was aching.

She sighed and took her time, absorbed in examining her own motives, her narcissism. 'Seemed the best way. You were so obsessed with that girl with the ridiculous name.'

'Kitty. Her name is Kitty.'

'It doesn't matter now.' Nothing had ever mattered so much. I could hear her, slurp slurp, stroke stroke, feel her twisting my hair in her hand. 'I need a cigarette.' I got up, stumbled to find the box, lit her Gauloise for her, 'And one for yourself.' I settled back down again, all without looking at her. She resumed playing with my hair. 'Frankly, I don't care what you did to Susannah. She probably deserved it. It's got nothing to do with her. You're so charming and so plausible, they're bound to acquit you, and I want you to come home.'

'Why do you think you saying those things will make me come home?'

'Because no girl will ever want you, now. You're damaged goods, if your own mother says so.' The smell of the smoke made me feel sick, watching it in the air, if you could call it air, trapped in that room. 'I want you to come home and stop chasing after other girls. They never make you happy.'

'But, Mummy—' Laboriously I forced my jaw to work, to make the words. 'I'll go to prison. I won't come home.' (At the time I hadn't realised it would be an institution for the criminally insane, I thought more of yobs doing Open University courses and getting on my nerves.) It was so quiet, my voice so loud. 'I'll go to prison. I won't come home. Get this absolutely straight.'

She waved her hand about, the cigarette lodged loosely between her fingers. 'If they do lock you up they can't keep you there for ever. When you come out you'll come home.'

'And you'll be the only one left for me.'

'That's right. I'm sick and tired of the other girls.'

'It was cruel of you.'

'Darling, try to understand. It was a means to an end. It had to happen.' She stopped stroking my hair and moved to stroke my cheek and throat, that place in the throat where I'd held buttercups for you, Kitty Kitty. She pressed her fingertips into my throat and before I could feel choked and afraid, put them in my mouth, tapped my teeth. 'I love your teeth,' she said. I bit her, bit down hard. She laughed. 'As playful as ever, I see,' she said.

In the morning the silence was more of a comfort than it had been the night before. She slept on her side beside me in the old bed as she always used to, and I didn't disturb her or open the curtains, creeping out of bed to go and make the coffee for her tray. I felt nothing except that I knew I was awake. My thoughts were slow, revolving. Words came. Greedy was one, unkind another, and then the child's favourite: unfair. I could have laughed at myself for the belief I'd always held so strongly, that we were partners in crime, for life. The loveliness of you, Kitty, your magnificence, struck me again and made me gasp. I let the colours of you flood me for a second and then I willed you to go away. In the cottage kitchen, on the cold tiles, I surrendered you, Kitty. That's what I tried to do.

We sat up in bed, her in the crook of my arm, looking out at the trees.

'What hurts me most is not even that you said I killed him, which I'd never have done –'

'You wanted to, though – don't split hairs.'

'The worst thing for me is Kitty losing our baby. I don't know why, but it hurts me the most. It would have been better if one pure thing could have come out of all this mess.'

She shifted, fidgeted, sitting up straighter, jealous, impatient. 'No, darling – she didn't lose it, it was aborted. She did it the day before she trapped you, trapped you by making you rape her.'

'What do you mean?'

'She's a clever girl. She wanted to be prepared, she told me. She went to the South of France before she came to see me. She put me up to talking to the papers – she said it was the best way of hurting you. She wanted to understand you, how to hurt you the most.'

'She told you to talk to the papers?'

'Yes. It was her idea. The most effective thing, she said.'

'And she had an abortion? She got rid of our child?'

'She never wanted your baby. She wanted you to feel, believe, that she loved you when she lost the baby. That it was your violence which destroyed it, which changed her mind.'

'She wanted me to hurt her?'

'Darling, I told you, it was all planned.'

It was all planned, Kitty, wasn't it? Even that Mummy would tell me like that when I was quiet, when I believed that the worst had happened to me. I had the small comfort then of thinking you were good and I didn't deserve you. But you and she wouldn't even let me own the idea of you, in the end. I think the strangest thing was that I had no anger, no tears, no passion left. She laughed at me, while I cried. She laughed and said, 'You'll get over it, and then we'll be happy again.'

It is true that I am mad, no fit father for your child. You made me mad. It was you. You and Mummy and Susannah. My three cruel women.